T0196846

The Body in the Apartment

Books by Judi Lynn

Mill Pond Romances
COOKING UP TROUBLE
OPPOSITES DISTRACT
LOVE ON TAP
SPICING THINGS UP
FIRST KISS, ON THE HOUSE
SPECIAL DELIVERY

Jazzi Sanders Mysteries
THE BODY IN THE ATTIC
THE BODY IN THE WETLANDS
THE BODY IN THE GRAVEL
THE BODY IN THE APARTMENT

Published by Kensington Publishing Corporation

The Body in the Apartment

Judi Lynn

LYRICAL UNDERGROUND
Kensington Publishing Corp.
www.kensingtonbooks.com

LYRICAL UNDERGROUND BOOKS are published by

Kensington Publishing Corp.
119 West 40th Street
New York, NY 10018

First Electronic Edition: March 2020
ISBN-13: 978-1-5161-1020-9 (ebook)
ISBN-10: 1-5161-1020-X (ebook)

First Print Edition: March 2020
ISBN-13: 978-1-5161-1023-0
ISBN-10: 1-5161-1023-4

Printed in the United States of America

I'd like to thank my usual suspects: Mary Lou Rigdon and my daughter Holly Post for their insightful critiques.

I'd also like to thank my good friend, Ralph Miser, for sharing so many of his ideas with me. He's a mine (mind?) of interesting clues for fixer-uppers.

And of course, these books wouldn't be possible without my wonderful agent, Lauren Abramo, and incredible editor, John Scognamiglio, and the entire support team I have at Kensington.

So thank you, Larissa Ackerman, Lauren Jernigan, James Akinaka, Rebecca Cremonese, Alexandra Kenney, Michelle Addo, and Alexandra Nicolajsen.

And thank you to Tammy Seidick for my wonderful covers.

Chapter 1

Jazzi had mixed feelings. Ansel's older brother, Radley, was moving out after staying with them for three months. She'd enjoyed getting to know him, and Ansel had enjoyed having him around. But it would be nice to have the house to themselves again. And it's not like Radley was moving back to Wisconsin. He'd found an apartment in the same building where Donovan, his work supervisor lived. He'd still pop in every weekend for the family Sunday meal, probably more often if he got hungry.

As he stalked through the kitchen on his way upstairs, he stopped to sniff. "What's in the oven?"

So much like his brother, a man who loved food. At six one, Radley wasn't as tall as Ansel, and his build was sinewy instead of pure muscle, but he was almost as good-looking. And he was more outgoing, making friends easily.

"Beef enchiladas. I made an extra pan for you to take with you. You can keep the glass dish. You might need it."

Radley came to give her a hug. "If I bring it back empty, will you fill it for me again?"

Yup, he and Ansel had a few things in common. She waved him away. "Dream on. But you're always welcome to drop in."

He gave her a quick kiss on the cheek before tromping up the steps. Inky and Marmalade chased after him. Her cats thought moving day was a new kind of entertainment.

When Radley had come for her and Ansel's November wedding, he'd liked River Bluffs so much, he left his family's dairy farm and started training at the furnace and air conditioning company where Thane worked. Thane was her sister, Olivia's, live-in boyfriend. The two had hit it off so well, he became a regular at Thane's Saturday night poker parties, along with Donovan and Walker, Thane's BFF.

None of this set well with Bain, Ansel and Radley's oldest brother. Their dad was furious. When Radley called to tell Bain he'd signed a one-year lease on an apartment here, Bain went ballistic. But what could he do about it? Radley didn't want to milk cows for the rest of his life.

Jazzi glanced at the kitchen calendar. The time had flown so fast. She couldn't believe the day had come for Radley's move—February twelfth. And five days after that, on the seventeenth, Franny's baby was due. She, Ansel, and Jerod flipped houses together. Her cousin was so nervous about Franny's pregnancy, he walked on pins and porcupine quills. Every time his phone rang at the fixer-upper they were working on, he jumped for it.

Ansel and Radley had taken bets on whether the baby would come before or after Jerod handed the buyer the keys to the finished house. It was almost done, so Ansel—who'd bet on *before*—teased Franny to get busy and push the baby out.

Franny was ready. Big and uncomfortable, she swore this would be their last kid. No more.

A loud thunk came from the basement, and Ansel grunted.

"Are you okay?" Jazzi went to the door to hold it open.

"This bench isn't heavy. I thought I could manage it myself, but it's awkward."

Jazzi went to grab an end and help him carry it up. She studied it and shook her head. "It's an old garden bench. I hope he paints it if he's using it in his living room."

Ansel laughed. "I promised to help him sand it and give it a coat of glossy blue. Either that, or he'd use it, as is. My brother doesn't care too much about matching furniture."

"He loves our house." She scanned the big open kitchen and sitting area they'd lovingly redone.

Ansel followed her gaze, as proud of their house as she was. They'd remodeled it with entertaining in mind. "Why wouldn't he? But if my brother doesn't marry a woman with the gift of decorating, we'll be sitting on hodgepodge couches and chairs for a long time."

"I heard that!" Radley called, coming to join them. He set down the two wooden chairs he'd carted from the attic. "And you're right." He nodded to his brother. "Let me help you carry that to your van."

Jazzi went to toss the salad she'd serve with the enchiladas. Glancing out the kitchen windows, she frowned at the white expanse of snow covering their backyard. When she and Ansel had tied the knot before

Christmas, they'd intended to go on their honeymoon the first week of February, flying to some place tropical during the Midwest winter. But then Radley had moved in with them and Jerod's baby was due, so they'd decided they didn't want to leave. They'd figure out a time to honeymoon once everything settled down.

Jazzi sighed. Life didn't always go according to plan.

The stove buzzer rang and she took the two pans of enchiladas out of the oven, putting them on the stainless-steel countertop to cool. While the men carted Radley's things to Ansel's van, she'd opted to stay out of their way and cook. When they returned to grab the small wooden table Radley had found with the chairs in the attic, they came to inspect her work.

"The cheese is all melted and gooey." Radley reached to snitch a bite, but she slapped his hand.

"It's too hot. You'll burn your fingers and your mouth. Yours will cool enough to eat on the way to your apartment."

He snitched a piece anyway and winced when he swallowed it. "Have I told you that Ansel did a good job when he married you? Thanks for putting up with me so long. It took me till now to buy a used van and find a place to live."

The used van rankled her. "It was tacky that your dad didn't send you the money he got when he sold your old car."

Radley shrugged. "It wasn't worth much. He used the money to pay for extra help until he and Bain got used to the new workload since I'm not there."

Right. He'd kept the money to punish Radley.

She put her hands on her hips. "Your dad wouldn't even send you your clothes."

"No loss there. Most were barn clothes. I had two good outfits for when we went to town, which wasn't often."

Radley was being more generous than his idiot father deserved. As far as she was concerned, Ansel's dad and brother were self-absorbed tyrants. Until Radley had gotten his first paycheck, all he had to wear were the clothes he'd packed to come for their wedding. He didn't even have much of a savings because the farm hadn't paid that well lately. Bain had kept most of the profits in an account to cover expenses.

"I think serfs got treated better than you. Your dad and Bain had enough money for *their* new vehicles."

Radley's crooked smile blossomed. "You're a great friend to have in my corner."

She waved him away. His blue eyes were twinkling and he was enjoying himself too much. "Do you have everything yet?"

"I only have one small load to go. Jerod drove to Walker's to get a recliner he's getting rid of. Thank heavens he decided to get a new one in his lower level. They'll meet me at 3F."

She pressed her lips together. "You're sure not starting out with much."

"Are you kidding? You're even giving me the queen-size air mattress you bought when the house was too full of people at your wedding, and Thane's donating an old chest of drawers from his bachelor days he's kept in his garage."

Jazzi tried to picture the hodgepodge of used furniture and shook her head. "Call me when you're ready to leave and I'll grab my coat."

This February had been mild compared to last year. So far, no ice. Lots of snow, but the city kept the streets cleaned, salted, and sanded. The stove buzzer rang again, and Radley paused before grabbing his clothes. He turned to see what she brought out of the oven this time, then came back to get a closer look.

"Is that a pie?"

She put it on a trivet to cool. "Could be. Ansel told me you loved cherry, so I made two of them. One for us, one for you."

He watched her take out the second one and turn off the oven. "You love to feed people, don't you?"

"That, and I like spoiling them, if I can." She'd gotten that gene from Gran. She'd spent many a weekend at her grandma's house, learning to cook. She wouldn't have even known how to boil eggs if she had to rely on her mother. Mom and Olivia would rather shop and eat out.

Radley picked off a small piece of piecrust. "You can spoil me any time you want to."

With a laugh, she shooed him away. "You'd better get the rest of your things, or Ansel will be in here wondering what you're up to."

The cats ran, one on each side of him, as he climbed the stairs one last time. George, Ansel's pug, guarded the house from his dog bed with his eyes shut, as usual. She went to look out the window to see what Ansel was doing just in time to see a black pickup park in front of the open garage. Its door flew wide and Bain got out. Oh, fudge! He started to the kitchen door, hands knotted into fists, his lips pulled into a snarl.

Ansel yelled and started after him. "Hey! Wait. What are you doing here?"

Bain reached the door first and banged on it. Jazzi waited until Ansel had caught up with him before opening it. They spilled into the kitchen together, both of them looking angry. Her Norseman didn't lose his temper often, but Bain pushed all of the wrong buttons for him.

Bain stabbed his finger in her direction. "Where's Radley?"

"Right here." Radley didn't sound a bit perturbed. He set his suitcase and clothes on their long farm table and faced his brother.

"This has gone on long enough," Bain barked. "We need you at home. Pack your things, and I'll drive you back."

"I have packed my things, and I'm moving into my new apartment. I'm not working on the farm anymore."

"I didn't ask you. I told you," Bain snapped. "Get your things and get in my truck."

"He's not going." Ansel moved between Bain and Radley. "He's staying here."

"You keep out of this. It's your fault. You encouraged him to stay."

"No, he made a choice. Unlike me. You kicked me off the farm, remember? And it was the best thing that ever happened to me. Radley can do better here, too."

"He's coming with me. Get out of my way." When Ansel didn't move, Bain drew back his fist and swung at him.

Ansel caught his wrist and held it. "I don't want to fight with you, but I will." And he'd win. Ansel was six-five of solid muscle.

Bain winced, obviously feeling Ansel's grip. "Okay, let go."

"Can you control your temper?"

"I have to, don't I? But I'm not leaving. Not until I get to talk to Radley."

"You'll have to wait till we move his stuff into his apartment. Walker and Jerod are waiting for us there."

"I'm coming with you, or you'll move Radley in and won't bother to tell me where to find him."

Ansel looked at Radley.

"Let him come. It's not going to change anything. Maybe he'll see how many friends I have and be happy for me."

Fat chance, but Jazzi kept her opinion to herself. Instead, she went to slip on her coat and load Radley's food into cardboard boxes to carry with her.

Ansel turned to his pug. "Stay, George. We won't be long, and you'll only get in the way."

George stretched and rested his head on his paws. It took a lot to excite Ansel's dog.

Jazzi rode with Ansel to Radley's apartment in West Central. Radley rode with Bain. "That way I can give him directions, and we can talk."

If Radley thought he could reason with him, Jazzi suspected he was wrong. But if anyone would give it a shot, it would be him. He was the most lighthearted of the three brothers.

Jazzi liked the idea of Radley starting out in West Central. When she'd met Ansel, she was renting the bottom floor of an old house there. She loved the neighborhood, within walking distance of downtown. Now, their good friends, Reuben and Isabelle, lived in the tall Victorian she'd called home. They'd restored it to its former glory and returned it to a single family house.

Ansel pulled to the curb in front of Radley's long, brick apartment building. "Bain must have parked in the back lot." Only tenants were supposed to park there, but Bain thought rules didn't apply to him. That was fine with Jazzi. When they left, they wouldn't have to walk out with him.

They entered the old building and climbed the steps to apartment 3F, carrying the bench between them. They'd come back for the rest later. Radley's door was open, and Jerod and Walker were angling a recliner so they could fit it inside. The chair was a brown tweed, out of date, but it looked worn and comfortable. Ansel and Jazzi carried the bench in behind them.

Radley put it against the wall in place of a couch. He arranged the chair at an angle beside it, facing his TV. Thane had already come and gone, and his chest of drawers anchored a wall in Radley's bedroom. There was a quick knock on the door and a man with wavy, sandy colored hair and liquid brown eyes came in, carrying a round coffee table. He reminded her of a cocker spaniel. "I used it as a nightstand, but bought a new one last week."

Radley gave a quick nod to him. "Hey, everyone, this is my supervisor at work, Donovan." He made quick introductions.

Jazzi had never met him, but she'd heard a lot about him. Both Thane and Radley rated him highly as a supervisor and friend. He sure looked like a nice guy. He'd make a great neighbor for Radley. If she remembered right, he lived one floor down.

"You sure you don't need this?" Radley asked. He sat in the chair and plopped his feet on the coffee table. When Donovan grinned, Radley gave him a thumbs-up. "Thanks."

Bain looked around the apartment and crossed his arms over his chest. "You're leaving the farm to live in this dump with a bunch of hand-me-downs?"

Radley let out a short laugh. "What did we have at the ranch house? Grandma and Grandpa's old furniture? The beds we slept in as kids?"

Bain's scowl deepened. "This is other peoples' rubbish. Open your eyes, Rad, and come home."

When Radley looked troubled, Donovan jumped in to defend him. "Give him a chance. He's just starting up. He makes enough money, he can buy a new piece of furniture a week if he wants to. Come to see him again in a few months, and this place will look good."

Bain glared at him. "First of all, I don't know you, and I don't care what you think. This is family business. You're not family, so butt out."

Radley pushed to his feet. "That's enough."

Donovan held up his hands in a placating gesture. "No worries. I know all about family drama, have plenty of my own. I'll leave you guys to it. But, Radley, you have a shot at a fresh start. It's your choice." He turned and they heard him walk down the hall and start down the stairs.

"Are you going to listen to him or me?" Bain demanded. "We've worked together since we were kids."

"I'm staying," Radley told him.

"Dad's getting older, slowing down. Are you just going to desert him when he needs you?"

"I've heard that my whole life. I'm staying."

Jamming his hands into his pockets, Bain started for the door, too. "Fine. Find out for yourself how much fun it is trying to make it on your own."

His footsteps pounded down the stairs, and Ansel frowned at Radley. "Are you going to be okay?"

Radley shrugged. "You know Bain's temper. He'll stew and grumble, then get over it in a while."

That's when they heard a gunshot. They all looked at each other, then raced for the top of the stairs.

Chapter 2

When they hesitantly made their way to the second floor, Jazzi pointed at Donovan stumbling out of his apartment, his hand pressed to his chest. Blood covered it and dripped down his arm. As he tried to walk toward them, his knees buckled and he fell.

They ran to him. Jerod and Radley knelt beside him, and Jazzi reached for her cell phone to call 911. Then she called Detective Gaff. She'd worked with him on previous murders. More of them than she should ever have had to deal with.

"A man's been shot at the apartments on Berry Street, apartment 2D," she told him. "He's in bad shape. I called 911. Are you on duty today?"

"I'm working a homicide not far away. Give me fifteen minutes."

Jazzi wasn't sure Donovan had that long. There was so much blood. It spread beneath him and oozed out of the exit wound in his back.

"We need to apply pressure to the wound." Radley pressed both hands to Donovan's back, pressing down hard. Relief flooded her when sirens approached the building and EMS techs hurried up the steps. Everyone stood back out of the way, to let them do their jobs.

Walker's voice shook when he asked her, "Is Gaff coming?" He'd worked with the detective when his dad, Darby, was killed. He respected him.

"He'll be here soon." She hoped it was only to solve a shooting, not a murder. She willed Donovan to hang on, to make it.

Walker leaned against the wall to wait. Ansel grabbed her hand, though, and pulled her after him. When she glanced back at the medics, Ansel tugged harder.

"What is it?"

"Where's Bain?" His voice cracked with tension.

"Bain? He left."

"Hurry!" He practically dragged her after him. They got out of the building before cops arrived. He headed straight to the back lot and found his brother searching through his pickup in near panic.

"Did you hear the shot?" Ansel asked.

Bain's face drained of color. "Someone must have seen me walk back to my truck to put our gun in the glove compartment. It's gone. Somebody stole it."

Ansel stared. "I told you it was a stupid idea to buy a gun."

"Dad bought it when we drove here for your wedding. He said every big city was filled with violence. He insisted I bring it to get Radley."

Jazzi studied the glove compartment. No marks on it. No marks on the truck's doors either. "No windows are broken or doors jammed. How did someone get in?"

Bain swallowed hard. "I never lock it. No need to on the farm or in our small town. I just forgot."

Ansel raked a hand through his white-blond hair. "There's no way to prove anyone took it."

Bain pressed his eyes shut, rubbed his forehead. "But why would I shoot anyone here? I don't know anybody in River Bluffs."

"It's Donovan, and you just argued with him. He's lost a lot of blood. You'd better come with us. Detective Gaff is going to want to question you." Ansel waited for his brother to follow him, but Bain stood rooted to the spot.

"This is going to look bad. I've heard about big city cops. They pin a crime on anyone to close a case. I just fought with Donovan. It was my gun."

Ansel frowned at him. "You've listened to Dad too long. Cops aren't like that, especially Gaff. It's going to look worse if you run. How far do you think you'd get? You'd be pulled over somewhere between here and home."

Bain gripped the truck's door handle. Jazzi tried to reason with him. "If you follow us in now, they can check your hands for any residue. If you'd fired the gun, they'd know."

Bain's gaze slid to the work gloves on his front seat. "Unless I wore gloves."

She sighed. He would have to have those right there, wouldn't he? But Ansel started to return to the building.

"They know where you live," he said. "Do you want them to arrest you on the farm in front of Mom and Dad?"

Bain's shoulders sagged and he trailed after Ansel. Jazzi brought up the rear. By the time they reached Donovan's hallway, the medics were carrying Donovan out on a stretcher. A sheet covered his face.

Jazzi's limbs felt numb. He'd died? They'd just talked to him, laughed with him. He was *nice*. Who'd want to hurt him? A tech strode toward his apartment and Jazzi watched him go inside. She froze. The door was open, and she could see that his couch was slashed open and its stuffing thrown everywhere. Books were knocked off shelves, furniture overturned. The door to his bedroom was ajar, and his mattress was cut open, too.

Ansel followed her gaze and grimaced. "Someone was looking for something."

Radley came to stand next to Bain. "I thought you left."

Voice low, Bain said, "Whoever shot him used my gun. They took it out of the pickup."

Radley's jaw dropped. He stared. "Geez, Bain, you couldn't have made things worse if you tried."

Jerod and Walker had heard him, too. Jerod took a deep breath. "Gaff's a good guy. All he cares about is finding the truth. Don't play games with him. Just tell him exactly what happened."

Bain nodded, but Jazzi wasn't sure he'd comprehended. His hands shook, and she thought he might be so shocked, he was only going through the motions. She turned to Ansel. "Stay with him. He needs support right now."

But when Gaff got there, he left them waiting to zip into the apartment to see the crime scene and talk to his men. When he emerged, he suggested they all go down to the building's lobby to talk. Once Bain was away from 2F, he looked a little more together than before. And Gaff kept his voice low and calm as he asked him questions. Still, when they finished, Gaff pinched his lips into a tight line. "We found your gun in the dumpster behind the building. We're taking it in for evidence. We're taking your gloves, too, to check for residue in case you wore them when you fired your weapon. Until we learn more, you're our chief suspect. So don't leave town until I tell you it's okay. We have to start somewhere, and right now, we don't have a lot to go on."

Bain held out a hand to brace himself on the back of a chair. "But Dad needs me on the farm."

"I'm sorry about that," Gaff said. "But there's no way around it right now."

Bain looked at Radley. "I can't afford to stay in a hotel."

Radley shook his head. "I don't have a spare room. I don't even have a couch."

Ansel's voice sounded strained. "You can stay with us until this is settled."

Jazzi's heart sank. She felt it shrivel and weep. Bain. Living with them. And he'd be in a worse mood than usual. But he was Ansel's brother. They couldn't just leave him on the streets. Could they? No. Shame on her. Would it look bad if she offered to pay for a hotel room for him? She grimaced. Yeah, Ansel might not appreciate that. But she wasn't looking forward to spending time with Ansel's oldest brother.

Chapter 3

Jazzi was ready to head home, but Radley said, "Why not come to my apartment and have a beer while I call Thane? He's going to be upset. Donovan and I were supposed to play cards with him tonight." He motioned to Walker. "You were going to be there, too."

Walker's shoulders sagged. "Should we drive to his house and tell him in person instead of over the phone?"

"No, he might not be home. He was going to run around with Olivia today. She's making one of their spare bedrooms into an office. That's why he couldn't stay to help more with the move."

"We still have a few things for you in the van," Ansel said. "Jazzi and I will carry those in while you make your call."

"I'll help you." Jerod started to file after them. "Can we make it in one trip?"

"I'll help, too." Bain followed them out of the building. Jazzi couldn't hide her surprise, and he growled, "The sooner we're done here, the sooner we're out of the building. I want to get away from here."

Soon, Jazzi was surrounded by men who towered over her. Every single one of them, including Walker and Radley, were six feet or taller. Jazzi suspected that, like her, none of them wanted to hear Radley's end of the depressing phone call or gauge Thane's reaction to it. She opened the back doors of the van and handed a huge tote to Jerod. "Pots and pans. We bought a new set when we moved into the house. I meant to take these to Goodwill but never got there."

She handed a heavy box to Bain. "Odd dishes and silverware, a few coffee mugs, more old stuff I've never bothered to get rid of."

Bain glanced inside it. "A can opener. He'll need that. He's partial to Dinty Moore stew and Chef Boyardee. That, and frozen pizzas."

She handed him a bag full of grocery staples. "I know." Canned food and soups filled half of it, along with flour and sugar. "I already sent milk and eggs with him earlier."

He shook his head and impatience colored his voice. "You're not his mother, you know."

"I know. She probably wouldn't have bothered."

Bain's jaw dropped. He stared at her, then turned on his heel and stalked away.

Ansel put an arm around her. "I appreciate everything you're doing for Radley. So does he."

"Your brother and I are going to bump heads. Are you okay with that?"

"Have at him. If he gets on my nerves, he has to get on yours, too." He handed her the bag of old towels she'd packed. "Hope Radley brought soap so he can take a shower."

"I put a bar in the bottom of the bag."

Ansel grinned and picked up the last sack filled with a pillow and a sheet set. "You think of everything. Let's hope Radley's off the phone when we take these in. This is going to put a damper on the family meal tomorrow."

She picked up the box loaded with the food she'd made. She cooked for her family every Sunday. That way, everyone could touch base and keep tabs on each other. Somewhere along the line, Walker had been adopted into their midst, and then Radley. She and Ansel had bought a second long, narrow fold-up table to seat everybody. Joined to their farmhouse trestle table, along with the first fold-up they'd bought, what had once been a long rectangle had become a big square.

They entered the building and climbed the stairs to 3F. Cops and crime techs still came and went from the second floor. At Radley's, Bain sat in the recliner, his head back and his eyes closed, while Radley put things in cupboards. Jerod leaned his long frame against the wall. "Supervising," he told them.

Radley's kitchen was small but big enough for one bachelor. He turned when they put their bags on his small wooden table. "Thanks, guys. I have everything I need to get settled in."

Jazzi rolled her eyes. "We didn't give you anything fancy. I hope you can replace most of it soon."

He motioned to the cupboard with mismatched glasses, cups, and dishes. "This is the kind of stuff I'm used to. It'll make me feel at home. I felt like I was staying at a topnotch bed-and-breakfast at your place, like I should mind my manners."

"I didn't notice you being on your best behavior," Ansel teased.

"I didn't say I did. I said I felt like I *should.*"

Ansel chuckled, but Jazzi quit worrying her bottom lip to say, "How's Thane? Okay?"

"He didn't take it very well. He and Donovan have been work buddies for a long time. He said Olivia's ordering in food tonight. He doesn't want to see anyone, but they'll be at the family get-together tomorrow."

Jerod grimaced. "Yeah, that's sure to be fun. Nothing like a murder every other month to cheer us up."

Jazzi glanced at her watch. "Talking about the Sunday meal, we'd better go. I have to cook something for everybody."

"You could pass on that if you want to." But Radley sounded disappointed.

"Don't be silly. It won't be anything special, though. I was planning on brats and sauerkraut."

"Love those. I've never left your table hungry." Radley motioned toward Walker. "What about him?"

Jazzi shrugged. "We've adopted him. He's officially part of the Sunday doings."

When Walker balked, Radley nudged his arm. "Come on, man. It's better than sitting home, brooding."

"I'll be there. I would brood. Can I stop and grab something on my way?"

"Nope, and you're welcome to come for supper tonight, too. I already made a cherry pie and we have lots of food. We won't starve."

Walker loved desserts as much as Ansel did, she knew. His gray eyes lit up when she'd mentioned pie.

"You sure?" he asked. "I can always stop to buy a pizza."

That sobered everyone. Pizza is what Thane served for poker night.

Ansel gave himself a small shake. "We'd better go. Quit fussing and come on over, Walker." He touched Bain's arm on the way out. "We're heading home. You coming?"

Bain pushed to his feet. "I'll follow you in my truck. I don't know the way yet."

He sounded lost in more ways than one. Jazzi had to feel sorry for him. Talk about plans going wrong. He came here to collect his brother and now he was stuck in River Bluffs as a murder suspect. Even Bain didn't deserve that.

"I could ride with you and give you directions," she volunteered.

"God, no, a little of you goes a long way."

Her spine stiffened. Bain wasn't that lost. He was still his unpleasant self. If he lost them on the way home, he had a cell phone. He could call Ansel. If he called her, she wouldn't answer.

Chapter 4

George perked up his head when they walked through the kitchen door, and Inky and Marmalade came running. The pets weren't happy they'd been left alone for so long on a Saturday. Usually, Jazzi and Ansel worked around the house and ran to the store. When they'd return, they'd throw empty paper bags on the floor for the cats to run in and out of. Their usual weekend routine, and the pets liked it.

Bain came in next, and George turned his head, ignoring him. Even the pug knew Bain was a party pooper. Jazzi called the pets into the kitchen to fuss over them, ladling food into their bowls, while Ansel took Bain upstairs to help him get settled. He'd be staying in the same caramel-colored room Radley had used. It was on the far corner upstairs without a direct view to their bedroom. Thankfully, Radley had tugged off the dirty sheets, and Jazzi had placed fresh ones on the chest of drawers.

While the men made the bed, Jazzi started supper. She covered the enchiladas with foil and put them in the oven to heat up. With a salad and pie, that was a good enough meal.

Raised voices upstairs caught her attention. "It's all your fault!" Bain shouted. "You lured Radley here with your stupid wedding. If he'd have stayed home, where he belongs, none of this would have happened."

"If I remember right . . ." Ansel's voice could freeze pipes . . . "I didn't want you at my wedding. I told you so. You came anyway."

"Mom wanted to see it. So did Adda. Our sister wouldn't leave it alone."

"So, send Mom with Adda and Henry. You and Dad could have stayed on the farm with your cows. You put them above anything or anyone anyway."

Hmm. Jazzi smiled. Her Norseman could hold his own. She stepped closer to the stairs to eavesdrop.

"If Mom came, Radley would come. If I'd stayed home, it wouldn't have changed anything."

"Maybe if you'd treated Radley better than you treated me, he'd have been happy on the dairy farm."

"We did treat him better. He got to stay and work with us."

"*Got* to? Or did you need him for cheap labor? Did he have any say in any of the decisions you and Dad made?"

"Dad and I know what's best for the farm."

"And what's best for you. Was it the best for Radley?"

Silence hung between them.

"I don't want to eat supper with you and Jazzi. I'd rather eat in my room."

"Fine with me. We won't miss your company, but don't think we're carrying food up to you like room service. If you want something, you know where the kitchen is, and you won't cook for yourself. You eat what we eat, or you stop to buy food someplace else."

Good for Ansel! Jazzi would dish up a plate for Bain to take upstairs. That way she didn't have to be around him.

"I've said all I want to say to you. You can leave me alone and go downstairs to play in the kitchen with your wife." A door slammed and Jazzi heard Ansel walking toward the stairs. She hurried to the table and started setting it so that it wouldn't look like she'd stopped everything to listen to them.

When he joined her in the kitchen, he wore a scowl. "Bain wants to eat in his room. He'll grab food and take it upstairs."

"If that what makes him happy." She kept her voice neutral.

He grinned at her. "You heard everything, didn't you?"

"Couldn't help it. Your voices were raised. The cats skedaddled down here to stay out of your way."

Just then, there was a quick knock at the kitchen door and Walker came inside. He sniffed. "It smells good in here."

"Is Radley settled already?" Jazzi started peeling apples for the Sunday dessert—apple crisps. She'd boil potatoes ahead, too. The baked beans could wait until morning.

Walker shook his head. "He's still sorting through things, but I've done all I can to help him. Thought I'd come here and pester you guys until supper's ready."

She loved having Walker underfoot. "In that case, I'm putting you to work. You can help me peel these. The enchiladas will be ready in ten more minutes."

He gladly picked up a paring knife and got to work. They were down to three apples when Ansel's phone buzzed. He frowned at the caller ID. "Didi," he told her.

Walker frowned. "Never heard of her."

Ansel's face colored as he pushed the button and said, "Hi, Didi, what's up?"

His shoulders tensed as he listened to her. "Lock your doors. I'm on my way."

As he jammed his phone in his jeans pocket, Jazzi stared at him. "Is something wrong?"

"Someone broke into her house. When she and River walked in the front door, whoever it was went out the back, but she's frightened. What if they'd walked in on the robber? I'm going to pick her up and bring her here. Do we have enough for her to stay for supper?"

"There's plenty. A robber? Like at Donovan's?" If Donovan had had a back door, would the robber have slipped away? Would Radley's friend still be alive?

"I sure hope it's not the same person." With a nod, he stalked out of the kitchen to his van.

Walker looked at her. "Who's Didi?"

Jazzi took a deep breath. "It's a long story. I'll tell you while we finish the apple crisps."

He pitched in while she talked.

"Last Halloween . . . "

"Before you two got married? When was that anyway?"

"November tenth."

"And Ansel's known her that long? He never mentions her."

"Well, it's sort of complicated, and it embarrasses him a little."

Walker's brows shot up. "This sounds juicy. I can't wait."

"It wasn't the best thing that ever happened to us." Jazzi finished the crumble topping and sprinkled it over the apples. Walker helped her put them in the built-in wall ovens. "It all started when we got a letter from a woman Ansel had a one-night stand with."

"A month before you tied the knot? And you still married him?" Walker let out a whistle.

"He was miserable and lonely when he first came to town, before we ever met. I can't fault him for something that long ago."

"You're a good woman."

She rolled her eyes. "His family had kicked him out. He moved to River Bluffs because his uncle promised him a job, but the sons let Ansel know he wasn't welcome. He had to go on his own as an independent contractor."

"He hadn't started working with you and Jerod?"

"Not yet. He wasn't in the best frame of mind. Brooklyn was close to hitting bottom herself. It's the only time they saw each other. But Brooklyn always remembered him as a decent guy."

Walker snorted. "That's not the only reason she remembered him. Let's face it. Ansel turns heads."

She couldn't argue that point. Her Norseman made knees buckle. "The thing is, last year, Brooklyn found out she had cancer and was dying. She needed someone to raise River, so she was desperate to find the father of her son."

Walker's brows shot up. "Whoa! Wait a minute. She got pregnant?"

"That's how babies are made." She wasn't comfortable telling this story. Reaching for a bag of potatoes, she started cutting them in quarters to busy her hands. "The thing is, Ansel wasn't the only guy she slept with. She didn't know who the father was."

Walker reached in the bag to help. "This is better than a soap opera. How old is the boy?"

"River's seven now."

"Has Ansel lived in River Bluffs that long?"

She scooped her pile of potatoes into a large pan of salted water. "Seven years."

"How long has he worked with you and Jerod?"

"Over two years now."

"It took you two a while to get together." He shook his head, looking baffled.

"When we first met, I was engaged to Chad. By the time we broke up, he was living with Emily."

"Ah, your timing was off. Got it. But what about this Brooklyn? She raised a kid by herself and never notified the dad?"

"If one man—Archie—was the father, she didn't want him around River. She decided to go it alone. A woman who lived across the street from them works from home and took care of River whenever Brooklyn couldn't be there. Didi was nuts about the boy, and he loved her. When the DNA tests came back, Ansel wasn't the father. Archie was. Brooklyn begged Ansel to protect River when she was gone, to make sure her son had a good life and not let Archie take him. She couldn't count on anyone else but Didi to be there for him."

Walker went to the fridge and grabbed a beer. He motioned to a wine glass for her and she nodded. When she put the potatoes on the stove to boil, he sat across from her at the kitchen island, and they sipped their drinks together. "How could Ansel keep Archie from demanding his own son?"

Jazzi sighed. "Brooklyn never told Archie the results of the test. She was pretty sure he wouldn't push to find out either. He was an addict. That's when things got complicated, though. When his drug dealer saw Brooklyn's lawyer stop at his place, he thought it had something to do with a plea deal. He killed Archie so he couldn't talk." The actual events had been even more complicated, but she'd told Walker the important points of what happened.

He ran a hand through his thick, chestnut-colored hair. "So, River's dad is dead."

Jazzi nodded. "And that's when Didi insisted on taking him in. She's supporting him on her own. We stop by to check on them once in a while, and she won't let us help with much. They're both happy together."

Walker took another sip of beer. "That's some friend to step in and raise Brooklyn's boy."

"Didi's wonderful. Ansel and I think the world of her, but you'll meet them soon. Ansel's bringing them here for supper."

And no sooner had she said that than the kitchen door opened and they walked inside with Radley not far behind them. She hadn't expected him. Thank heavens her lasagna pan held a lot of enchiladas. This should prove to be an interesting supper. There were enough people with different things going on, there'd be plenty to talk about. But then she looked at Walker, and the man's face looked like he'd been gobsmacked. He could hardly take his eyes off Didi. Jazzi smiled. Interesting wasn't going to be the half of it.

Chapter 5

When River saw Walker, he reached for Didi's hand. Walker was tall and muscular. He probably looked a little intimidating to the boy, so Jazzi gave him a big smile. "Hey, kid. How's it going? Let me introduce you to a good friend of ours. River, this is Walker. Walker, this is River and Didi."

Didi tilted her head and studied him. Her wavy, ebony hair fell in a curtain past her shoulders. "Ansel's told me about you. You own a cement company, don't you?"

"Yup." His gaze locked on the boy. "Maybe someday River can ride along with me in one of our dump trucks."

River's dark eyes gleamed. "Do you drive cement trucks, too?"

"Sure do."

Didi's generous lips curved in a smile. The girl wasn't beautiful, but with her creamy complexion and vivid coloring, she was eye-catching. "I buy River a Hot Wheels car or truck every time we go to the grocery store. He has a thing for vehicles."

Walker grinned and held out his hand to give the boy a high five. "Then he has good taste."

River laughed and slapped palms with him. With one quick conversation, Walker had caught his interest.

Walker's attention, however, returned to Didi. "What do you do for a living?"

"I work from home, doing medical transcripts. I'm always there, so I can walk River to the bus every morning and wait for his bus after school."

"Nice." Walker's brows furrowed. "Ansel said someone broke into your house."

She shivered and rubbed her arms. "He went out the back door while we came in the front. I've never been so frightened."

Radley, who'd stayed in the background until now, blurted, "Someone broke into my friend's apartment today, too." Thank heavens, he didn't add that the intruder shot and killed Donovan. He looked around the kitchen. "Where's Bain?"

"He doesn't want to eat with us." Ansel went to count dishes and put them on the dining room table.

"That's too weird. What's he going to do, hide upstairs and pout? I'm going up to get him." Radley headed to the stairs.

By the time she and Ansel loaded the food on the island so that people could serve themselves, buffet style, Bain followed Radley into the room. He grimaced and looked at Ansel. "Radley told me to get my butt down here. He said to grow up and be glad you're letting me stay here."

Jazzi rolled her eyes. Not exactly an apology and not really saying that he appreciated it, but it was better than nothing.

Ansel blinked, surprised. Finally, he shrugged. "No problem."

Bain noticed Didi and River. "More people?"

Ansel followed his gaze. "Didi got broken into today. A few weeks ago, someone must have had too much to drink and banged on her door at three in the morning. She's pretty shaken up." He made quick introductions.

Bain glanced at the crowded kitchen. "I'm not up for company right now. Mind if I take my plate upstairs to eat?"

"Be my guest." Ansel handed him a paper plate and a fork.

Once Bain left, Walker asked, "Someone banged on Didi's door a few weeks ago?" When Ansel nodded, he said, "She has every right to be worried." Walker looked worried himself. When River started to fidget—nervous, too—he bent to say, "Bet you're hungry by now. Want me to carry a plate for you and help you load it up?"

The boy nodded and came to peek over the countertop to point at what he wanted. The rest of them grabbed plates and got in line.

Once everyone was settled, Walker returned to the robbery. "You know, it seems like too much of a coincidence that someone tried to get in your house a few weeks ago and you had a break-in today. Maybe he was only checking things out the first time."

Didi nodded. "I think so, too. I live in a working-class neighborhood, but I've never had any trouble before. Not once."

"It might not be safe for you to go home. What if the guy wasn't finished with his search? What are you going to do tonight?"

She flicked a nervous glance at River. "I can't afford to stay in a motel. I guess I'll sleep with my cell phone right next to me."

Walker shook his head, obviously not satisfied with her answer. "Too risky. Why take chances? Look, Ansel and Jazzi can vouch for me that I'm a good guy. I live alone in a tri-level. Why don't you stay at my place tonight? If you want to hang out and sleep in the family room in the lower level, you won't even see me."

She frowned. "Why would you do that? You don't even know us."

"A while ago, someone killed my dad. I just lost a good friend. Life doesn't feel as safe as it used to. I'd blame myself if something happened to you and the boy when I could have helped." Walker's gaze settled on River. "If you go back to your place, I won't get any sleep. I'll worry about you. If you don't want to stay at my house, I could sleep on the couch at yours."

Ansel interrupted. "If you're worried about Walker, we all heard him make the offer. If he does anything that bothers you, we'd all give him grief. And the robber might come back again. You'd be safer at his place."

She pursed her lips, studying Walker, then nodded. "If you're sure. I didn't really want to go home, but I didn't know what else to do. I need to get my laptop, though. All of my work's on it. I don't know if the robber didn't want it or didn't have time to take it, but I can't lose it."

"Fair enough. I'll drive you over and you can grab clothes and anything else you need. I'm supposed to come to Jazzi and Ansel's for lunch tomorrow, but I can stay home and cook instead." He glanced at Jazzi.

She knew an unsubtle hint when she heard one. "Don't be silly. I've made plenty. Bring them along."

Grinning, Walker relaxed his shoulders. "I was hoping you'd say that." He turned to Didi. "After the Sunday meal, you can decide what you want to do next. You're welcome to stay at my place as long as you need to, though."

River wiggled with excitement. "Can I see some of your trucks?"

"You can even sit behind the steering wheel. How's that?"

Didi threw up her hands in surrender. "I guess we'll take it one day at a time, but thank you. It's going to take a while before I feel safe in my house again."

They got serious about eating, and it was quiet for a while. When they finished, Jazzi stood to collect dirty plates and Ansel helped her carry them to the sink to rinse. Then they brought paper plates and the cherry pie to the table. The slices were smaller than usual when she cut it, but she hadn't known there'd be so many people. She served it with vanilla ice cream to make it more filling.

When supper was over, Radley stood and circled the table to give Jazzi a hug. "Thanks for another good supper."

"Any time." She had a soft spot for Ansel's brother.

He laughed. "You'd better quit telling me that or I'll be here every night."

"Wouldn't bother me," she said.

"It would bother me. Every night's too much." Ansel bent to give the last slice of bratwurst he'd cut to George. If he had his way, he'd pull a chair up to the table for the pug.

Radley laughed. "Maybe I'll come over one night and grab Bain, and we can go out for supper."

Ansel's blue eyes lit up. "Even better."

They all stood then and got ready to call it a night. Radley left to return to his apartment, and Didi and River left with Walker.

Once the house got quiet, Bain came down to put his dirty fork in the dishwasher. "Great supper. Thanks."

The man was trying. Jazzi didn't know what Radley had said to him, but it must have made an impression. "Would you like to take my laptop up with you? There's no TV in your bedroom, but you could watch something on the computer screen."

"You wouldn't mind?"

She got it to hand to him. "Ansel has a laptop, too. We can share for a while. Use mine as long as you're here."

She'd caught him by surprise, she could tell. He gave a brisk nod and left them.

Ansel stayed to help with the cleanup. "There'll be even more people here tomorrow. Today was eventful enough. I hope everyone's in a good mood."

So did Jazzi. When her family got cranked up, you never knew what would happen.

Chapter 6

As usual, Jerod and his family were the first ones to arrive for the Sunday meal. Gunther and Lizzie dropped on the kitchen floor to pet George. The pug wasn't a huge kid fan, but he tolerated their attention. Jazzi's cousin came to toss an arm around her shoulders. Almost as tall as Ansel and huskier, he made her feel small. "What are you doing for Valentine's Day tomorrow?" he asked. "If my wife doesn't pop, I'm fixing her a special supper. Bought filet mignons and a box of her favorite chocolates."

Franny pressed a hand to her back—a common pose these days. "I'm not going to pop. But I hope I don't go into labor until Tuesday. If the baby wouldn't come out before I got as big as a Hummer, he can wait another day."

Jazzi tried not to stare. Every time she saw Franny, she looked bigger. Her stomach looked so stretched, she was surprised her skin didn't just split open and let the baby tumble out. She struggled to remember Jerod's question. What were they doing for Valentine's Day? "Ansel and I have reservations at the Oyster Bar. It's going to be crowded, but we love the food and atmosphere."

"Pricey," Franny said.

Jerod laughed at her. "We can afford it. You just don't like to go anywhere without the kids."

She wrinkled her nose. "We go to the movies once in a while when my parents babysit."

He removed his arm from around Jazzi to wander to the kitchen island and the cheese ball she put out every Sunday. "I'd take my wife out more often if she didn't spend half the time we're gone wondering if the kids are all right."

Jazzi smiled. It was fun listening to the two of them. Jerod might fuss, but he was as big of a homebody as Franny. His whole world revolved around his family. "You're never going to get her out of the house when the baby's here."

The back door opened and Mom and Dad entered the kitchen, along with Jerod's parents—Eli and Eleanore. Mom beamed when she saw Franny.

"I wondered if you'd make it this week. The baby's due any day now, right?"

"On the seventeenth," Jerod answered.

Dad's brows rose. "Only four days away. Keep us in the loop when you head to the hospital."

Eli patted his son on the back. "Have you picked out a name yet for our new grandson?"

"We have two choices. Franny wants to look at the baby and see which one suits him better." That's all he'd say about it. Ansel had tried to finagle the names out of him, too.

Walker, Didi, and River walked into the kitchen next. They came to hang around the snacks on the kitchen island with everyone else. Soon, Radley came, then Gran and Samantha. Gran took a long look at Franny and said, "Wednesday."

"You're sure?" Franny asked.

"Late in the afternoon." Then Gran went to the refrigerator to pour herself a glass of red wine. She liked it cold. Every week, she drank a glass before the meal and at the end of the meal.

Didi frowned at Walker, and he hurriedly explained, "Gran has the sight. If she says Wednesday, Franny will have the baby then."

Gran returned and took a sip from her glass before leveling her gaze on Didi. "Gil made poor choices of friends. He made poor choices in prison, too, and that's part of what got him killed."

Didi gasped, and her hand went to her throat. Walker frowned, confused. Everyone turned to study her.

Flushing, Didi said, "Gil was my ex-husband. Someone murdered him in prison."

Oh, crap. This was the first time poor Didi had met her family, and Gran's announcement wasn't the best way to start things off. Jazzi was trying to think of something to say to smooth things over when Olivia and Thane straggled into the house. Huge smiles were plastered on both of their faces.

Ansel stared. "Okay, spill. What's up?"

Yeah, what was the deal? Thane had been crushed when he'd heard about Donovan. Jazzi had expected him to be depressed and brooding today.

Olivia held up her left hand with a chunk of diamond on her finger.

Mom let out a happy squeal. "Have you set a date?"

"April second." Olivia held out her arms, and she and Mom hugged each other.

"Is that a Saturday?" Walker asked.

"A Sunday." Thane grimaced. "We didn't want people to think our wedding was an April Fools' joke."

"You're not wasting any time." Ansel went to bring him a beer and clinked glass bottles with him.

Thane shrugged. "Olivia's had the itch ever since you and Jazzi did the deed. I thought we should wait till the glow was off your wedding, but then Donovan was shot, and it shook me up. It kind of made me think I shouldn't hold off on doing the things that are important to me."

"Well, we're happy for you." Radley raised his beer bottle in a toast, too.

People lined up to slap Thane on the back and congratulate Olivia and him. Jazzi grabbed her sister in a fierce hug. Olivia had been more patient with Thane than she'd thought possible. Her go-get-'em sister had dated the man forever, moved in with him, and still given him time to decide to commit. Jazzi was thrilled for her. When everything calmed down, Ansel said, "I'm hungry. Let's eat."

Everyone laughed. The man loved his food almost as much as his pug did. Jazzi put two platters of brats and sauerkraut on the island, the crispy potatoes and baked beans, along with toasted buns and apple crisps. "Dig in," she said.

Walker helped River fill his plate while Jerod helped Gunther and Lizzie. Then the adults got in line. Buckets of ice held beer and wine bottles.

It took a while for everyone to find a spot at the table, and then conversation flowed again. Radley looked around the group. "Where's Bain?"

"He came down and got a plate of food earlier. He wasn't ready for such a big crowd," Ansel said.

Mom couldn't stand not knowing. She returned to Olivia and Thane's wedding plans. "Do you know what you want yet—a church wedding, a reception, big or small?"

Olivia glanced at Jazzi. "We'd like to have a small church wedding so that I can wear a long wedding gown. Then we'd like to have the same kind of reception Jazzi and Ansel had. Maybe here? With a little different food? Not quite as expensive?"

Dad smirked. "You mean you want Jazzi to make it all."

Olivia hesitated. "If Jazzi doesn't mind. I can help out."

Ansel shook his head. "We've seen you cook. I'll help out in the kitchen. And yes, we'd love to have the reception here."

"Is that all right with you, sis?" Olivia asked.

Jazzi was glad Ansel was on board with the idea. "That will be our wedding present to you."

Olivia let out a long breath of relief. "Good, then the rest should be easy."

River finished his bratwurst and reached for his soda, then pointed a finger at Mom and Dad. "You're married, right?"

Mom nodded.

"And you?" The finger pointed at Eli and Eleanore. They nodded. "You?" He moved to Jerod and Franny.

"Yup," Jerod told him.

He came to Ansel. Ansel wrapped his arm around Jazzi's shoulders. "Very."

"And you're getting married?" he asked Olivia and Thane.

"As soon as we can." Thane sounded so proud, Olivia blushed with happiness.

He turned to Radley. Ansel's brother shook his head. "So far, no woman will have me."

Jazzi rolled her eyes. Radley was six-one and almost as handsome as Ansel. If he put himself on the market, there'd be a lot of takers.

When he got to Gran and Samantha, he frowned.

"Both widowed," Samantha told him. "But we had long, happy marriages before our husbands died."

That seemed to satisfy him. He laid his hand on Walker's arm. "You?"

"I haven't been lucky enough to find the right girl."

Then the boy looked at Didi.

She pinched her lips together. "I got married when I was twenty, but Gil was gone more than he was home. He hung out with his friends a lot when we were dating, but I thought that would change when we got married. It didn't. I didn't like his friends. When they decided to rob a drugstore, they all went to prison together. That was it for me. I divorced him and I've been marriage shy ever since."

River's eyes shone with fierce concentration, trying to put all of that together.

"There are lots of good men out there," Olivia told her.

"I know. I just don't seem to pick them." Didi fidgeted, obviously uncomfortable.

Ansel stood and started gathering dirty plates. "Pretty soon, Jazzi starts making cookies and homemade candy, one or two kinds a week, and freezes them for Easter. I get to sample them to make sure they're good. I can't wait."

"Is that your way of trying to change the subject?" Jerod stared at him.

Ansel made a face. "I thought we should talk about something happier over dessert."

"Crappy technique," Jerod told him, "but good idea." He turned to Jazzi. "You make the sugar and spice cookies for Easter, don't you?"

Why did he even bother to ask? "Have I ever *not* made your favorites? But I don't make as many as I do for Christmas. I make more candy instead." She loved making mounds of cookies for the Christmas tins she delivered every year.

Didi leaned forward, excited. "I've always wanted to learn to make candy. Could I come sometime and watch you?"

Jazzi stood to gather plates, too. "If you come, I'll put you to work."

"Can I come? Please?" River asked.

How cute was this kid? How could she say *no*? "Why not?"

People started back to the kitchen island for dessert and Ansel took his place in front of gallons of ice cream and a scoop. "Tell me what you want."

Jazzi loaded the dirty plates in their deep sink and stopped to stare at George on her way back to the table. Ansel's pug had found a nearly empty beer bottle someone set near the recycle bin. It must need emptying. Using his paws, he had the bottle tipped back and was drinking the small amount in the bottom. She shook her head. "Your dog's drinking beer again," she told Ansel.

"Good boy!" Ansel patted his head on his way to the freezer to put away the leftover ice cream.

The rest of the meal settled on small talk and catching up, and by the time people left, Jazzi had invited Didi back on Tuesday night to make chocolate crinkle cookies and cashew brittle.

Alone during clean up, Ansel shook his head. "This meal was more eventful than most."

"I feel sorry for Didi." Jazzi rinsed the last plate and handed it to Ansel to load into the dishwasher. "Her husband went to prison, then got murdered. And now someone's breaking into her home."

"Hopefully the two aren't connected." Ansel folded the dish towel and draped it over the handle.

Jazzi tried to shut off thoughts of prison and murder and went to settle on the sofa across from Ansel's to relax and enjoy TV. They'd relax for the rest of the day. Tomorrow, they'd be back in New Haven, working on the Victorian house they were restoring. But she couldn't stop thinking about Gil's murder and Didi's break-in. Were they connected? Was that a possibility? She'd have to mention it to Gaff.

Chapter 7

On Monday, George sat by Jazzi's feet in the kitchen while she made sandwiches to pack for lunch at the New Haven Victorian they were flipping. The pug had a soft spot for deli ham. He liked beef and turkey, too, but when he smelled ham, she was his new best friend. The cats wound around her ankles, too. They never turned down scraps of ham either.

Ansel took a bag of chips out of the cupboard to add to the cooler and shook his head. "They have you surrounded. You might as well surrender."

She handed him a slice of meat to tear into bites for George while she fed the cats. "Our pets would leave us if we became vegetarians."

He laughed. "I'd have to sneak out for meat fixes myself." Her Norseman wasn't a fan of meatless Mondays. She could be satisfied with spaghetti with sun-dried tomatoes and artichokes or noodles with mushroom sauce, but not Ansel. He'd tolerate them on rare occasions, but then he'd be hungry for a steak the next night.

The cooler packed, she lugged it outside to his work van while Ansel carried George. They'd told Bain they were leaving and offered to make him a sandwich for lunch, but he was in a foul mood, so they'd left him to his own devices. He wasn't used to sitting around a house all day. What he'd do to occupy himself, they had no idea.

The wind had a bite when they trudged from the van to the Victorian. Snow was expected. Jazzi was hoping it would wait until after their Valentine dinner at The Oyster Bar, but they'd celebrated plenty of Valentine's Days in crappy weather.

The old house felt warm after being outside. As always, Jazzi scooted the cooler into a corner of the gutted kitchen, out of their way. The first thing they'd done was remove old cupboards, haul out dated appliances, and knock down walls. They'd installed heavy support beams to open up the entire ground floor. They were going to start hanging drywall today and finish the seams before moving upstairs and doing the same. Nothing in the house was worth saving except for the woodwork.

Jerod came when she and Ansel were nailing up the first sheet of drywall. "Sorry I'm late. I served Franny breakfast in bed and got the kids ready for preschool and drove them there before coming here."

"Nice." Jazzi was impressed.

Jerod looked pleased with himself. "Since Gran said the baby was coming tomorrow, I thought Fran had better enjoy her last peace and quiet while she could."

After pounding in his last nail, Ansel turned to him. "Are you still making her supper tonight?"

"Yup. The kids aren't filet fans, so I bought a bag of frozen chicken tenders to make them."

Jazzi laughed. "When the kid food stage ends, they're going to be more expensive to feed."

"Don't I know it?" He tossed his winter coat over the stair railing and came to pitch in. The entire back wall was done when Jazzi's cell phone rang.

Pulling it from her back pocket, she blinked. "It's Gaff."

The detective surprised her by saying, "I'm going to visit Donovan's parents. I asked them a few questions when I told them about their son's murder, but I'd like to talk to them again. Sorry, but they asked me to bring you with me."

"Me? I didn't know Donovan and I've never met his parents."

"But you were there when Donovan stopped by Radley's apartment, and you were the one who saw him stumble out into the second floor hallway after he'd been shot. *And* you know everyone else involved that day, *and* if I can solve this case, it would clear Bain. Besides, people seem to talk more when you're with me. You're able to make connections I can't."

If he thought she might help, and it would clear Bain so that he could leave and go back to the farm, why not go with him? "Sure. When are you leaving?"

Jerod and Ansel exchanged glances, and she knew they'd gauged what his call was about.

"What if I pick you up at four?

She covered the mouthpiece and asked, "Are we leaving here early tonight for Valentine's Day? Gaff wants to pick me up at four."

Jerod nodded. "We'll scoot out of here at three thirty. He can grab you from your place."

"I heard that," Gaff said. "Works for me."

So much for covering her phone. "I have to be home by five thirty. Ansel and I have dinner reservations at seven."

"We'll make this quick. I'm taking my Ann out for Valentine's Day, too."

"Good. See you then." She ended the call and shared Gaff's information with the guys.

Jerod glanced at the clock. "We have plenty of time to finish the side wall if we hustle."

"Then let's hit it." Ansel grabbed a piece of drywall, and they got busy again. By the time three thirty rolled around, the long side wall was done, and they called it a day. Jerod hustled to get to his van. It was cute how excited he was to cook for Franny.

On the drive home, Ansel warned, "Don't get so involved with Donovan's parents you don't give yourself time to change into something sexy for going out with me."

She grinned. "I'm ahead of you. I bought a new red dress for tonight."

"Red?" His blue eyes lit up. "You look good in red."

"I thought it worked to celebrate Valentine's Day. I bought new heels, too. No snow yet, so I can walk in them." She never wore the super high stilettos her sister Olivia sometimes did. She wasn't graceful enough. She always felt like she might topple over. Ansel was tall enough that she could wear four inch heels if she wanted to and still be shorter than him *if* he held her elbow every minute to steady her.

"Glad you don't need boots this year." The man had a thing about her legs. Last February had been so icy, she didn't take risks. And it had been so cold, she'd worn dress pants so she wouldn't freeze. Ansel would like this year better.

"Is the dress low cut?"

"Low enough."

He let out a happy sigh. "Life is good."

Maybe they could start out with a little touchy-feely before she left, but that idea was dashed when they approached their house and Gaff's car was already in their drive. She grimaced. "Gaff's early." Then she reconsidered. "Maybe that's a good thing. I should get home sooner."

Ansel must have been thinking along the touchy-feely lines, too, because he didn't look happy either. "Oh, well, I'll get to spend some time with Bain."

He didn't sound thrilled about that. She didn't blame him. Bain had been in a mood this morning. Hopefully, he'd settled down by now. She petted George and hopped out of the van. When she slid in beside Gaff, he waited for Ansel to pass him on his way to the garage before backing up to leave. "Thanks for going with me. I got the impression Donovan's parents wanted someone to buffer my asking them questions."

"I can't blame them. It has to be hard to talk about your son's death."

Gaff drove to the southeast side of River Bluffs to a small subdivision of long ranch style houses. Everything was well kept, the homes and the yards. They pulled into the drive to a white house with a white stone front and black shutters. Jazzi followed Gaff to the door.

A woman opened it before they rang the bell. She wiped her hands on her jeans. "I'm glad you got here so soon. The waiting makes me nervous." She motioned them into a living room with pale green plush carpet and formal furniture. It didn't look like anyone used it; it was so pristine.

"The kitchen and family room are a mess," she told them. "I just couldn't make myself clean them. I feel so empty right now."

Jazzi reached out to touch her hand. "We're so sorry for your loss."

The woman blinked back tears. She walked to a chair next to the recliner her husband was sitting in. "Thanks for coming with Detective Gaff. I'm Maureen and this is my husband Ray. I work as a school lunch lady and Ray drives a truck."

"I'm Jazzi Zanders." She took a seat next to Gaff on the sofa across from them.

Maureen had the same sandy colored hair and brown eyes as her son, but Donovan got his size from his dad, who looked to be five ten with a medium build. Ray didn't have the sweet expression Donovan had, though. His mouth and eyes had a sharpness that made him look like someone to steer clear of.

Narrowing his eyes, he looked Jazzi up and down. "You're a looker. Wish Donovan would have fallen for you instead of that piece of trash he lived with for a while. Glad she dumped him. Heard he'd found someone new, but he didn't bring her to see us."

Jazzi wasn't sure what to say. "I only recently met Donovan. He was the supervisor and trainer for my husband's brother. Radley thought the world of him."

Sneering, Ray was ready with another snarky comment. "Radley—yeah, we heard that name. Hung out with another guy Don worked with, a Thane, right?"

Disliking his tone, Jazzi stared and said nothing.

Gaff pulled out his notepad and pen before jumping into the conversation. "It would help me to know some background on Donovan. Who were his friends? Was there anyone he didn't get along with? Did he run into trouble somewhere—have a gambling problem or anything like that?"

Maureen's eyes went wide. "Donovan was a good boy. He never gave us trouble. His older brother went through a rocky streak before he moved to South Carolina. Got himself together, and now we never see him."

"Our Donovan was a real do-gooder, didn't approve of how much I drink. No wonder his first girl moved out on him." Ray's lips turned down. "She was a wild child, stayed with him until she got back on her feet, and then the minute her first boyfriend got out of prison, she went back to him."

Maureen dabbed at the edges of her eyes. "Donovan thought he could help her, thought she'd change. You know how that works."

Jazzi thought about her ex-fiancée, Chad. After they'd moved in together, he'd thought he could change her, too, talk her into staying home and raising babies. They broke up soon after that. Ansel was happy with her just the way she was. Of course, it was mutual. Who'd want to change Ansel?

The tap of Gaff's pen filled the silence as he thought. "How long were Donovan and this first girl together?"

"They didn't move in together right away," Maureen said. "But she kept giving him her sad stories, and finally, he took her in. That lasted about a year."

"How long since they broke up?"

Ray scratched his chin. "Maybe five months. He's been seeing the new girl the last two months. Donovan couldn't stop talking about how nice she was. We never met her, just heard about her. Heck, anyone would seem nice after Miss User."

"Got any names for me?" Gaff poised his pen over the page.

"Brianne Buckley was the first one," Maureen said. "Elspeth Smythe, with a y and an e, was the second."

"Did Donovan have any friends who got into trouble?"

Maureen shook her head. "He chose friends a lot better than girlfriends."

"Anything else you can think of that might help me?" Gaff asked.

They looked at each other and shrugged.

Pushing to his feet, Gaff motioned for Jazzi to join him. "Well, we'd better go now. And thanks for your time."

Maureen grabbed hold of Jazzi's hand as she walked past her. "We heard you're the one who called 911 to get help for our boy. Thank you. You tried."

Jazzi's throat tightened again. She could still see Donovan stumbling into the hallway, bleeding heavily. "I wish I could have done more."

Maureen's voice hitched, ending on a high note. "You tried. There wasn't anything anyone could do."

Gaff put his hand at the base of Jazzi's back and led her out of the house. "Thanks for coming with me. It helped them."

"Did we get anything that might help you?" She slid onto the passenger seat and Gaff shut her door for her, then walked to the driver's side.

"Maybe. Interesting that Donovan's ex had a boyfriend who went to prison."

She'd noticed that, too. As he pulled away and started back to the north side of the city, Jazzi asked, "Will you let us know what you find?"

"Be glad to. We might have a jump off point. Didi's ex-husband went to prison, too, didn't he? Maybe there's a connection. Now I start digging. I'll question anyone and everyone I can." He raised an eyebrow. "How's Ansel's brother holding up, stuck at your house?"

Jazzi rolled her eyes. "He's a peach. He can make you want to throttle him when he's at his best. The longer this goes, the worse he's going to be."

Grinning, Gaff said, "I'll try to hurry for your sake."

But investigations went at their own speed. She'd learned that the hard way. She put that thought behind her and decided to change the subject. "I hope you and Ann have a great dinner out."

"Thanks, I always enjoy time with my Ann." Gaff glanced at his watch. "And remind your Viking, I'm getting you home in plenty of time to look scrumptious for him. He isn't too happy with me when I mess up one of your date nights. And he can look intimidating."

Ansel's bark was worse than his bite, but when he crossed his arms over his chest and scowled down at someone, he *did* make an impression. "He doesn't even have to try, but he's usually easygoing."

"Yeah, and I'd like to keep him that way. So you two have a great night, too."

They made small talk the rest of the drive, and when she got out of the car and started to the house, Ansel threw open the door to tug her inside. Yup, her Norseman was tired of talking to his brother and was ready for a fun night out.

"Radley's coming to pick up Bain and take him out to eat," Ansel told her.

"That'll be good for both of them." Radley had just lost a good friend, and his brother was the number one suspect for killing him. They could commiserate with each other.

She and Ansel hurried to shower and dress up for their celebration. When she came down the stairs, Ansel was wearing black dress slacks and a red shirt. The red was almost a perfect match for her dress. She laughed. "Did you do that on purpose?"

"Sure did. I want the world to know we're a couple." His gaze slid over her. The dress's boatneck collar set off her long neck. It fit snugly until it passed her hips and flared in soft folds past her knees. "You look wonderful."

"So do you." They were both blond with blue eyes. Both dressed in red. Was that overkill? Who cared? She pulled on her black, wool coat and Ansel offered his arm to walk her to her pickup.

"I don't want to talk about anything serious tonight," he said on the drive into town. He flipped on music instead.

As always, the Oyster Bar was crammed full of people. A waitress led them to their reserved table, and they sipped wine while they waited on their food. Jazzi always ended up getting the same thing each time she came here—the almond-crusted walleye. Tonight, Ansel ordered the cioppino. Afterward, they shared a decadent slice of dark chocolate cake. When they paid and left a generous tip, they were both feeling spoiled and replete.

It didn't start snowing until they were leaving the restaurant. It didn't accumulate until after they got home. The Fates had given them decent weather for their celebration. They didn't stop there. While the world was blanketed in white, they closed the pets out of their room and enjoyed more time together. It was way past their bedtime before they invited George and the cats to sleep with them.

As she drifted into slumber, thoughts of Donovan and Didi flitted into her mind, but she pushed them away. She could worry about murder and ex-cons tomorrow.

Chapter 8

On Tuesday, Jazzi and Ansel got off to a rough start. Too little sleep made them sluggish. They finally loaded the cooler full of sandwiches and chips into the van, and Ansel carried George to the back seat so the pug could supervise their work for the day. On the drive to the Victorian in New Haven, they didn't talk much. They were both still a little groggy.

Road crews had cleared last night's snow, and hopefully, today's was only supposed to amount to a fine powder. Ansel cranked the heater higher to ward off the chill. The temperature had dipped during the night and more foreboding clouds hunkered over River Bluffs. "Are Gran and Samantha coming tonight to help you bake and make brittle?"

Gran had helped her make Easter bags for everyone in the family for years. "If the weather holds. Neither of them drives in bad weather anymore. Didi and River are coming, too."

"Are we feeding them supper?"

"Sort of." She wasn't much in the mood to make anything serious after how much she ate last night. "I bought a lot of pot stickers for people to nosh on."

"I like those. Will they be enough?" Ansel had a hefty appetite. He frowned, obviously anticipating near starvation with no formal supper. "Since Walker's bringing Didi and River, I'll grab him, and we'll run to buy some egg rolls and crab ragoon."

That meant Walker would be staying, too. She shrugged. "Whatever. You guys can't eat every cookie we make. I need enough to freeze for presents."

They turned onto the street toward the Victorian. "Give us a number. We'll count them out and make sure to leave yours alone."

She held in a sigh. This was getting complicated. Most years, Gran and Samantha came to help with a batch of cookies or two, and then she did the rest. She'd already made the dough for the chocolate crinkles and put it in the freezer. It was so sticky, it had to be cold before they could handle it. But even baking worried her. She hoped she didn't get distracted and burn something with so many people underfoot. She'd have to set every timer she had in the kitchen.

Ansel pulled into the driveway behind Jerod's pickup.

"Franny must still be biding her time." Jazzi grabbed the cooler to carry in while Ansel picked up George. The minute they walked through the back door, Jerod's anxious energy hit them.

Ansel put George on the dog bed he took to each work site and tossed his coat over the stair railing. "How did your supper go last night?"

Jerod leaned the piece of drywall he'd carried against the front wall. "Great. Franny loved it. She ate too many of the chocolates, though, and got heartburn. When I left this morning, the baby had dropped. Franny promised me she'd sit on the couch most of the day and take it easy. She's really uncomfortable now."

"Call us for D-Day," Ansel told him. Her hunk had started calling Franny's delivery day that.

Jazzi tossed her coat on the railing next to his and strapped on her tool belt. "And if you need anything, let us know."

"Thanks, I appreciate that." Jerod pushed the drywall into place and Jazzi grabbed her nail gun. The yakking stopped and the work began, but he kept pulling out his phone to check for calls.

Finally, Jazzi said. "If you've checked your cell once, you've checked it a hundred times. Why don't you just go home and stay with her? You're a nervous wreck."

"I wanted to. She wouldn't let me. She said I'd drive her nuts." Jerod ran a hand through his thick brown hair. Her cousin had beautiful blue eyes rimmed by long lashes. Jazzi hoped the baby inherited those.

"Smart woman. She sent you here to drive us nuts." Ansel laughed at him.

With a grunt, Jerod lifted another piece of drywall. He was almost as tall as Ansel but with a beefier build. "Let's get this done."

He threw himself into the job, and by the end of the day, the drywall was up. Tomorrow, they'd start taping the seams and mudding it. Hopefully, Jerod wouldn't join them. He'd be at the hospital, holding his new baby boy.

After a quick sweep, they pulled on their coats and headed to their vehicles. Jerod hopped behind the steering wheel of his truck and took off, in a hurry to get home. Ansel loaded George onto the backseat of the van and shook his head. "I sure hope Franny has that baby before we have to sedate your cousin."

"He got this nervous with the first two," Jazzi said, "and Gunther came late. I thought he was going to lose it."

On the drive home, a few snowflakes swirled past the van's windows, but once they hit the pavement, they melted. Good. All Jerod needed was bad roads when he had to drive Franny to the hospital. And she didn't like the idea of Samantha on slippery streets.

When she walked inside their stone cottage, the cats raced to her, winding around her ankles. She stooped to pet them before she opened a can of food to split between their dishes. Ansel carried in George, and footsteps sounded on the stairs. Bain came down to join them.

"I have to do something," he said. "I can't stand sitting around the house another day. Dad called and he's having trouble getting everything done on the farm, even with the neighbor kid coming to help out. I sit here and worry about the milking and feeding times. I need something to do. Can I help you on your fixer-upper? Tell me what to do, and I'll do it."

Ansel locked gazes with Jazzi. He wouldn't drag Bain along with them if she didn't like the idea. She didn't like it, but she understood how Bain must feel.

With a grimace, she nodded. "There are always plenty of small things that need to be done, but if Jerod's there, you have to take him in stride. He loves to poke fun. He won't stop just because you're Ansel's brother."

"I won't blow up. I'll keep my mouth shut, but I can't stand looking at these four walls anymore. I'm used to working from early morning until the last chore's done."

"Okay, we leave at seven thirty every morning. Be ready." Ansel gestured around the kitchen. "We're going to be invaded soon by people coming to help Jazzi bake and make candy. We're making pot stickers for supper. Are you up for that?"

Bain's expression looked pained. "How often do you guys entertain?"

"Lots more than you do. We like people. The women will be fussing out here, but you're welcome to join Walker and me in the living room."

Bain nodded. "I've met Walker. He's okay. I'll eat with you guys."

That settled, Ansel went up for a quick shower while Jazzi went to the cupboards and started putting out the ingredients they'd need for their group cooking tonight. Then she put a huge pot of water on the stove to boil. When everyone got here, all she'd have to do was pop the pot stickers in the pot while Ansel and Walker ran to get the rest of the meal. She'd taken the easy way out and bought the dipping sauce.

When Ansel returned, she hurried upstairs to shower and get ready. Walker got there first with Didi and River. He came in and immediately told them, "I drove Didi to her house this afternoon while River was in school. She wanted to pick up more stuff to keep at my place. While she was grabbing clothes, I bundled up her mail to take with us and a car slowed way down in front of her house, casing it. When the driver saw me, he sped away."

"Did you tell Gaff?" Jazzi asked.

Walker nodded. "Something's still going on over there. I don't want Didi staying there until we're sure it's safe."

River spotted the cats and bent to pet Marmalade. The orange cat purred, but when he reached for Inky, her ebony fur brat arched his back and hissed.

"He's a naughty one," Jazzi told the boy. "But if you pull a string for him, he'll chase it until you're too tired to play with him."

"Do you have a string?"

Jazzi took a long one out of the kitchen junk drawer. "We had them declawed, so he can't scratch you."

Flicking the string, River took off and the cats chased after him. Jazzi watched them for a while. She might have been wrong. Little boys had more energy than she did. The cats might wear out before River did.

Ansel, Walker, and Bain left to buy the egg rolls and crab ragoon before Gran and Samantha stepped into the house. After hanging her coat on the coat tree by the door, Gran went straight to the refrigerator to pour herself a glass of wine. Gran was spry for eighty years old, a little senile, but plenty savvy. Her shoulders stooped a little, and her blond hair had turned white. She pulled it into a loose bun. Her blue eyes sparkled with curiosity. When she was stressed, she always thought Jazzi was her dead sister, Sarah, and she slipped into the past, but other than that, she didn't miss much.

"I need inspiration while I cook," Gran told them. "How was Jerod today?"

Jazzi put a cheese ball and crackers on the kitchen island. It was safer not to drink on an empty stomach. "He was a mess. You know how he gets."

Gran smiled. "His Peter will come at three tomorrow. Then he'll be a happy man."

"Peter?" Samantha cocked her head at Gran.

"The new baby. Franny will take one look at his blond hair and blue eyes and think of *Peter and the Wolf.*"

Peter. Jazzi savored the name and decided she liked it.

Gran grimaced. "Jerod's going to call him Pete, though. Franny will have to get used to that."

Samantha laughed. The short, plump widow who'd moved in with Gran had become part of their family. "She loves that man. She won't mind."

Everyone got drinks and a few crackers before Jazzi heard Ansel's van pull back into the drive. She dropped the pot stickers in the boiling water. They didn't take long. Then she put out paper plates. She was keeping things easy tonight.

Once the food was loaded on the kitchen island, people grabbed plates and got started.

Gran studied Didi and asked, "Tell us about your Gil. He was a good man, wasn't he? Even if he wasn't much of a husband."

Didi's wavy black hair was pulled back in a hairband tonight. She pushed at a strand that had worked free and pinched her lips together. Finally, she said, "He was a good man. That's the part that was so sad, but he ran with a rough crowd. And he'd rather spend time with them than me. He kind of treated a younger guy in their group, Ronnie, as a kid brother. He did his best to keep him out of trouble, but Ronnie was attracted to it like a fish to a red worm."

"How much trouble?" Walker asked.

"He ended up going to prison for sneaking a gang into a warehouse he worked at. He helped them load refrigerators into a truck to sell somewhere."

Walker stared. "And he didn't think he'd get caught?"

Didi rolled her eyes. "I didn't say Ronnie was smart. He was as gullible as they came, and one of the guys talked him into it. I tried to tell Gil that watching over Ronnie was only going to get him in trouble, but he felt responsible somehow. He always chose them over me. Made me feel pretty undesirable."

Walker snorted. "You don't have to worry about that."

Didi blushed, but looked pleased. She took a deep breath, "Eventually Ronnie decided to help some friends rob a drug store. Gil went along to drive the getaway car and get Ronnie away from there as fast as possible. They all got caught."

"And then you divorced him?" Ansel asked.

"I was tired of playing second fiddle and I didn't ever see that changing, but it really bothered me when a cop showed up on my door and told me that Gil was murdered in prison. They suspected his cellmate, Gavin, but could never prove it."

An idea popped into Jazzi's head. "Is Gavin out of prison now?"

"I don't know. I lost track of all of them. I wanted them behind me."

Jazzi made a mental note to share what she'd just heard with Gaff tomorrow. Silence hung in the air for a minute until Jazzi rubbed her hands together. "Let's start cooking."

The women stayed in the kitchen and the men grabbed seconds of everything and disappeared into the living room.

They started with the cookies since those would take the longest to bake. Gran was a huge fan of chocolate crinkles. Jazzi took the dough out of the freezer for them to roll into balls and dip in powdered sugar. That guaranteed cookies to chomp on in half an hour or less. The recipe made five dozen, so she could let people eat the first batch or two.

While those were in the first set of ovens, they started making the dough for both the snickerdoodles and wedding cake cookies—her favorites with all of their chopped pecans. With the two wall ovens still available, she could bake a lot of cookies at the same time, and they could go a lot faster than in her old apartment.

The minute the first sheet of chocolate crinkles came out of the oven and cooled slightly, Gran snitched one and handed it off to River.

"Do you mind if he eats cookies this late at night?" Jazzi asked Didi.

"Who can say no to warm cookies?" Didi reached for one, too, and the men all came in to wipe out another sheet.

Jazzi raised an eyebrow at Gran when she put her hand behind her back to sneak River one of the snickerdoodles when that sheet came out of the oven. "Gran! He's going to get sick, and I need forty cookies to make up my gift trays."

She should have known. The minute the number left her lips, Ansel and Gran started counting to put forty of each in dishes to put aside. The remainder on the counter tops were fair game. The counting must have made Gran thirsty, because she went to the fridge to pour herself another glass of red wine and sneak River one of the wedding cake cookies. He wrinkled his nose at that one, not one of his favorites. Most kids that Jazzi had met, especially Jerod and Franny's, went for the super sweet goodies.

While the rest of them sorted cookies, Jazzi put three heavy pots on the stove burners to make three batches of brittle. "I usually make pecan, but I have cashews and peanuts, too, so we can make a pot of each."

She attached three candy thermometers to the pots and started instructing people on what to do as she went. After the ingredients were ready to reach 310 degrees on the thermometers, Didi said, "Did I tell you guys that I was having a security system installed at my house so I can return sometime?"

Walker's hand froze in midair as he reached for a cookie. "When?"

"Sometime next week, that's as soon as the company could work me in."

He frowned. "I still don't like it. If the guy breaks in while you're there, it could take fifteen minutes before anyone reaches you. A lot can happen in fifteen minutes. Why not just stay at my place until you know who's ransacking your house?"

River ran to stand beside Walker, nodding vehemently. Walker had made a true fan.

Didi bit her bottom lip. "Okay, I didn't think of that. You're right."

River turned to Walker and raised his hand for a high five.

Didi glanced at the candy thermometer and said, "Oops, it's up to temp."

They each dropped in one cup of cold butter and stirred until the temperature reached 290 degrees. Then they removed the pots from the heat to stir in the salt, baking soda, vanilla and nuts before quickly spreading the brittle onto greased, rimmed cookie sheets.

Didi's grin almost rivaled River's. "I just made candy, didn't I?"

Gran laughed. "Sure did, hon. And Walker's right. Don't go home. You don't want to be there when Gil's prison mate comes again."

Didi hugged her arms. "Gavin?"

Gran frowned, concentrating, then shrugged. "Can't tell. But he sure disliked your ex-husband. Not sure he likes most anybody, though. A lot of negative, nasty energy surrounds him."

Walker came over to wrap an arm around Didi's waist. "That's settled it then. You stay with me until this guy's behind bars again."

Chapter 9

Jazzi's cell phone rang at three a.m. She fought to rouse herself enough to reach for it.

Squinting at the caller ID, she told Ansel, "Jerod." She tried to sound awake. "Are you and Franny at the hospital this soon? Gran said the baby would come at three this afternoon."

"She called last night to say she got the message—a.m., not p.m. And Franny and the baby are perfect!" Jerod's voice boomed into her ear. "Ten fingers and ten toes. Lots of blond hair and blue eyes. Franny saw him and thought of *Peter and the Wolf.* We named him Pete."

She huffed out a breath. "We? I don't think so. Franny named him Peter, but you'll never call him that."

Jerod laughed. "You gotta come see him. Don't let Ansel hold him, though, or he'll want one of his own."

She glanced at her Norseman. He was already sitting on the edge of the bed, scratching his head—naked from the waist up, ready to get dressed and go. She'd never get tired of the sight. Jerod might be right, though. Ansel wanted kids sooner rather than later. She preferred to wait. They'd had that discussion. He'd agreed to give her a few years.

"Viking boy's getting dressed now. We'll be there soon."

"Hurry. Mom and Dad are already on their way. You know my mom. If Ansel wants a turn with him, he'll have to beat her to it. Franny's parents are coming, too."

Their family was like that. People showed up for every big event. And there was no bigger draw than a wedding or a baby.

Franny had birthed at the hospital on the southwest side of the city, so it took them a while to get there. And true to Jerod's words, his mom was already cradling Peter in her arms. She tore her gaze away from the baby when they entered the room and smiled. "Jerod said I have to share. Would you like to hold him?"

Ansel shot out his arms and snuggled the baby close. A lump caught in Jazzi's throat as she watched her blond giant cuddle little Peter. His whole expression turned mushy, totally enthralled by the infant. What would he be like if he were holding his own son? He crooned to the baby in a soft voice. "I'm your Uncle Ansel, and we're going to have lots of good times together."

Finally, Jerod cleared his throat, saying, "Jazzi might want to hold him, too."

Did she? She'd oohed and aahed over Gunther and Lizzie when they were born, but she'd been single. A baby of her own didn't tempt her. Ansel lowered Peter into her arms, and a warm, deep yearning flooded her body. No, no, no. This wasn't the right time. She didn't want to rush into parenthood. But when Franny's parents showed up with Gunther and Lizzie, she had a hard time passing the baby to Franny's mother.

Gunther tugged on her arm. "I'm a big brother now. I'm going to help Mom take care of our baby."

Jazzi smiled at the word *our*. Jerod sure had neat kids. Thane and Olivia trickled into the room next, and Thane couldn't wait to take his turn with Peter. When he offered him to Olivia, she raised an eyebrow and said, "I'll pass. Let Eleanore hold him again."

Jerod's mom didn't need a second invitation. She cuddled the baby close.

They stayed another half hour before Franny started looking tired, and then they took their leave. "Cute baby," Ansel said, driving home.

"Blond hair. Where did that come from?" She, Mom, and Olivia were all blondes, but she couldn't think of anyone on Jerod's side of the family with that coloring.

"Has to be Franny's side," Ansel said. "We haven't met them all, have we? He got married before I started working with you."

"I know Franny has three sisters, but I don't remember much about them." Had any of them had freckles and carrot orange hair like Franny? She didn't have a clue.

At home, they crawled back in bed until the alarm went off at six thirty. They dragged through their morning routine, but by the time Bain stalked into the kitchen, they were ready to go.

He was dressed, too. "I'll do my best to help out. I'm no contractor, but I can help with any lifting or pounding. I'm going crazy hanging around here, doing nothing."

Ansel glanced at Jazzi. "You still okay with that?"

She nodded. "We'll be short Jerod today. We can use an extra hand."

That made it just Ansel, Jazzi, and Bain at the old Victorian today, with George supervising from his dog bed in the corner. Ansel showed Bain how to tape the drywall seams and they all got to work.

"Did you hear us leave the house this morning?" Ansel asked his brother. "Jerod's wife had her baby, a little boy."

Bain grunted a reply. Clearly, babies didn't excite him. "Jerod had better learn how to use birth control. He makes good money, but he's not rich, and kids are expensive."

Ansel's blond brows pulled together as he studied him. "You're thirty-four, nine years older than I am. Do you ever plan on getting married and having kids?"

"What for? I hardly have any free time, as is."

Ansel just looked at him and shook his head. Bain worked on taping the long, side wall while she and Ansel started on the next one. When Ansel's cell phone buzzed, he frowned at the ID. "Didi."

Jazzi didn't make any bones about listening to his side of the conversation, especially since it worried her. "You went there alone?" And then, "No, don't call Walker if he's out of town. I'll send Jazzi to meet you."

When he shut off his phone, he pressed his lips together in a tight line. "Walker's in Columbia City, making estimates on a new cement job for spring. Didi decided to go to her house after she dropped River at school, and she found it trashed. The guy's long gone, so she's not worried about him coming back, but she's pretty shaken up. She wants to sort through a few things but doesn't want to stay there alone."

Jazzi nodded. "I'm on my way. Do you think I should call Gaff and see if he can meet us there?"

"It wouldn't hurt. Somebody's looking for something, and it didn't sound like he'd found it."

Jazzi grabbed her coat and started for the door. "I'm taking the van, so you guys are stuck here until I get back. I'll make sure I'm here by five."

Ansel shrugged broad shoulders. "Don't worry about it. We have plenty to keep us busy if you're a little late."

Bain shook his head. "I don't get you two. You don't have to go out of your way for Didi. If I understand it right, you're not even River's dad and you never met this woman until your one-night-stand partner died. It was one night, Ansel, and she came on to you instead of the other way around. You don't owe the dead woman anything either."

Ansel stared at him, clearly annoyed. "I know I don't owe either of the women anything, but that doesn't mean Didi doesn't need help. And I can still care about what happens to her."

Bain sniffed. "You've turned into a bleeding heart, that's what. You've got it too easy up here, so you think you can be Mr. Do Good."

"No." Ansel glared. "That happened when I went home to help you and Dad on the farm when you got yourselves in a bind. I didn't owe either of you anything either."

Bain's face turned mottled red, but he tamped down his temper. "Let's get back to work."

Jazzi grimaced. Another unpleasant exchange. Did Bain think of anyone besides his dad, himself, and the farm? She wondered if Bain ever missed Radley's company, or if he only missed the work he'd done. She stood on tiptoe to kiss Ansel's cheek as she went out the door. She was proud of her man. On the drive to Didi's house, she called Gaff and explained what had happened.

"I'll get there as soon as I can. I suppose Didi has already touched everything that was disturbed, but I'll send a fingerprint person anyway."

"Okay, see you later." When she parked at the curb and walked to Didi's narrow two-story, it took a minute before Didi unlocked the screen door.

"Sorry, I was hiding in the kitchen in case whoever did this came back and I had to make a break for it. This spooked me out." She wore old jeans and a flannel shirt today. Her black hair was scraped back in a knot. "Look at it. It's a mess."

The front door was kicked in and the house ransacked. The couch and chairs were slashed, every drawer spilled, and the kitchen cupboards open with their contents scattered across the floor. Some floorboards were even pried up.

Jazzi stared. "What do you think he was looking for?"

Didi sagged onto a wooden rocking chair and shook her head. "My house doesn't exactly scream money. Does this look like some place valuables would be hidden?"

"Sorry, but no. It does make me think of Donovan's apartment, though. His place was trashed like this, too."

Looking around, dazed, Didi said, "I don't see any way that Donovan or I would be connected."

Neither did she, but it was too much of a coincidence. "Can I help you with anything while we wait for Gaff?"

"I was going to gather up the rest of River's and my cold weather clothes, and I meant to take all of the groceries in the freezer and veggie drawer to Walker's place. I didn't want them to go to waste." She let out a long breath. The refrigerator doors hung open. "I suppose everything's ruined by now."

"I'm sorry. Want me to help you throw them away? Then we can bag up your clothes."

They were filling the trash can in the kitchen with defrosted chicken breasts and wilted lettuce when Gaff walked in. He glanced around the house and grimaced.

"Someone sure was thorough. Did Gil leave anything here when you two got your divorce?"

"No, and if he would have, he'd have come for it. We had a friendly separation. I didn't want anything from him, and he didn't ask me for anything either."

Jazzi motionied toward the loose floorboards, saying, "Do you think it's just a fluke that two places have been broken into and searched, or are they connected somehow?"

"Let's find out." He asked Didi to make a list of Gil's old friends, especially the ones who went to prison with him.

She sat at her empty work desk and wrote down names. When she handed them to Gaff, he skimmed them. "I'll look these guys up to see where they are and what they're doing now. If they're in town, I'll stop in to visit them. I'll let you know what I find out."

A knock sounded at the door, and Ben, one of the crime scene techs, came to join Gaff. He nodded when he saw Jazzi and shook his head. "You're involved in another one?"

"Unfair. Ansel and I know Didi, that's all."

He grinned. "Well, you know better than to touch a lot of stuff, so maybe I'll get lucky with fingerprints."

She sure hoped so. And if someone who'd served time in prison with Gil did this, she was sure his fingerprints would be in the system.

"Mind if I bag up the rest of my winter clothes to take to Walker's house?" Didi asked.

Gaff looked surprised. "You're still staying there?"

"He hasn't kicked me out yet, and he doesn't want me to come back here until whoever's breaking in is caught."

Gaff nodded. "Can't blame him for that. He's a good guy. Get your clothes, and we'll get busy. I'll let you know if anything turns up."

Jazzi went with her to help, and then they both parted at their vehicles. Didi drove back to Walker's place, and Jazzi returned to Ansel and Bain at the Victorian.

Chapter 10

When Jazzi walked into their fixer-upper, she blinked, surprised. Ansel and Bain had taped every seam and were working on mudding them. George wagged his tail when she went to toss her coat on the stair railing, so she bent to pet him.

"We've got this," Ansel told her. "Bain and I are a good team. What if we take a coffee break, you tell us about Didi, and then you can rip off woodwork in the bedrooms upstairs while we work down here?"

"Sounds like a plan." She went to the kitchen and poured three mugs of coffee while the guys washed up in the bathroom upstairs. Everything on the ground floor was gutted—no sink.

They sat in folding chairs around the card table they'd brought, and she passed out sandwiches.

"How's Didi?" Ansel asked.

Jazzi explained about the utter wreckage at her house and Gaff's idea to question all of Gil's old friends.

Ansel drained his coffee cup and went for a refill. The house was warm enough while they were working, but drafty when you sat down to take a break. Hot coffee hit the spot. "If this is the same guy who shot Donovan, he doesn't mind killing to get what he wants. I'm glad Didi's staying at Walker's."

"River, too." Jazzi would snatch the boy and hide him at her place rather than have him put at risk. "I've never seen Gran latch onto a kid so fast. Makes me wonder if she's met Peter yet."

Ansel grinned. "I think Gran likes kids better once they can walk and talk. She has a thing for the naughty ones. She'll like our kid when we have one."

Jazzi's jaw dropped. "You're assuming our kid will be naughty."

"If he takes after his mother . . . " He let that hang.

"I was NOT . . . " She couldn't in good conscience finish that sentence, and his grin widened.

Bain shook his head. "Kids today have too much free time. Put them to work early and they learn some discipline."

She bit her bottom lip. Better not to say what she was thinking. Kids, to his dad, meant free labor with few benefits. Heaven forbid he should offer them hugs or praise.

Bain scowled at her. "What? No comment?"

She met his gaze. "Do you want one?"

He might be an idiot, but he wasn't stupid. "Maybe not." He drained his coffee cup and rested both elbows on the table, suddenly serious. "If Detective Gaff thinks maybe one of the men who went to prison with Didi's husband is behind the break-ins, does that mean he thinks I'm in the clear? That maybe I can go home?"

"I doubt it." She finished her coffee, too. "He's still in the beginning stages of his investigation, making lists and checking them twice."

Bain grunted. "I don't need clever answers."

"She's right," Ansel said. "It's too soon for you to get crossed off the list, but Gaff's making progress. There's no use getting antsy. Let's get back to work."

The guys went back to mudding, and she went upstairs to yank trim off every wall. With the help of her crowbar, she'd finished by the time the guys called it quits and closed everything up to go home. The ride across town was quiet. Bain's brooding put a damper on any small talk. They'd just walked in the kitchen door and Ansel had lowered George into his dog bed when his cell phone buzzed. Jazzi fed the pets while Ansel took the call. Bain trudged upstairs to his room.

"I'm going to take a shower and watch a little TV on your laptop," he called to them.

Fine with her. The less of Bain, the better. When Ansel finished his conversation and hung up, he turned to her. "Walker asked if we could stop by his place tonight. He offered to buy pizzas. I said we'd be there."

She loved pizza, and she had a soft spot for Walker. "Is he okay?"

"He's worried about Didi. Wants to brainstorm a little."

"Not a bad idea. I don't have any leftovers for Bain to heat up, though." Inky threaded in and out between her ankles, and she stooped to pick up the cat and snuggle him. He was a brat, but he loved attention. She glanced at the bouquet of flowers she kept in the crockpot by the kitchen sink.

He'd bitten off three more heads. When he got bored by himself during the day, he did things to purposely annoy her.

Ansel followed her gaze and raised a blond eyebrow at her black cat. "You know we could lock you in the basement while we're gone."

Inky narrowed yellow eyes at him, and Ansel laughed. "He's incorrigible."

Marmalade came to Ansel to be picked up. Ansel scooped him into his arms, stroking his orange fur while he walked to the corkboard on the wall to glance at the list of restaurants they called when they wanted delivery. "We'll order something in for Bain."

"Whatever he picks is fine with me." And it was, even though Ansel's brother hadn't paid for one thing since he moved in with them. Cheap, cheap, cheap! But she wasn't doing this for Bain. She was doing it for Ansel, so she kept her opinions to herself.

Ansel huffed. "He's not picking. I am. He'll eat whatever shows up on the doorstep." He decided to play it safe and order pizza. "I know he eats that. He almost died when we had Chinese, too exotic, so we'll stick to something simple."

After he'd placed the order and put money on the kitchen island to pay for it, they went upstairs to shower and change before they drove to Walker's house. This time of night, traffic was heavier than usual and it took them longer to get there. It had snowed a little during the day, and the roads were a little slippery, so everyone drove with caution. Gaff called Jazzi on the way.

"Mind if I drop in to talk to you tonight? I thought you might want to keep in the loop of what's going on. If you hadn't called me about Didi's place, I wouldn't have followed this lead."

"Thanks. We'd really appreciate it. We're almost to Walker's house right now. Want to meet us there? He has pizzas coming."

"Even better. Didi will be there, too. I'll see you in a bit." She could hear the smile in his voice. "I can only nab one slice, though. My Ann's got bean soup waiting for me at home—one of my favorites."

"Ansel's too. See you soon." Ansel especially liked beans in white chicken chili. She'd have to remember to make a pot for him. That and potato soup with big chunks of ham. She decided to cook both of those on Saturday to have on hand.

When they pulled into Walker's drive and started toward the door, River flew out of the house to greet them.

"Did you bring any cookies?"

She bit her lip. "I sent extras with your mom last night." Then she got flustered. "Not your mom. Sorry, I meant Didi."

River laughed. "I call her Mom. She doesn't care." His face fell. "No cookies?"

"Sorry, I put the rest in the freezer for Easter." Ansel had grumbled about that, too. He hadn't gotten as many as usual to snack on. Next week, they'd make oatmeal raisin and sugar cookies and peanut butter fudge. She'd make double batches of cookies this time. Oatmeal raisins were his favorite.

River sighed and linked his arm through hers. "That's okay. Are you making chocolate chip cookies next week? I think you should make more of those so there's lots of leftovers."

Ansel's other favorite. "Maybe we'll make those instead of the sugar cookies, a double batch."

"Yes!" With a skip in his step, he led them into the kitchen.

Walker had completely remodeled his house. They'd spent a weekend helping him, along with Jerod and Thane. Now, a soft gray sofa and two chairs circled a coffee table in the living room and a huge deep blue sectional could be seen in the lower level TV room. In the kitchen, new white kitchen cabinets gleamed with black granite countertops. A heavy round oak table was surrounded by six chairs.

Didi opened a bottle of wine and poured a glass for Jazzi while Walker handed Ansel a beer. She smiled. "Thanks for coming."

Jazzi explained that Gaff would arrive soon, too.

"Good." Walker sounded relieved. "Maybe we can figure out what the heck's going on."

The pizzas arrived before Gaff did, and they waited another five minutes before he got there. Then they opened the boxes and dug in.

Gaff didn't waste time since his Ann was at home waiting supper for him. "I checked on every name you gave me, Didi, and every one of the men Gil went to prison with is out on the streets again, including his cellmate."

Didi blinked. "That means no one's ever going to get blamed for killing him, doesn't it?"

"I'm afraid so. No one ever talked, and there was no way to prove who did it."

She looked upset, and Walker reached to place a hand on her shoulder.

Gaff went on. "Not only are they out, but three of them are back in River Bluffs. I went to see them, and I'd guess they'll be back behind bars soon. Not a repentant body in the lot of them."

Walker's grip on Didi tightened. "Did you get a feel for who might be behind the break-ins?"

"They're all as shoddy as the next one. Gavin, the cellmate, came back here to take up with his wife again. She visited him every week in prison, bringing him cigarettes and news about their two kids. He works with his dad on a roofing and painting crew, so he always has a job to come home to."

"Why didn't he get along with Gil?" Walker asked.

"Now that's interesting." Gaff finished his pizza and grabbed for a napkin. "Gavin hated Gil for the same reason Jarrett did. Ronnie—the kid Gil protected, even in the joint—kept stirring up trouble. He'd have been pounded to mincemeat if it hadn't been for Gil. No one really wanted to tangle with your ex. He was too smart and was known for biding his time to set things right."

Didi pressed her lips together in an unhappy line. "Ronnie would throw his grandmother under the bus to save his own skin. Gil was wasting his time trying to help him."

"Talking about grandmothers…" Gaff looked at Jazzi. "Ronnie's living with his grandma. I'd like to visit her tomorrow, but Ronnie asked me to bring you along to make her more comfortable. He said she gets nervous around cops."

Who didn't?

When she didn't give a quick answer, Gaff said, "The kid talked to Donovan's dad, Ray, and Ray said his wife was a lot more at ease having you with me, so Ronnie wanted that, too."

Jazzi frowned. "Ronnie knows Ray? That's a stretch, isn't it?"

"They worked together at a warehouse when Ronnie turned eighteen. Ray still works there, but Ronnie got fired and visited prison for the first time when he helped himself to a few refrigerators to sell on the black market."

"What about this Jarrett?" Ansel asked.

"Works at a garage as a mechanic. He's been in and out of prison for breaking and entering and robberies. That's all I know about him so far. Not an easy guy to talk to." He glanced at his watch. "I'd better get going. What do you say, Jazzi? Can I pick you up at ten tomorrow morning?"

"Sure. Why not?"

Walker looked dazed. When Gaff left, he shook his head. "I was hoping Gaff would find someone to investigate. I didn't expect *three*. Heck, there might even be more."

"At least he has someone who's suspicious besides my brother." Ansel folded his empty paper plate to toss in the trash. He looked at his watch. "We have an early morning tomorrow. Thanks for the supper, but we'd better get going, too."

"Thanks for meeting Gaff here." Walker reached for Didi and River's plates to throw away with his own. "It's no fun being in the dark, wondering what's going on. Will you share what you learn when you visit Ronnie's grandmother tomorrow?"

Jazzi heard the stress in his voice. "Will do. And I'm glad Didi and River are staying here with you. I think this is the roughest crowd we've ever met."

"Prison cronies." Ansel nodded and held out her coat for her. As he slid into his, he locked gazes with Didi. "Stay safe. If you need anything else in your house, wait until one of us can go with you."

She looked near tears.

"You going to be okay?" Jazzi asked.

She nodded. "It's just that it was Ronnie again. It was *always* Ronnie. He's probably the reason Gil got killed."

On the drive home, Jazzi twirled her ring around and around on her finger. Ansel reached over and took her hand. "I wish I could have put a big diamond in that setting. Your ring isn't much to brag about."

She held it up and smiled. "It's exactly what I wanted, and it matches yours. We're in the wrong line of work for anything clunky."

He snickered. "Most women wouldn't consider a diamond clunky."

"Then they're not banging it on gutters like I do. This ring's a lot safer."

When they got home, the cats rushed to greet them and even George sauntered over to beg for a snack.

Ansel hung up his coat and bent to scratch the pug behind his ears. "You're out of luck, bud. But I'm hitting the couch soon. You can watch TV with me."

Jazzi glanced at the kitchen island. An empty pizza box sat on top of it. Bain could at least have thrown it in the trash. Ansel followed her scowl and said, "I'll get it. He's my brother."

She let him while she hung up her coat, too, and slid out of her shoes and into her house slippers. They were settling on the sofas, across from each other, when Bain came down to join them.

"Did you get enough to eat?" Ansel asked.

He nodded. "I called Dad after supper, but he was working in the barn. He's having to keep late hours since I'm not there. I talked to Mom instead. She's wearing out faster lately. I'm starting to worry about her. We can't afford to hire a cook or cleaner."

Jazzi reached for the throw blanket on the back of her sofa so that Bain couldn't see her face. He always had to ruin everything by making it all about money and the farm.

Ansel sat up to talk to him. "You should take Mom to the doctor. It might be something that's easy to fix. Maybe she's anemic or needs B12 shots. It could be a lot of things."

"Dad won't do it. He's afraid it will be something expensive, and our insurance won't cover it."

"Then do it yourself," Ansel said.

"Mom won't go if it makes Dad mad." Bain sat down on the other end of the couch. "Dad doesn't love any of us, does he? Not even Mom."

Ansel blinked, caught off guard. "I thought he loved you. You were always his favorite."

"No, he just always expected a lot out of me. Always has. And I tried not to disappoint him. That, and I love the farm as much as he does."

Bain's comments surprised Jazzi. "Did he love your mom when he married her?"

Ansel shook his head. "Not like I love you. You're at the top of everything that matters to me. For Dad, the dairy farm came above all of us. Always. And lately, it's like he's written Mom off. The less she can do, the less he thinks about her."

Bain nodded. "He wants her there, but more like a backdrop, an old habit. And she cooks meals. Not the best meals, but there's always food on the table. If I ever get married, I want more than that. I want what Adda and Henry have, what you two have."

Ansel looked at his brother as if he didn't know him. "I didn't think you even considered getting married. I didn't think the thought crossed your mind."

Bain grimaced. "What do I have to offer a woman? I'm not good-looking like you or Radley. I don't have an ounce of charm, not much money, and most of the time, I'm downright grumpy. I worry about the farm all the time."

Ansel stared at him. "Have you ever thought it's not worth it?"

"Never. If I could, I'd put more time and money into the place. There are lots of things I'd like to do, but Dad keeps dragging his feet. I'd like to start beehives near our fields and make honey. I'd like to add orchards on the side of the pasture close to the house and farm the fields on the other side ourselves. That way, we'd have more ways to make money than just milk, so that when the milk prices drop, we have other things to fall back on."

Ansel's blue eyes lit up, and the men started talking farming. The more Jazzi listened to Bain, the more she thought he might have possibilities after all. Bain finished with, "that's why I was hoping Radley would come home. If Dad would let us, we could do a lot more than we're doing now."

There. He'd done it again. Ruined it.

Ansel shook his head. "He's not going back with you. He's not into farming like you are. Maybe you should partner up with someone else."

Bain let out a frustrated breath. "If I ever get to go home. Gaff can't keep me here forever, can he?"

Ansel shrugged, "I don't know if there's a time limit."

Bain rubbed his hands over his face and stood. "Well, I'll go with you guys to work again tomorrow. I might as well do something. Anything's better than sitting around all day."

"Jerod's coming in tomorrow, too," Jazzi told him.

Bain snorted. "Babies don't let you get much sleep. He'll be too tired to hassle me much."

"You don't know my cousin." She watched him climb the steps to the guestroom, and she and Ansel stretched out on their sofas again. They needed to relax before calling it a day. The sooner Gaff found Donovan's killer, the sooner Bain could go home and the sooner Didi would be safe. And she and Ansel could finally have their house to themselves again.

Chapter 11

Jazzi packed more chips and sandwiches than usual on Thursday morning. She and Bain carried the coolers to the van while Ansel carried George. With the three men and her sanding walls together, they should be able to finish them. If they got all the dust and dirt cleaned up before they left, they could prime them tomorrow.

She was going out with her sister, Olivia, tonight—their weekly girls' night out. Radley, Thane, Ansel, and Bain had plans to meet at the Tower Bar and Grill on State Street. Walker usually joined them wherever they went, but he'd decided to stick close to Didi and River right now.

Jerod's pickup wasn't in the driveway when they reached the fixer-upper. Babies threw off the best routines. The three of them turned on the coffee pot and got busy. Jazzi wore a baseball cap to keep most of the dust out of her hair. She didn't want to run out to Gaff's car looking like she was wearing a powdered wig. Ansel didn't bother to wear a hat, but when he ran his hand through his white blond hair, a cloud of fine white powder surrounded him.

When Jerod showed up an hour later, they all stopped for a coffee break. Her cousin had dark circles under his eyes.

"Pete wakes up every three hours and takes an hour to suck down his bottle. Doesn't leave much room for sleep."

Jazzi made a mental note. If and when she had a baby, bottles were the way to go, then Ansel could get up for feedings, too.

Ansel frowned. "I thought Franny was going to nurse."

"She is," Jerod said, "but she makes enough milk that we bottle some, so I can give her a break when she's dragging."

Jazzi studied him. He looked like he could win a walking dead contest. Her cousin was a good man, determined to do his fair share with the baby. "Gaff's coming for me at ten," she told him. "He's found three more suspects to interview, maybe four if he counts Donovan's ex-girlfriend."

Ansel filled Jerod in.

Jerod grinned at Bain. "Looks like you're moving farther down the list. That's a good thing, right?"

"I hope I get crossed off soon and can go home."

"And leave all this fun? Who else shows you a good time renovating like we do?"

Bain studied the house. "I like this place. It has character."

"You should drive back to see it when it's done," Jerod told him. "It's going to be a beauty."

"Not gonna happen." Bain drained his cup. "Spring and summer are extra busy on the farm. I won't be able to get away."

The way he said it made Jazzi think he'd consider returning to look at the house if he could. They finished their coffee and got busy again. By the time Gaff knocked on the door, one wall was smooth.

Jazzi usually heard the detective pull in, but she'd missed it with all the sanding noise. She took off her baseball cap and slapped it against her jeans. Dust went everywhere. She brushed herself off, then got her heavy coat and went out to meet him.

Once they were heading into town, Gaff said, "With the walls knocked out in your fixer-upper, it looks a lot bigger. You guys take rundown houses and make them into something special."

She smiled. "Thanks. That's the plan." The more Gaff saw their remodeling, the more interested he got in it.

"What are you going to paint the exterior?"

"My friend Reuben's going to help us pick out colors. He's a designer and has a special love for Victorians."

"He's the guy who bought the house in West Central where you used to rent, right?"

"I only had the bottom floor. He rented the top."

"And now the house is lavender. Are you sure you want him to help pick colors?"

She laughed. "I think the lavender's pretty, but Ansel won't go for anything too out there. Neither will Jerod."

"Good." Gaff turned onto Creighton Avenue and headed to the section of town people read about in the paper every Monday morning—lots of gunshots and dead bodies each weekend.

Jazzi frowned. "Ronnie's grandma lives over here?"

"Her place is a few blocks from Pontiac. Ronnie claims it's pretty quiet."

"I hope so."

Gaff pulled in front of a cement block two story. The gray rippled blocks had never been painted. They looked strong and solid. The screened porch door was open, so they entered the airy room to knock on the front door. A small withered woman with crinkly gray hair opened it and motioned them inside. She was so bent and tiny, Jazzi wanted to slide an arm under her to support her, but the woman cracked a smile and moved spryly to a velveteen sofa. She nodded for them to take the two chairs across from it.

"You're here about my Ronnie." Bright dark eyes studied them.

Gaff looked around the room. "He said that he'd meet us here while we talked to you."

"Boy got in late last night. Got home from washin' dishes about one in the mornin', then stayed up playing on that game box of his half the night."

Gaff gestured to Jazzi. "This is Jazzi. Ronnie asked if she'd be here when we visited you."

"A nice lookin' girl. Nice o' you to come. S'pose you want to know about my grandson."

When Gaff took out his notepad and pen, she said, "His mama left the boy with me when he was just a baby. Took off with some guy. I've raised him ever since. He was a good boy, never got in trouble, till he fell in with the wrong crowd in high school. Ain't been nothin' but trouble ever since."

"Are those the men he went to prison with?" Gaff asked.

"This last time. Been a few short trips before that." She shook her head. "Not sure what his mama took when he was inside her, but he didn't come out smart enough to get a good job. Not attractive enough to catch a good girl either. He swears this time he learned his lesson, though. Swore he wouldn't cross the law again. Says if he has to wash dishes for the rest o' his life, at least he'll be in this house with me and get plenty o' love."

Gaff raised an eyebrow. "Do you believe him?"

She cocked her head to one side and pursed her lips. "He means it for now. He'll get the house when I'm gone. At least he'll have a roof over his head if he wants one."

"I need to talk to him," Gaff said. "Mind if I go upstairs and wake him up?"

"I'll get him. He's a might grouchy at first. No need for you to see him like that." She grabbed the stair railing to make her way to the second floor. A short while later, she returned with a man in his early thirties, a couple of inches taller than Jazzi, with lank, drab brown hair, colorless eyes, and a flat face. He had a weak chin.

Gaff poised his pen above his notepad. "I came to ask you who helped you rob the drugstore that sent you to prison."

Ronnie sagged onto the other side of the sofa and leveled a look at Gaff. "You already looked it up, but I'll tell ya anyway. Gil drove the getaway car. Me, Jarrett, and Boscoe went inside. Boscoe kept gettin' in fights in prison, or he'd have got out with Jarrett and me. Gil got knifed. I don't ever wanna go back to the big house again."

A car backfired outside and Ronnie jumped. So did Jazzi and Gaff.

Grandma frowned. "Did something happen?"

"It's fine, Granny." He shook his head at them. "Going deaf. Can't see too well either. Glad I came back to keep an eye on her."

Gaff asked him about other robberies he committed.

"Small time stuff. In and outta old peoples' windows. Stole a car once for a joyride. Nothin' big."

"What made you decide to try something bigger?" Gaff asked.

"Jarrett thought we was ready. We was, too, but we both think someone snitched on us. Jarrett's pretty sure he knows who."

"Care to share?"

Ronnie shrugged. "I ain't got a clue. Not sure Jarrett's right either."

Gaff looked up from his notes. "You must have some idea who killed Gil."

His grandma put her hand to her throat. "Gil's dead?"

Ronnie pressed his lips together. "He died in prison, Granny."

She shook her head. "That poor boy, he was always nice to you."

"Sure was. He and this big guy got into it in the workroom when they were on laundry duty. The guy told Gil that I wasn't pullin' my weight, that maybe I needed a little extra motivation, but Gil said no one touched me, or they'd regret it."

"So he stuck up for you," Gaff said.

Ronnie nodded. "Gil always had my back. When we went out in the prison yard, though, the guy bumped into Gil on purpose to get stuff started. Big mistake. Gil knows how to box. Smart people left him alone."

That's what Didi had said, too. "What happened?" Jazzi asked.

"Everyone crowded around, tryin' to get a better view. No one saw who did it. There was too much pushin' and pullin'. Couldn't be sure it was Gavin since Gil got shanked in the side."

Gaff studied him. Maybe Gaff didn't believe him any more than she did. Ronnie had had a front row seat, a clear view of Gavin and Gil. He must have seen something. "Did you get picked on once Gil was dead?"

Ronnie shook his head. "Jarrett went to prison with us, and he let everyone know he was takin' Gil's place. Jarrett's one big, mean gorilla of a man. People left me alone."

Gaff leveled a stare at Ronnie. "Where were you last Saturday during the day?"

"The day Donovan was killed?" Ronnie put a hand on his grandma's knee. "Workin' on my car in the garage. Ask Granny. She brought lunch out to me. My spark plugs needed changed."

"Is that right, Mrs. Reynolds?" Gaff asked.

Ronnie's grandma glanced at Jazzi, looking confused. "Last Saturday? I recollect that's right."

She didn't sound sure. Jazzi smiled at her. "Did you go to church the next day?" Maybe that would help her put the days in the right order.

"Mighta. Can't quite remember."

Gaff turned his attention back to Ronnie. "Do you and Jarrett get together now that you're both out?"

"Nuh-uh. I don't want nothin' to do with the old ways. I just wanna work and keep my head down."

Gaff stood and held out a hand to help Jazzi to her feet. "Thanks for talking to us. If I think of any other questions, I'll give you a call."

Ronnie shrugged, then patted his grandma's shoulder. "I'm goin' back to bed. I'll get up in time for supper."

She smiled and watched him climb the steps, then stood to lead Gaff and Jazzi to the door. "It was nice seein' you, folks. You come again, ya hear?"

On the walk to his car, Gaff shook his head. "A nice woman, but age is getting the better of her. I hope Ronnie stays clean to help her out when she needs it."

Jazzi wondered how much help Ronnie would actually be. She wouldn't want to have to count on him in a pinch. She even wondered if he knew who killed Gil but knew his options were better if he kept that information to himself. He seemed the type who would always put himself first.

Chapter 12

Gaff drove Jazzi back to New Haven. When she pushed inside the Victorian's kitchen door, Jerod, Ansel, and Bain were still sanding. She went to the staircase and tossed her coat over the railings, then donned her white work mask. Dust clogged the air.

"Any luck?" Jerod asked.

"Not much. Only learned that I wouldn't trust Ronnie any farther than I could punt Ansel in a strong wind."

Jerod laughed. "Don't give my Franny any ideas." He finished one strip of tape and moved to the next. "Where's everyone going tonight for Thursday night out?"

"Thane, Radley, Bain, and I are going to the Tower Bar on State Street," Ansel said. "Walker's coming, too."

"He is?" Jazzi didn't think anything could pry him from Didi and River.

Ansel grinned. "Didi told him he either did what he usually does and stops fussing over them, or she's taking River to a hotel."

Jazzi liked Didi more the longer she knew her.

Jerod waggled his eyebrows. "Five big, strapping guys walking in to drink beers with no women on their arms. Good thing I won't be there, or we'd have to fight women off."

"I'm wearing a ring," Ansel said.

"Like it matters. Sometimes, that's a turn on." Jerod ran his hand over the wall to check to make sure the seam was smooth. "Walker's hooked good, isn't he?"

Ansel finished his seam and moved to the next one. "It took one look. That's all."

"That's how it was with me and my Franny," Jerod said. "Actually, I didn't fall until she opened her mouth. I knew I'd met a woman who wouldn't put up with my crap."

Jazzi rubbed her forearm across her forehead to shake dust off loose strands of her hair. "What's Didi going to do while Walker's out?"

Ansel's grin widened. Her man's grin could melt hearts. "She's loading up all of the dishes and glasses in Walker's cupboards. He wants to give them to Goodwill and buy new ones with her."

"Oh, boy, that proves he's hooked." She'd asked Ansel to help her choose things for their house when they were renovating it, and he hadn't even moved in yet. But she wanted him to like how everything turned out. Yeah, looking back, she'd already fallen for him. She just hadn't realized it.

"Walker says he never noticed what a mishmash of kitchen stuff he owned until he couldn't come up with three matching plates for supper."

Jerod laughed. "Wait till he has kids. Dishes and glasses get dropped and chipped. We use a lot of plastic now."

Jazzi wrinkled her nose. She had a thing for table settings. She'd have to be desperate before plastic plates graced her table.

Bain finished the seam he'd been working on and before he could start on a new one, Jerod nodded to the kitchen clock. "It's almost five. We only have one more wall to go. Let's call it a night."

They pitched in to clean up, then headed to their vehicles. Jazzi carried an empty cooler to the van. She made a mental note to pack more sandwiches for a while. The guys had saved her one for lunch, but the rest were gone. Jerod had gone to grab another one at three for an afternoon snack. That made her think. Jerod and his family were probably eating quick, easy suppers right now. She needed to make a pot of soup and a couple of casseroles for them. Then all they had to do was reheat supper. But not tonight. Tonight was girls' night out, and she was looking forward to it.

Chapter 13

When Jazzi walked in the Dash-in, Olivia was already sitting in a booth, waiting for her. She was holding her hand in front of her to admire her engagement ring. Jazzi had to laugh. She found herself doing that, too.

"Not too shabby, huh?" Jazzi's sister wiggled her fingers at her.

"Gorgeous. Have you and Thane made any more decisions about the wedding?" She slid onto the seat across from her. No reason to glance at the menu. She knew what she wanted.

"We're having the ceremony at the small church his parents used to go to before they retired to Phoenix. I already ordered my gown. I saw it in a bride magazine. And I was hoping you and I could get some ideas for the reception while we ate."

Lord, her sister was a lot more organized about her wedding than Jazzi had been. Probably a good thing. April second wasn't that far away. "Did you bring a pen and paper like Gaff always carries?" Jazzi teased.

Olivia reached into her purse and put a small yellow notepad and pen on the booth's table. Yup, she was ready.

The waitress came and Jazzi ordered her usual duck burger and Olivia her usual flatbread pizza. Funny how they often ordered the same things over and over at the restaurants they went to. After the waitress returned with their glasses of wine, the sisters got down to business.

"Shrimp?" Jazzi asked.

Olivia wrinkled her nose. It was cute when she did it. Not everyone pulled it off so well. "Cocktail shrimp gets expensive, doesn't it? Thane and I were thinking about those shrimp flatbread pizzas you made once."

Jazzi nodded. "Those would work. We could cut each flatbread in fourths so they're easy to hold."

"We like crostini with chicken salad, too, and Thane loves the beef satays you make."

"All affordable." Jazzi used flat iron steaks to make the satays. "What else?"

"I love your sausage parmesan palmiers."

Jazzi smiled. If she wrapped anything in puff pastry, her sister couldn't get enough of it. "Any dips or veggies?"

"I like your warm broccoli 'n' cheddar dip."

"That's easy to make. What about my jerk vegetables on bruschetta?"

"Mm, I forgot about those. They're good." Olivia wrote them down.

"Asparagus spears wrapped in prosciutto?"

"I like those, too."

By the time the waitress brought their food, they'd finished the list, along with their glasses of wine.

Between bites, Olivia asked, "Do you think you can make us a few different kinds of sheet cakes? We'd rather not have to pay for a wedding cake."

"That's no problem." Jazzi stopped to lick her fingers clean where mayo had squeezed out of her sandwich. "But they'll look like sheet cakes. I'm not good at fancy decorations."

Olivia shrugged. "Just as long as they look yummy. What can you come up with?"

"German chocolate sheet cake and a coconut sheet cake. I've made both of those. They're good. I'll have to try out a couple more. If you'd go for cake rolls, I could make sponge cakes with cream cheese fillings and different fruit toppings."

"Let's do it." Olivia tucked her notepad and pen back in her purse. Then she smiled. "Our wedding's going to be great, and we won't have to go in debt for it. We put most of our savings on the house when we bought it. We should have kept a little on the side."

"What for? This will work." Jazzi took a sip of wine. "Is Thane getting pretty excited?"

"He can't wait, and I'm glad, or else he'd be depressed over Donovan's death. It bothers him enough, as is. It just doesn't make any sense. Donovan was such a good guy. Everyone liked him."

"What was his family like? I met his mom and dad, and I got the feeling their marriage was a little strained. But that could have been because they just lost their son."

Olivia finished her first square of pizza and reached for another. "No, Donovan's home life wasn't very good. His dad's a bully, loves to throw his weight around. Plays fast and loose with ethics. His older brother got out of town as fast as he could. He kept in touch with Donovan, called him once a week, and they got along, but he had no desire to see his folks. His mom's a chain-smoker, always nervous. Donovan loved her, but wouldn't go home to visit her. He'd meet her places instead. Thane thinks she tries to keep her distance from Ray, doesn't trust him anymore."

"Because he cheats?"

"Not the way you're thinking, not with other women." Olivia drained her wine glass and pushed her empty plate away. She was a careful eater most of the time—always watching her calories—but not when they went out. "Donovan didn't go to Thanksgiving at his parents' last year because he thought his dad borrowed the company truck to make some money on the side, moving suspicious stuff for some guys he knew."

Jazzi felt herself tense. "For Ronnie, Jarrett, and Boscoe?"

Olivia shrugged. "Donovan never mentioned names, but he worried his dad pulled shady deals every once in a while. He didn't want to get caught in the middle of any of it."

"Did his mom know?"

"She suspected, but when she tries to talk to Ray about anything, he just tells her to mind her own business."

"But that *is* her business! She's married to him."

The waitress came with their bills and Olivia handed across her debit card. Jazzi paid cash and added a generous tip. When the waitress left, Olivia gave Jazzi a knowing look. "Ray doesn't much care what his wife thinks."

Jazzi leaned closer and kept her voice down. "Could Ray have done something that got Donovan in trouble?"

Olivia pursed her lips, considering the idea. "I don't see how."

"I don't either." But Jazzi wasn't ruling it out. "Can I share this with Gaff?"

"If it helps solve who killed Donovan, sure."

The waitress returned with Olivia's tab and card, and after Olivia finished signing it, they left. On the way home, Jazzi kept thinking about Donovan and his parents. Ronnie had gone to prison for stealing refrigerators from a company he worked at. Had Ray driven the truck to move the stolen goods? Even if he had, how would that affect Donovan?

When she got home, she couldn't wait to share her ideas with Ansel, but when she opened the garage door, his spot was still empty. He and "the boys" must be having fun. She parked her pickup on her side of the space and started toward the house. She'd only gone a few steps when a cat meowed at her. Had Inky or Marmalade slipped outside somehow?

She glanced at the side of the building, and hidden in the shadows, a gray cat crouched over an empty plastic bowl. A stray? Where had he come from? And who'd fed him?

Just then, Ansel's van came down the drive, so she waited for him. When he and Bain walked toward her, the cat stared at Bain and yowled. Bain glanced at Ansel and her, looking guilty.

"Is he yours?" Ansel asked.

Color crept all the way to Bain's hairline. "He was so thin, I felt sorry for him. I've been putting food out for him when I take my evening walks around the pond, but if you don't want a stray hanging around, I'll quit."

Jazzi bent and the cat let her pet him. "Poor thing, it's so cold, he probably needs to be fed twice a day. We should give him dry food when we leave in the mornings, too."

Ansel nodded. "I'll buy a bag to keep in the garage so Bain can just scoop it in his bowl."

Bain smiled. A rare sight. "Thanks. He's a scrappy little guy. I kinda like him. If I ever get to go home, I might take him with me. We could use fresh genes for our barn cats."

Ansel's blond brows rose in surprise. He'd told her their dad didn't believe in coddling the cats on their farm, said they had to earn their keep or starve. Jazzi had a feeling Bain snuck them food on the side. Jazzi was starting to like the man a little more.

When they bundled into the kitchen, their own pets came to greet them. While Jazzi and Ansel fussed over the cats and George, Bain carried a large bowl of cat food out for his stray. Once everyone got settled, Jazzi shared what Olivia had told her about Donovan and his family.

"It makes me wonder if Ray's shady deals put Donovan in jeopardy."

Ansel shook his head. "I keep thinking that Didi and Donovan are connected somehow. I don't see how Donovan's dad would fit in for either of them."

Jazzi had no idea, but she decided to run the idea past Gaff tomorrow.

Chapter 14

Ansel, Jazzi, Bain, and Jerod were sanding the last wall on Friday when Gaff gave a quick knock and walked inside the old Victorian.

"Did I time it right for a sandwich?" he asked. "It's almost noon."

"Sure. Have a seat." Jerod grabbed an extra lawn chair and pulled it to the card table. Their lunch was nothing fancy. Jazzi had made a lot of tuna salad when she got up in the morning and brought bread to heap it on so that the sandwiches wouldn't get soggy sitting in the cooler. And wouldn't you know it? The men oohed and aahed and ate every last bite. Sometimes, she could go to a lot of bother and only get good reviews and then make something simple that they raved over. She'd have to make tuna salad more often.

Gaff reached for a few more chips before saying, "I went to see Jarrett this morning—the guy who got out of prison with Ronnie. He's working as a grease monkey, getting free rent in an apartment above the garage."

Jerod took car repairs seriously. His dad was a mechanic, so he'd grown up poking under hoods or on a dolly, rolling under chassis. "Has he got credentials?"

"He tinkered with his dad all the time in their garage."

Jerod shrugged, unimpressed.

"Learn anything interesting?" Ansel asked.

"He went to prison for moving stolen goods out of state."

Moving them how? Jazzi couldn't hide her excitement. She told him about the conversation she'd had with Olivia.

"Donovan's dad, huh? So far, his name hasn't come up in any of the conversations I've had with Gil's old friends."

Ansel shook his head. "Walker went out with us last night. He said Gil didn't count any of those guys as friends. The only person he was close to was Ronnie."

Gaff didn't look surprised. "Jarrett didn't strike me as a good friend for anyone. I asked him about Ronnie, if he was part of the stolen goods job, but Jarrett said he only did small stuff with him—hot wiring cars or muggings. Nothing big. Said the boy wasn't smart enough for anything elaborate."

That's the impression Jazzi had gotten when she met him. "Ronnie might not be smart, but he struck me as sneaky."

"I asked Jarrett about someone ratting him out, and he swore no one would do that. But he would say that, wouldn't he? He wouldn't let on that he suspected someone." Gaff took a few more chips, then washed them down with Pepsi.

"Do you think he'll go after whoever tipped the cops on him?" Ansel asked.

Gaff looked thoughtful. "My cop intuition tells me there's more to it than that. The man's nursing a grudge. He can hardly keep his voice calm when he talks about his old group. Something's festering, but I'm not sure what, and Jarrett's not the type to let bygones be bygones."

Jazzi collected the dirty paper plates to throw away. "Did he know Donovan? Did you ask about him?"

Gaff nodded. "I asked. He played dumb, asked if Donovan was in the pen, too. When I mentioned Didi, he laughed, said Gil sure knew how to pick 'em. Said Didi dumped Gil the minute he landed in the pen; whereas, his girlfriend fiddled around with another guy until he got out, then she dumped the loser and ran to him."

Ansel frowned. "So Donovan's first girlfriend had a connection to Jarrett? And Jarrett was the guy who took over protecting Ronnie when Gil died?"

"Interesting, huh? Brianne was there when I talked to him, and boy, did she look like a piece of work!" Gaff got quiet for a minute, then said, "I asked him if he'd heard that Didi's house kept getting broken into and he asked if she was all right, said it wasn't safe for a pretty girl like her to live in a rundown neighborhood, that she should know better."

"So he knows where she lives." Jazzi pressed her lips together in an unhappy line.

"I told him the neighborhood wasn't posh, but it was usually safe."

Jerod leaned his elbows on the table and hunched his shoulders. He could be protective of his friends, and he didn't look happy with where this conversation was going. "Jarrett doesn't know Didi's living with Walker, does he?"

Gaff shook his head. "And I think we should keep it that way. She needs to stay away from her house so no one can follow her."

"I'll remind Walker of that," Ansel said.

With a nod, Gaff stood. "I'm going to see Gil's cellmate on Monday. He's out of town right now, got permission from his probation officer to visit his sick brother. I'll let you know how that goes."

Bain perked up when Gaff mentioned special permission for someone to leave town. He hurried to say, "It sounds like you have enough suspects now that I might be lower on your list. I talked to my dad last night, and he's having a hard time without me. If I'd wear an ankle bracelet, could I go home and help him on the farm?"

Gaff gave him a long look, then sighed. "Let me talk to a few people first. I'll give you an answer on Monday."

Bain didn't push it, probably knew better.

When Gaff left, all four of them went for a cup of coffee and looked at each other.

"Is this one depressing mess or what?" Jerod asked.

No one could disagree, so they drank their coffee, then got back to work. By the time they left the house that night, every wall was sanded and the work site picked up and clean.

Chapter 15

On their drive home, Ansel wore his brooding look. When her Norseman fretted, he reminded Jazzi even more of a Viking. She wouldn't want to be on the other end of that scowl. Sleet pelted the windshield and the streets were slippery. It would be March soon, and February had decided to go out with a roar, not a whimper, but that obviously wasn't what was on Ansel's mind. He said, "It's too much of a coincidence that all of these guys knew each other and crap started to happen when they got out."

She'd been turning those ideas over and upside down in her mind, too.

Bain spoke up from the back seat. George was lying with his head on his lap, and Bain mindlessly petted him. "Everything's connected somehow, but Donovan doesn't seem to be a part of any of it. I wish we could follow the dots that tied him to one of these guys."

Jazzi knew from experience that connecting dots took a lot of work and patience. "Do you think we're trying to connect two crimes that aren't tied to each other? Didi and Donovan don't seem to go together."

"They have to," Ansel argued. "Prison has to be part of it. We just don't see how yet."

He was right. They *had* to be.

A car skidded through a red light into the intersection and Ansel had to slam on the brakes. He'd been driving at a snail's pace, but the van still slid sideways, so he feathered the brakes to correct it. They all heaved a sigh of relief when their front tire bumped against the curb and stopped.

"We're staying home for supper tonight," Jazzi announced. "No use going out in this." She loved their Friday nights out, but not enough to risk life and limb.

"Did you thaw something?" Ansel eased through the last intersection before turning onto their street.

"I have plenty of things I can nuke enough to cook. It might not be gourmet, but we won't go hungry."

Bain snorted. "Anything you make has to be better than Mom's."

Jazzi's eyes flew wide. She'd never heard Bain complain about his mother's cooking. Ansel laughed. "Poor Mom, she tries."

"Not very much." Bain patted his stomach. "You guys have spoiled me. It's going to be hard to go back to meatloaf with no flavor once a week and spaghetti with a can of tomato sauce poured over it."

"We Herstad boys appreciate good cooking. We'll help you in the kitchen tonight." Ansel volunteered his brother, too, and Bain nodded. He slowed almost to a crawl to turn into their driveway and park in the garage. He was carrying George to the house and Bain was carting the cooler when the stray cat flew out of the woods, running full speed toward them. His tail was gone. A coyote came to an abrupt halt at the edge of the tree line when it saw them. A furry tail hung from its lips.

Bain put down the cooler and held out his arms. The cat leapt right into them, and Bain turned to glare at the coyote. It slunk away.

Jazzi picked up the cooler. "You might as well bring your cat inside. He's not safe out here."

"You don't mind?"

"My cats might not be nice to him, but they won't eat him. That coyote will." She turned to Ansel. "Should we take him to the vet to do something about his tail?"

Bain shook his head. "A couple of farm cats lost their tails and healed just fine. He'll be okay." He took the cat straight to the laundry room to show it where the litter box was. The cat clung to his wool coat with its claws, and it took a lot of petting to calm it down. Inky and Marmalade hissed at it for a few minutes, then wandered into the kitchen to weave around Jazzi's ankles, begging for food.

She laughed and bent to stroke their fur. Mealtime was more important than upping a rival. Inky was all smooth silky sleekness. Marmalade was heavy fluff. After they were satisfied with enough attention, she opened a can of tuna and split it between them. She carried two paper plates to Bain along with the bag of dry food and another can for his stray.

Bain frowned at Inky and Marmalade. "They're going to give Stubs a hard time. Maybe I should keep him in the basement."

"Stubs." She smiled. "I like that. The basement's a good idea. When he feels more comfortable, he can come up and brave my beasts. We have an extra pet bed if you want to take it down there."

Bain and Stubs disappeared down the basement steps, then he returned to get all of the pet supplies. She noticed he took an antibiotic salve with him, too, and smiled. He gave a sheepish look, then asked, "Do you have another litter box and more litter?"

"They're in the basement pantry where we keep extra supplies. We bought a spare box when we weren't sure our cats would share, but they didn't need it."

Bain disappeared again. She and Ansel headed upstairs to take quick showers and change into sweat pants and loose sweaters. Then they returned to the kitchen to see what they could scrounge up. There were smoked sausage links and a head of cabbage. She always stocked cans of diced tomatoes.

"Sausage-cabbage soup?" she asked. "We have a round of crusty bread we can thaw."

"I love soups." Ansel licked his lips.

That reminded her. "I want to make some big pots to share with Jerod and Franny so they don't have to cook for a while, and I thought I'd dish up plastic containers for Radley, too."

The kitchen door had opened while she talked and Radley stepped inside. "I'm all for that. I'll pitch in if you need me. We'll help you cook as many as you want if you have what you need."

"What are you doing here?" Ansel asked. "I thought you were going to Walker's tonight for supper."

"He lives way out south. He called to say the roads are worse on his side of town. Thane and I worked on a furnace about ten minutes from here, so I thought I'd stop and beg for food from you guys instead. I knew you'd have to feed Bain."

"There's an extra bed if you want to spend the night." Jazzi grabbed handfuls of potatoes to put on the countertop.

Radley grinned. "Just like the old days. I might take you up on that. The sand and salt trucks will have things in better shape tomorrow morning."

Bain came up to join them, and they all settled around the kitchen island and got busy. While she started the sausage and cabbage soup, Ansel and his brothers worked on potato soup, chopping potatoes, carrots, and celery, along with an onion. They tossed those in the pot. Once they got it simmering, Bain opened a package of diced ham and stirred it in.

Ansel frowned. "I like my soup a little thicker."

Jazzi pointed to the pantry shelves. "Add some instant potatoes until it's how you like it."

Radley blinked. "You don't add flour or cornstarch?"

Jazzi was stirring the chunks of sausage links she'd put in the Dutch oven. "Nope, with instant potatoes I don't have to worry about lumps."

All three men stared as Ansel tilted the box over the soup and stirred it in. They all grinned as the soup thickened.

Jazzi rolled her eyes. It was too easy to impress the Herstad boys. "One soup down, two to go. Now you can finish this one while I start on the white chicken chili. I already have all the cabbage and onions chopped for you to add to the sausage."

"Did you soak beans and thaw a chicken?" Radley asked.

He overestimated her dedication to cooking. "I'm lazier than that. You should know that by now." Jazzi opened the freezer and pulled out a bag of shredded chicken. "I bought three rotisseries chickens and bagged the meat I pulled off them." She went to the pantry and put three cans of northern beans and two small cans of mild diced green chiles on the counter. "The beans turn out perfect every time."

Radley shook his finger at her. "Now you're teasing me."

"Don't bet on it. Start opening cans."

Bain laughed at the look on Radley's face and began melting butter and stirring in flour to make a roux.

"Look at you." Radley took out his cell phone and snapped a picture. "Mom will never believe you helped in the kitchen."

"Don't send that to her. She'll expect me chop and dice at home."

Jazzi only half-listened to their banter while she snuck George a piece of chicken. Sheesh! She was getting as bad as Ansel.

Radley shook his head, smiling, when they finished cooking fifteen minutes later. "That was quick. I thought it would take forever."

"I use shortcuts. Once in a great while, I'll make a bean soup from scratch with dried beans and a ham hock for Ansel, but only once in a while." Jazzi went to get four bowls. "Choose any soup you want. There's bread and cheese on the table."

Radley ladled out a large helping for each of them. They pulled chunks of bread off the crusty round to dip in the soup. Ansel passed out drinks.

Once they'd settled at the table, Ansel asked, "How's your cat, Bain?"

Radley's brows practically flew up to his hairline. "You have a cat?"

"I had to rescue it from a coyote. The poor thing was starving."

Radley stared. "You never worried about that on the farm."

Bain made a face. "Shows what you know. I kept feeding the barn cats dry food after you left. They'd grown to depend on it."

Radley smiled. "Your growl is worse than your bite."

"It just made sense," Bain argued. "We need all those cats or the barn would be overrun with mice."

"That's true." Ansel went for a second bowl of soup. "Will your cats accept Stubs?"

"Stubs?" Radley's lips curled as Bain explained about his cat losing its tail.

Jazzi had taken a bag of cookies out of the freezer before they started cooking. She poured cups of coffee and passed the tray around. Radley gave a contented sigh. "You're so nice to me, Jaz. I don't suppose you'd like to do me another favor."

She pursed her lips. She'd learned the hard way to never say an automatic yes. "What is it?"

He grimaced. "Donovan's mom called me last night. She asked me to clean out Donovan's apartment for them. She can't bring herself to do it. She said I could keep anything I wanted and then give the rest to Mustard Seed."

Jazzi liked Mustard Seed. The warehouse stored used furniture for people whose houses had burned or been damaged. "They only take furniture. You know that, right?"

Radley nodded. "She said to give the rest to the Salvation Army."

"Fair enough. Sure, I'll help you. When are you doing it?"

"Tomorrow, if that works for you."

"The house can go another week without dusting," Ansel told her. "You got pretty thorough last weekend. I'll clean the floors while you're gone."

"Thanks." She was a lucky girl. Her hunk didn't mind pitching in on housework.

Radley's shoulders relaxed. "I appreciate your going with me. I didn't want to do it by myself. Every time I look at something, I think of Donovan."

"You'd have to. He was a good friend." Radley had spent a lot of time with him and Thane, and Donovan had been patient when he was training him.

They all worked together cleaning up, so it went fast. Then they found comfortable spots to watch TV and rented a movie. Even Bain stayed to watch it with them. Jazzi looked around during a lull and George was snuggled beside Ansel, Inky and Marmalade were with her, and Stubs was curled next to Bain. Happiness swelled inside her. She never thought she'd grow fond of Bain, but she was beginning to like Ansel's brother. His parents hadn't made his life all that great either.

Chapter 16

A big tree limb had fallen near their garage during the night, so the three men went out to saw and stack it, since Ansel was playing with the idea of building a firepit in their backyard. Luckily, the limb had missed Radley and Bain's vans. While the guys worked in the yard, Jazzi made two nine by thirteen shepherd's pies. Jerod's kids loved anything with hamburger, even if it held vegetables and especially if it had mashed potatoes on top. She figured they'd like the casserole.

By the time the men came in for lunch, she let them dig into the one she'd made for them. Then she and Radley loaded Jerod's food into her pickup, and Radley grabbed his soups in plastic containers. They drove separately to his apartment. The snow plows and salt and sand trucks had been busy last night. The roads were messy but safe. When she finished helping Radley, she'd drive the food to Jerod's and then go home.

Radley gladly stored his soups in his refrigerator before they walked down the steps to Donovan's. Radley had a key. It felt odd to walk into a dead man's apartment. They both looked around nervously, trying to shake off the feeling that they should call out to let him know they were there. They were stripping the bed and tossing used towels and dirty laundry in a bag when someone called from the living room. Frowning, Radley went to see who was there.

"Who are you?" she heard him ask.

Jazzi's heart lurched. Had the burglar returned? She hurried to stand beside him.

A girl with dyed black hair with bright blue streaks stood in the center of the room. Her eyes were rimmed with black eyeliner and she wore black lipstick. She might be pretty without the sneer. She raised her chin. "I'm

Brianne. I lived with Donovan for a year. I heard about what happened to him and came to get a few things I left here before they changed the locks on the apartment."

Radley stood so that she couldn't pass him. "There's nothing here for you. Donovan boxed it all up and sent it to you, like you asked him to."

Jazzi stared. She'd never heard Radley use such a harsh tone of voice.

Brianne narrowed her eyes. "I might have forgotten a couple of things."

"You might have, but Donovan made sure there was nothing of yours left here. He didn't want anything that reminded him of you."

The girl's brows rose in amusement. "Some men can't handle rejection."

Radley snorted. "You did him a favor. He wanted you gone but was too nice to toss you out. He said you were a lesson learned. No more taking in riffraff."

Her eyes shot fire. "He begged me to stay."

"No, he didn't. I was here when you came with Jarrett's luggage to pack your things, remember? We went out to celebrate once you left the parking lot."

Whoa! That was purposely mean. Radley wanted to put this girl in her place. Come to think of it, Ansel didn't mince words when he didn't like someone.

Brianne jammed her hands on her hips, visibly angry. "He was jealous I was going back to Jarrett."

"Funny, he told me you'd found your proper level. That you and a prison thug should have a lot in common."

Jazzi couldn't believe he'd just said that. Radley was Ansel's funny brother, the one who made her smile. She'd never heard him insult anyone.

Brianne moved to slide past him, but he sidestepped her. "You're not welcome here. You don't respect Donovan's memory. You're probably just trying to nab some of his things to sell. It's not going to happen. Leave."

"You have no right . . . "

He cut her off. "Leave or I call the building super."

"Go ahead." She crossed her arms, smirking, calling his bluff.

He took out his cell phone and started punching numbers.

She turned on her heel and stomped out of the building.

Jazzi went to Radley when his body started to shake. She slid her arm around him. "Are you okay?"

"That girl did everything she could to play games with Donovan and milk him for more money. When her hoodlum boyfriend got set free, she couldn't ditch Donovan fast enough."

"Did it bother him?"

"Not that she left, but he told me he felt dumb as a box of rocks for falling for her sad story in the first place. He figured he'd give her a small break and then she'd move on, just like she did."

"He was a nice man."

"Too nice for her." Radley let out a deep breath, visibly worked to calm himself, then started back toward the bedroom. "Let's finish this up."

It took all afternoon to empty drawers and pack belongings in boxes to drive to the Salvation Army. Then Radley called Mustard Seed and two men came to collect the furniture. Jazzi helped him bag the food in Donovan's cupboards to take to the soup kitchen. When they finished emptying the last kitchen drawer, the apartment was empty. Radley's shoulders slumped and he heaved a sad sigh. Then he locked the door as they left and gave the superintendent the key.

He hugged Jazzi as she got ready to leave. "Thanks for being here."

"No big deal. Want to come for supper tonight? Need some company?"

"Not tonight. I'm not in the best mood."

"Will you be at the Sunday meal tomorrow?"

"What are you making?"

She laughed. It was always about the food. "I bought everything for chicken and noodles with mashed potatoes, sautéed green beans, a Waldorf salad, and coconut cream pies."

"A feast. I'll be there. I love anything with noodles."

So did she. She could probably eat pasta every other night and be happy. Ansel—not so much.

When she left Radley's, she headed to Jerod's house.

Her cousin met her at the door. He was still wearing his pajamas. So was Franny. He saw the tote bag, and his eyes lit up.

"Did I come at a bad time?" she asked.

"Nah, but if we get a chance for a quick nap, we take it," he told her, carrying the tote straight to their big dining room table. Dirty pans filled the sink. "Haven't gotten to those yet. Pete hasn't been a happy boy." He pulled the foil off the shepherd's pie and Gunther and Lizzie came running.

"I smell food!" Gunther cried.

Jerod tossed two paper plates on the table and dished the food up for them. The kids dug in.

"We ate a late breakfast and haven't started supper yet. You saved us from more hot dogs."

Franny came to eat, too. "Peter kept us up all night. Had a touch of colic. Thank you so much for the food. I couldn't work up the energy to cook."

Jerod nodded. "Our little boy's kicking our fannies."

The words flew out of her mouth before she could stop them. "What if I take Gunther and Lizzie to our place and they spend the night? That way, if Peter sleeps, you can, too."

Jerod stared at her. "Do you mean that?"

"You always thought they were too young before. They're old enough now."

"Please, Daddy! Please." Lizzie jumped up and down.

Jerod squeezed Jazzi to him. "You're the best, cuz. Thank you. You do enough for us all the time, I didn't want to inflict babysitting on you, too." He turned to the kids. "Get your pajamas and toothbrushes. Your mom and I will see you at the Sunday meal, then bring you home."

Both kids raced upstairs and returned in a few minutes. Franny tossed their things in a grocery bag and hugged them goodbye. She looked like she was ready to drop. The kids never shut up all the way home. Jazzi decided to take the easy way out and stopped to buy a bucket of fried chicken and all of the sides for supper. By the time Jazzi led Gunther and Lizzie into the house, her ears hurt. Her head throbbed. What had she been thinking?

Ansel took one look at them and grinned. "I smell children."

He knew they watched *Hocus Pocus* every Halloween. They giggled and ran to him. Even Bain got into the act, dropping down on his hands and knees so that he and Ansel could be in a "horsey race." Jazzi watched them, shaking her head. Who knew? The Herstad boys both had a thing for kids.

Chapter 17

She told Ansel and Bain about meeting Brianne while they ate their chicken. The kids surprised her by each eating a leg and a biscuit. They'd just eaten before they came here, but she got the idea they were really hungry. Either that or they had a thing for fried chicken.

While Ansel and Bain watched *The Incredibles* with Gunther and Lizzie, Jazzi roasted two chickens, one for each soup pot in the morning. While those cooked, she sautéed sliced mushrooms, diced carrots, celery, and sweet onions with minced garlic and seasonings to add to the base. It would make life easier tomorrow.

When she started on the pie dough, Bain wandered out to see what she was doing. "I always wanted to learn how to make pies."

She told him how much flour to add to the food processor and when they'd added the salt, diced butter, and cold water, he stared in disbelief.

"That's it?" he asked.

"We have to let it rest for half an hour before we roll them out."

Bain went back to the movie, and she started on the fillings. He returned to roll out four bottom crusts, then disappeared again. By the time the movie was over, the pies were cooling.

"We can do the rest tomorrow," she decided. It had been a long day.

Bain went upstairs to call his dad, and Jazzi went to sag on the sofa in front of the TV. No luck. Gunther was sprawled on it, sound asleep. Lizzie was asleep in the recliner. Ansel met her gaze and smiled.

"Cute, aren't they?"

"An aunt couldn't do much better." She went upstairs and returned with two pillows and two blankets. "They can sleep down here. We'll leave the light on over the kitchen window. If they wake up, they shouldn't be scared."

They got the kids tucked in, then she and Ansel went upstairs to bed. He carried George, and Jazzi led Inky and Marmalade. Stubs watched and rushed after them. He found Bain's bedroom, and everyone got settled in their own spots. Jazzi read for half an hour to relax, and then she snuggled next to Ansel and drifted off.

* * * *

Kids' running and playing woke her in the morning. She opened one eye and glared at the alarm. Seven o'clock. Ansel sat up, rubbing his eyes.

"When do kids start sleeping in?" he asked.

"When they're teenagers?" She had no idea.

Bain couldn't sleep through them either. Except for him, seven o'clock *was* sleeping in. Dairy cows demanded early attention. They all padded downstairs to find Gunther and Lizzie playing tag in the kitchen.

Ansel groaned. "Maybe your idea of waiting for a while to enjoy being a couple isn't such a bad one."

Ha! Kids always looked better when they weren't yours. She went to turn on the coffee pot, and Lizzie came to cling to her.

"I'm hungry."

Jazzi opened the pantry and pointed to the row of cereals. Ansel ate them as snacks late at night. Each kid wanted a different one, which was fine with her. Once she had them settled at the kitchen island, the coffee was done, and she and the guys carried their mugs to the living room coffee table.

Peace ruled for another half hour, and then Gunther said, "Let's play a game."

Ansel was awake now. His blond hair was mussed and his chin was scruffy. He looked more delicious than her pies. "I get to pick. Yahtzee."

They bickered for a few minutes, but Gunther caved when he figured out it was Yahtzee or Monopoly. Jazzi vetoed that game. "Everyone will be here before you're finished."

Jazzi cooked while the guys entertained the kids. She hadn't planned it that way, but it gave her time to start the Sunday meal. She was finishing the Waldorf salad when the phone buzzed. When she heard Gaff's voice, she braced herself.

"I know your family will be there soon, but I wanted to give you the bad news to get it over with."

"What bad news?"

Ansel jerked his head up to listen.

"Ronnie never came home from work last night. His grandmother called to report him missing this morning."

"Could he have gone home with someone else and didn't want to wake her in the middle of the night?"

"Maybe. He left work at one in the morning after washing all the dishes. Two cooks saw him get in his car and drive away, and no one's seen him since."

Jazzi's good mood tanked. "You think he's dead, don't you?"

"Either that, or we rattled him when we stopped at his house to question him. He'd been smoking pot. I could smell it—a violation of his parole. I talked to the officer he's assigned to, and he stopped at the restaurant Ronnie was working at and saw him outside on his break, drinking from a brown paper bag—another violation. Maybe he ran. His grandma told me he never wanted to go back to prison."

"Would you send him back for that?"

"I doubt it, but he didn't know that."

Jazzi bit her bottom lip. She didn't care much for Ronnie, but she really liked his grandma. "When you learn something, tell me, will you?"

"Sure will. Have fun with your family."

She squared her shoulders and told Ansel the news, then she put Ronnie out of her mind. Gran had told her once not to worry until you knew you had to. "It will save you a lot of gray hairs." After careful thought, she'd decided Gran was right. There wasn't anything she could do about Ronnie, so she'd concentrate on having a good time.

As usual, Jerod and Franny were the first to arrive, carting a baby carrier with them. They both looked more rested than they had yesterday. Gunther grabbed Ansel's hand and dragged him to his dad. "I beat Uncle Ansel in Yahtzee. I got two Yahtzees and he only got one."

"Good for you!" Jerod bent down to whisper, "Ansel didn't turn you upside down and shake you for beating him, did he?"

Gunther whirled on Ansel. "Would you? Please! Please?"

In answer, her Norseman grabbed both of the boy's ankles and flipped him into the air. Bain was doing the same to Lizzie when Radley walked through the door. "Is this an interrogation? I'll admit I did it, whatever it was. Just don't hang me by my toes."

When they flipped the kids upright again, Gunther was giggling so hard, he fell on his fanny. Mom and Dad came at the same time as Olivia and Thane.

Jazzi stared at her sister. "You're always late. Are you okay?"

Olivia laughed. "We're hungry. We wanted to get here before Jerod ate everything."

Gran and Samantha came next, followed by Walker, Didi, and River. Jerod's parents were the last to arrive, and Eleanore went straight to see the baby.

Jazzi and Ansel loaded all the food on the kitchen island. After people lined up to fill their plates, they settled at the long tables. The meal took longer than usual since everyone was in a chatty mood. At three thirty, they were gathering dirty dishes to serve dessert when Gaff knocked and peeked inside.

"Can I interrupt for a minute? I knew everyone would be here."

Peter started crying and Franny got up to nurse him in the other room. Jerod motioned to her empty chair. "Want some coffee?"

Jazzi loaded the dirty dishes in the sink to rinse later and returned with the pies—two coconut cream and two chocolate. "We're just starting dessert."

Gaff shrugged his coat off and came to join them while Ansel carried a piece of pie to Franny in the other room. Gaff waited until the meal was over before saying, "Thanks for letting me join you. Thane and Radley worked with Donovan, so I thought they could tell me if he'd ever known Ronnie."

Thane shook his head. "Not that I know of. He never mentioned him."

Gaff looked at Didi. "Gil liked the kid, didn't he?"

She pushed her empty plate away. "I'm not sure he liked him, but he felt sorry for him. He said life had given him a bad hand."

"Did you like him?"

Didi shook her head. "No matter what happened, Ronnie made sure he came out looking good, even if he had to throw someone else under the bus. I wasn't a fan. He wasn't crazy about me either. Gil's group thinks I filed for divorce the minute Gil got behind bars, but that was Gil's idea. He told me he'd only mess up my life, that I didn't need to be stuck with a con, I deserved better. He chose Ronnie over me."

Gaff nodded. "So, Gil was stuck with Ronnie, and Donovan was stuck with Brianne. Did they know each other?"

Didi looked surprised. "They might have. Gil said that Ronnie knew Donovan's dad. They'd worked together in a warehouse or something. And Ronnie worked with Jarrett once in a while. And Brianne lived with Jarrett, so . . ."

Excitement buzzed in Jazzi's mind. Were these the dots that connected Donovan and Didi? Had they found the thread of a trail?

Thane shook his head. "The difference is, Gil would still be standing behind Ronnie, but Donovan recognized Brianne's pattern and cut her loose."

Radley agreed. "Donovan had met a nice girl, Elspeth Smythe. He was ready to get serious with her."

That news depressed Jazzi even more. Donovan had a shot at happiness and someone took it away from him.

"Gil didn't deserve to die." Didi squared her shoulders, ready to defend him.

Walker looked at her and smiled. "I like how loyal you are."

Gran snorted. "You like everything about that girl."

Walker's cheeks flushed, but he didn't deny it.

Gaff turned to Jazzi. "Want to come with me to see Brianne and Elspeth tomorrow? Elspeth isn't a suspect, and I don't want to make her nervous. You could help soften my visit. And Brianne ... well, she'll be a pain either way, but she sure isn't fond of me."

"I thought you were going to interview Gil's cellmate."

"I am, but I don't want you around the likes of him. You might make the women open up, though."

Jazzi wasn't so sure. "I've met Brianne. She didn't like me much."

"Even better!" Gaff rubbed his hands together. "I don't want you anywhere close to Jarrett, so we'll meet her at Donovan's apartment instead. I got it approved by the super."

"Works for me." Jazzi would love to see Brianne's expression when she realized everything there was emptied out.

That settled, Gaff got up to leave and the rest of the guests were close behind. People were collecting their coats when someone pounded on the front door. Jazzi frowned. Who in the world could that be? Friends and family always came to the kitchen door. She went to answer it, and a big, bulky man pushed his way inside. His coffee colored hair was pulled back in a long ponytail. His steel gray eyes glinted with temper. He stabbed at her with his finger. "What right did you have to keep Brianne out of Donovan's apartment? You're the same blonde who went to see Ronnie, too, aren't you? Why are you sticking your nose in my business?"

Before Jazzi could answer, Ansel came and stepped in front of her. "Threaten her one more time, and that finger won't ever be the same." Then Jerod, Thane, Walker, and Bain came, too. All big men. Last, but not least, Gaff sauntered to the door with a smile.

"Hi, Jarrett, what brings you here? I thought you didn't know Donovan. Did you suddenly remember him?"

Jarrett's lips pulled back in a snarl. "Brianne told me about going to Donovan's apartment. Seems he was the sap she lived with while I was in the joint. She told me how the blonde here treated her."

Radley pushed his way to the front of the group. "Jazzi didn't say anything to Brianne. I did. Brianne must have realized I live in Donovan's building. And the only way you could have found this house is if you followed me here. What were you hoping to accomplish?"

Jarrett relaxed his stance. He had to. If he didn't drop the aggressive crap, Ansel would toss him out. "I was hoping she could tell me where you sent Donovan's furniture."

Gaff looked curious. "Why?"

Lies rolled smoothly off the man's tongue, because Jazzi didn't believe a word he told them. "Brianne was fond of a night table he owned. She was hoping to take it as a keepsake."

"It was already spoken for," Radley said. "Everything in the apartment is gone."

Jarrett tried to hide his irritation. "I guess I'm too late then."

Gaff's expression shifted into cop mode. "If you came here to intimidate Jazzi into telling you what you wanted, I wouldn't be happy. Neither would her husband or any of her friends. I wouldn't come here again if I were you."

"No worries. Brianne wouldn't be happy if I spent time with a bombshell blonde. She's the jealous type." Jarrett looked toward the kitchen. His gaze settled on Didi. "Why is she here?"

"Because I invited her," Gaff said. "She doesn't want to see you, so you can leave now."

"And not say hello to Gil's wife?"

"His ex," Gaff said. "And she has no fond memories of Gil's old friends."

Jarrett made eye contact with her. "Do you still live in the old neighborhood?"

"When she's in town." Gaff answered for her.

"Does River still go to the same school?"

The little boy looked alarmed and scooted closer to Didi.

"How do you know River?" Gaff snapped. "Gil was in prison when Didi adopted him. They didn't keep in touch."

Jarrett looked confused for a minute, then shrugged. "News spreads in the joint. Not sure who I heard it from."

"Because you didn't. Didi's house was broken into. You wouldn't know anything about that, I suppose."

"Why would I?"

"That's the million dollar question, isn't it? And why would you be here looking for a night table?"

"Hey, are you accusing me of something?"

"I'm putting you on the suspect list, that's for sure."

Jarrett's angry expression returned. "I dealt with you enough before I was arrested. I don't have to bother with you now."

Gaff held out his hands, unperturbed. "I didn't come to you this time. You came to me."

"Maybe you should be looking at Gavin instead."

"Gil's cellmate?"

"He knew Gil still had a thing for Didi. And he couldn't stand Ronnie. He and Gil bumped heads more than once."

"I'll be sure to let him know you mentioned him."

Jarrett's teeth bared in a smile. "You do that. I'd love to see good old Gavin outside of the pen."

"Did you want to see Ronnie, too? You've heard he's disappeared, haven't you?"

Jarrett shrugged. "Nothing to me. I only protected him when he was in prison." With that, he turned and left. Jazzi watched him climb into a rusted white Chevy.

"Isn't that the car that slowed down in front of your house?" she called to Didi.

Didi came to look, too. "Sure is."

Gaff's expression turned serious as he watched Jarrett drive away. "If I pull him in for questioning, he'll tell me he was checking up on you for Gil, that he'd promised him to keep an eye on you."

"Bull pucky." Jazzi let out a frustrated sigh. "I wish he hadn't seen Didi here."

"Me, too." Walker came to watch his car pull out of the drive. "If I see that Chevy anywhere near our house, I'm calling you, Gaff."

Our. He'd called it *our* house. Didi noticed it, too. Jazzi smiled.

Gaff's mind was still on Jarrett. "If you see him anywhere you go, let me know."

Walker put a protective arm on River's shoulder. "I think it's time River changes schools. There's a good one closer to my house."

Didi glanced at her son. "He has friends where he's going now."

"I can make new ones," River piped up. "Would I ride a school bus?" The idea clearly appealed to him.

"We'll check into it, but he's not going to school tomorrow." Walker glanced at Didi for her okay, and when she nodded, River looked relieved.

There wasn't much anyone could do at the moment. People started out the doors again.

Jerod and Franny took Gunther and Lizzie with them, but not before Gunther ran to give Jazzi a hug. "Can we stay here again sometime? Please?"

Eleanore looked offended. "What about your grandma? When are you going to come stay with Grandpa and me?"

Gunther licked his lips, nervous and surprised. "You usually take us places. And we stay at the lake with you."

"It's too cold for the lake now," Eleanore said. "We'll have to think of something closer to home."

The boy's eyes lit up, and Jazzi could almost see him calculating all of the places he could spend the night and be entertained. So could Jerod. He patted his son's head. "You're not ditching us every weekend. We'll figure something out."

By the time everyone had gone, Ansel, Jazzi, and Bain sagged onto barstools and had one last drink.

"I like everyone that was here," Bain told her, "but I never realized how much work having a close-knit family was."

"Anything worthwhile takes some effort," she said.

"Well, I'm not putting any more effort into anything tonight," Ansel said. He went to the living room and stretched out on a couch. Bain took his usual recliner, and Jazzi curled up with Inky and Marmalade on her sofa. She'd never realized how much work kids were. She had to give her cousin credit. He was a good worker *and* a great dad. Ansel would be like that someday. And her? She might drag and give it her best, like Franny.

Chapter 18

On Monday, the guys decided to wait to prime the downstairs until Jazzi went to see Brianne and Elspeth. Instead, they all trooped upstairs to the third floor attic to decide how to make it into a bedroom and bath. Even though it had windows, it had that musty, seldom used, attic smell. Jerod started a checklist.

"It needs insulation, drywall, and plumbing. I already bought the insulation. We can start on that today."

Jazzi hated working with the pink rolls. They always made her itch, but the two-by-fours were bare. It would be the easiest way to finish the room. With Ansel and Jerod working on the ceiling, and her and Bain installing it in the walls, they had it almost finished when Gaff arrived.

When she slid into the car next to him, she asked, "Where to first?"

"To visit Elspeth. I've stopped at Jarrett's to question him before, and Brianne doesn't get out of bed until late afternoon."

"A good thing," Jazzi mumbled. "She needs all the beauty sleep she can get."

Gaff laughed. "I like it when you're catty."

"I can sharpen my claws with the best of them, but I try not to do it too often. Donovan was right, though. Jarrett and Brianne deserve each other."

The ride to Elspeth's wasn't long. She lived in an old brick apartment building close to River Bluff's downtown. The trim all needed repainting, giving the building a rundown look, but it was sturdy enough.

"It's close to her job," Gaff said. "She works at the insurance company near the ball diamond."

There'd been a big debate, but River Bluffs had decided to build a ballpark downtown, and it had been an immediate success. Restaurants and hotels sprang up around it. Before, downtown had been failing. Now, between the ballpark, the event center, and Headwaters Park, the city was alive again.

Gaff parked at the curb, and they entered a small foyer with steep stairs leading to the higher floors. They climbed to the highest one and turned left to apartment 3A. The stairs and hallways were downright shabby, but when Elspeth opened her door and invited them in, they entered a warm, cozy space. The aroma of tomatoes and garlic hovered in the air.

"Something smells good," Gaff commented.

"Vegetable soup. I make a pot to take for lunch instead of eating cafeteria food."

She smiled when she saw them look around her apartment in surprise. "We're allowed to paint our rooms any color we want as long as we repaint them white before we leave." Oak floors softly gleamed and area rugs added charm. The sitting room and attached dining room were a warm peach. Glancing through the arch to the kitchen, which was a decent size, Jazzi saw a robin egg blue tile backsplash. She had a thing for that color.

"Your apartment's lovely." The furniture was flowered and overstuffed. The girl was as pretty as her living quarters with long light brown hair and gray eyes.

"Thanks." Elspeth motioned them to a love seat and two armchairs. "You came about Donovan?"

Gaff removed his notepad from his shirt pocket and clicked his pen. "Did you go to his funeral?"

She looked down and shook her head. "I didn't know anyone there, not even his parents. I didn't want to break down when I looked in the coffin. I took the day off work, though. I knew I wouldn't be able to concentrate. I'd finally met a good guy and then . . . " She couldn't finish the sentence.

Gaff nodded toward Jazzi. "This is Jazzi Zanders Herstad. She's Thane and Radley's sister-in-law. At least, soon now, she'll be Thane's sister-in-law."

Elspeth grinned. "Donovan was close to both of them. He talked about them all the time."

Gaff poised his pen over a clean sheet of paper. "We've heard that he wasn't close to his father."

Elspeth grimaced. "They never clicked. Donovan didn't like to talk about him. He loved his mom, but they weren't close either. I got the feeling he didn't approve of his father but knew his mom would never leave him."

"What was his problem with his dad?" Gaff asked.

"Ray shared news with his family on a need to know basis. That worried Donovan. He always thought his dad was involved in stuff he shouldn't be."

"Did he have anything solid to base that on?"

"Only tidbits he'd overhear once in a while when his dad talked on the phone and thought no one was around. Nothing specific."

"Did he ever mention names of his dad's friends?"

She shook her head. "Sorry. He really tried not to think about his dad too much or spend time with him. That's one of the things he and Radley had in common. Neither of them was overly fond of his parents."

Since she'd mentioned his name, Jazzi said, "Radley's worried about you. He thought Donovan was lucky to find you."

Elspeth gave a gentle smile. "He's that type, isn't he? Such a nice person."

"He's taking Donovan's death pretty hard," Jazzi confided. "It might be nice for the two of you to get together and talk about him."

Elspeth's gray eyes widened in surprise. "Do you think he'd like that?"

Jazzi nodded. "Very much."

"It would help me," Elspeth admitted. "I don't have anyone to share my feelings with about Donovan."

"Would you mind if he called you?"

"Mind? I'd welcome it."

Jazzi turned to Gaff. She hadn't meant to hijack his interview, but he didn't have any more questions.

"If you think of anything, will you give me a call?" He handed her one of his cards.

Elspeth stood to see them out, and Jazzi grinned to herself as they made their way downstairs.

"Playing matchmaker?" Gaff sounded amused.

"I know better than that," Jazzi said. "But it wouldn't hurt to throw them together and see what happens, would it?"

Gaff shook his head but helped her in the car before driving to Donovan's old apartment. He stopped for the key from the super on their way up, and Brianne showed up ten minutes later.

She stepped into the room and glared at Jazzi. "What are you doing here?"

"I invited her." Gaff leaned against a wall. All of the furniture was gone. Brianne walked to the kitchen countertop and hopped on it.

Brianne raised her hand to check her freshly painted fingernails and wrinkled her nose. "I always smudge one of them, no matter how careful I am."

Gaff's look conveyed how he felt about that. "I want to talk to you about Ronnie and Gil."

She frowned. "What have they got to do with Donovan?"

"That's what I want to know." Gaff opened his notepad. "All I've come up with is that Ronnie knew Donovan's dad. They worked together at a warehouse once. And Ronnie knew Gil. We think he's the connection."

"If he worked with Donovan's dad, then they were involved in a scam of some kind. That's all Ronnie was any good at."

"Did Ronnie work with Jarrett?"

They already knew he had, so she didn't bother denying it. "Off and on. He was a gofer. Jarrett couldn't count on him for much of anything. And if anyone scared him enough, he'd blab everything he knew, so Jarrett didn't give him much information."

"And Gil?"

"Jarrett never worked with Gil. Those two didn't get along. Gil had a grudge against him for something personal. That's all he'd say."

"Something personal?" Gaff scribbled that in his book.

Brianne shrugged. "I figured it had something to do with Didi. Jarrett had the hots for her, but she didn't want anything to do with him."

"But you didn't mind that Jarrett was a criminal? That never bothered you?"

She unzipped her purse and searched until she found a stick of gum. "It's not like I go to Sunday school, is it? Jarrett was always good to me."

"And Donovan wasn't?"

"Donovan thought he was doing me a favor, letting me live with him. Who needs that? Jarrett loves me the way I am."

She had a point. Jazzi still didn't like her, but she understood her a little more.

"Was Jarrett with you Saturday night and Sunday morning?"

Brianne quit fiddling in her purse and stared at Gaff. "Why?"

"Ronnie didn't come home from work Sunday morning. He left the restaurant he worked at around one a.m. and disappeared. His grandma's worried about him."

"Is that old lady still alive? She should be dead by now, shouldn't she?"

Gaff's tone grew sharp. "She's alive and worried."

Brianne shrugged. "Maybe Ronnie got in hot water again, and he's hiding out."

"You didn't answer my question. Was Jarrett with you Saturday night and Sunday morning?"

Brianne ran her hands up and down her body. "He sure was, and we hardly got any sleep."

"Right." Gaff waved her to the door. "If I have any more questions, I'll let you know."

Brianne jumped off the counter and looked at Jazzi. "Jarrett says you have one big, ugly boyfriend."

Jazzi chuckled. "Big, yes. Ugly? Hardly."

"Does he look like his brother, the guy who lives in this building and knew Donovan?"

"He's better looking. And taller."

"Doggone, girl. You got lucky."

"Don't I know it."

Brianne paused at the door. "If he gets tired of you, let him know I'm not married. Jarrett and I don't have any strings attached."

"I'll tell him."

Brianne laughed. "That means you're not worried. He's all wrapped up, isn't he?"

"When we put our rings on our fingers, his options were over. He's stuck with me."

"Stuck with you. I like that." Brianne winked at her and left.

The girl was being too chummy. What was up? It made Jazzi suspicious.

Chapter 19

Tuesday morning, Gaff called when they were putting up drywall in the attic. "Hi, Jazzi. Can I talk to Bain?"

She handed her phone to Ansel's brother. He listened, then grinned from ear to ear. "And I don't have to wear an ankle bracelet?" A pause, then, "You're right. The sheriff and his deputies know where to find me."

When he handed the phone back to her, Bain looked at Ansel. "Gaff says I can go home."

"Now?"

"If you drive me to your place at lunch, I'll pack my pickup and take off. Gaff's keeping my gun for now. Evidence. But the sooner I get to the farm, the better. Dad needs me. Every night I call home, things have gotten a little worse."

Dalmar would make sure it sounded that way. He was a pro at guilting out his boys.

Ansel hesitated. "You're going to stick up for yourself this time, aren't you? Make Dad let you make the changes you want on the farm?"

"I'll try. And I want to check on Mom, maybe take her into town to the doctor."

Ansel nodded. "We'll take you home after we eat here. We'll both want to see you off."

Bain shook his head and turned to Jazzi. "If it's okay, I'd rather not have to say goodbye to you. It'll depress me. I know you didn't really want me here, but you were nice to me anyway, so thanks for taking me in."

He'd surprised her, so she surprised him with a hug. "Come back anytime. We'll miss you."

He barked a laugh. "Hardly. I'm not easy to like, but I'll miss you. I'll miss Radley, too. I've missed him ever since he left the farm."

She shook her finger at him, suddenly serious. "Start being nicer to yourself. You love the farm, but there's more to life than milking cows."

"I get that now. I'll try to remember it."

The next hour was awkward while they worked, and Ansel took mercy on them by grabbing two sandwiches for him and Bain to eat while he drove him home. "I'll be back soon," he told her and Jerod.

The two of them ate a quick lunch and finished the three walls before Ansel returned. Her Norseman looked sad.

"I usually want to punch Bain, but I feel a little sorry for him this time." He motioned toward the stairs. "I need another sandwich. Are there more?"

They trotted down to the kitchen with him and Jerod and Ansel ate a second round of lunch while Jazzi drank more coffee. They were getting ready to return to the attic again and plumb the fourth wall for the bathroom when Radley called.

"I'm not going to make it to your house for supper tonight," he told Ansel. "I called Donovan's steady, Elspeth, to check on her, and she invited me for supper at her place instead."

"So you're cancelling on us to go to Elspeth's?" Ansel's blue eyes sparkled as he studied Jazzi.

She pressed her lips together, trying to look innocent, and he grinned.

When he hung up, he cocked an eyebrow at her. "Radley said you mentioned that Donovan's girlfriend, Elspeth, was struggling since she lost him. Radley's going over there to comfort her."

"That's nice. They've both missed him, and she could use a friend."

Jerod smiled, too. "My cousin, the altruistic matchmaker. You must have liked her."

"I did. I think Radley did, too, so why shouldn't they cry on each other's shoulders?"

Laughing, Jerod started up the stairs. "If she feeds him, she'll never get rid of him. He's like a stray. One bowl, and he comes to your door every night."

A stray reminded her. "Did Bain take his cat?"

"Even took a leash for him so that he could stop on the drive home to let him do his business."

Stubs had never gotten friendly with Inky and Marmalade. "I hope Stubs is happy on the farm with the other barn cats."

"He's an outdoor cat. He'll have a barn to live in, fields to roam, and free food. I'm guessing he'll get preferential treatment, too."

Feeling a little smug, Jazzi left the guys to the plumbing and started taping the drywall seams they'd installed. She couldn't do the ceiling drywall herself. It was too heavy.

By four, they were more than ready to call it quits a little early. Even George kept walking to the door and looking back at them, ready to be carried to Ansel's van. People were coming to bake cookies and make candy tonight. Jazzi had made a pot of Manhattan clam chowder before they left in the morning, and she had a variety of crackers and cheeses to go with it.

Ansel had just settled George on the backseat when Jazzi's cell phone buzzed.

Radley sounded upset. "Could you and Ansel meet Elspeth and me at Donovan's parents' house? His mom's shaken and scared. Ray doesn't know she called us, and he won't be happy to see us, but she doesn't know what to do."

"What happened?"

"I'm not sure. She was crying and hard to understand, but I think Ray's had an accident."

Jazzi wasn't sure why Donovan's mom would want them there for that, but she agreed to meet them and gave Ansel directions to their house. When they got there, Donovan's mom was holding the door open for Radley and Elspeth, and Ray was yelling in the background. They all looked at each other, a bit leery, but his mom saw Jazzi, reached for her hand, and pulled her into the house. The rest followed.

"You're that detective's friend. I couldn't call him. Ray would have my hide, but someone's hurt him, and he won't admit it. Says that a refrigerator started to slide off the back of the truck, and when he tried to catch it, he got the wrong end of the deal."

Ray stomped into the room to glare at his wife. "Maureen had no business calling anybody. I did something stupid and ended up with a black eye and broken fingers."

Jazzi stared at his hand. His left eye was swollen and bruised. All four fingers on his left hand were splinted and wrapped tightly. "Good, you saw a doctor."

"Had to, didn't I? I told the doc what I'm telling you. I caught the refrigerator wrong and barely kept it from hitting the ground. Broke my fingers and bumped my face doing it."

Either that, or someone broke his fingers for him. Jazzi took a deep breath. "If someone did this to you, and you didn't give them the answers they wanted, they can do it again."

He grimaced. "Don't go making something out of nothing. You've been hanging around with that detective too long. I had an accident. That's all, but my fool woman got all crazy on me."

"You're taking a few days off and staying home, aren't you?" Maureen asked.

"Will that make you happy so you quit harping at me?"

She nodded.

"Then I'll take the rest of the week off. I have plenty of vacation days."

Maureen calmed down a little. She sniffed and wiped at her eyes. "I'll stay home with you."

Ray groaned. "If you have to."

She gave him a look and he shrugged. "Are we good now?"

She turned to them. "Thank you for coming. I saw Ray and panicked."

Jazzi would have panicked, too, and she didn't believe Ray's story any more than Maureen did. She tried one more time. "If you have a problem and talk to Gaff, he could help you."

Ray waved them away. "No problem. No cops. We're going to be okay."

There wasn't much more they could do. They turned and started to their cars. Elspeth put a hand on Jazzi's arm. "Thanks for coming. I wasn't sure what to do."

Radley nodded. "I'd never met either of Donovan's parents. He said his dad wasn't easy to work with, so I was worried."

"Happy we could help. Are you going to have supper now?"

Elspeth laced her fingers with Radley's. "I made meatloaf and mashed potatoes. He swears that's his favorite."

Everything was Radley's favorite, but Jazzi didn't mention that. They walked to their vehicles and went their separate ways. Jazzi had to hurry to take a quick shower and be ready when everyone came. She had to push thoughts of Ronnie and Ray out of her mind to concentrate on her friends. But it was too much of a coincidence that Ronnie was missing and Ray had been beaten up.

Didi and River came with Walker, then Gran and Samantha arrived. Gran, as usual, went for her red wine, then stopped and stared into space.

"Jarrett and Gavin are both violent men," she told them. "Stay away from them."

With luck, Jazzi intended to never meet Gavin. Jarrett was enough. She wondered if Ray had worked with both of them. When they all stood in line to ladle clam chowder into their bowls, she asked Didi, "Did Gil know Gavin?"

"He knew *of* him. He warned Ronnie that if he got involved with him, he was on his own. Gil would wash his hands of him. Gil wasn't happy Gavin was his cellmate. He and Jarrett had reputations for being violent. Rumor was Gavin killed two people, but no one ever found the bodies."

Jazzi shivered. Would anyone ever find Ronnie?

Ansel slipped an arm around her waist. "What are you baking tonight?" A subtle hint to lighten up.

Jazzi smiled. "I thought we'd make a few different kinds of chocolate chip cookies."

"Yay!" River bounced up and down until Didi laid a hand on his shoulder.

"First supper, then baking," she told him. "Are we making a candy?"

"Peppermint bark with Rice Krispies."

Everyone seemed pleased, so they ate quickly. Walker and Ansel cleaned up after supper, and the women started mixing cookie dough. When they finished, they'd made ten dozen cookies, so there were plenty for people to take home. Not that River needed any more. Gran kept slipping him cookies while they baked. When Jazzi gave her a look, she said, "a cookie's at its best when it's still warm."

By the time the last person left, Ansel and Jazzi sagged against each other on the sofa.

Ansel turned his head and listened. "It's quiet. There's no one in the house but us."

She let out a long sigh. "Maybe we made a mistake when we designed this place for entertaining."

He laughed. "Entertaining means you wine and dine people, then send them home. We've run a boarding house since Christmas. We're finally alone. If I weren't so tired, I'd carry you upstairs and have my way with you, but when my head hits the pillow, I'm done for."

She snuggled against him. "That's the nice thing about being married. I'll see you again tomorrow night. And the night after that."

He lowered his head to rest it on top of hers. "Until we're old and gray. It's all good."

She couldn't agree more. They sat like that, simply enjoying each other, until they couldn't keep their eyes open. Then they finally called it a night.

Chapter 20

Wednesday blew in, starting March with its trademark winds. Small limbs littered the yard. Tree branches whipped back and forth in the woods behind their house. Jazzi packed ham and cheese sandwiches in the cooler, then added her panini maker to heat them at the fixer-upper. A warm lunch would taste good today. Before Jazzi and Ansel walked out the door, Gaff called.

"I'm going to check in on Ronnie's grandma today. Mind coming along? She could use a friendly face."

Jazzi had worried about the old lady. "When will you pick me up?"

"Two in the afternoon? I have a few things I have to do first."

"I'll be ready." She explained to Ansel as they got ready to go. Ansel had decided that George was shivering more than usual, so he'd dressed him in a doggie sweater for the day. If the dog sneezed, Ansel worried about him. Her tough looking Norseman was a marshmallow inside.

When they reached the house, Ansel carried George up the steps to the attic, so that he could be with them while they worked. She, Jerod, and Ansel spent the entire morning lifting and nailing drywall in place for the ceiling. Along with the insulation, the area already felt more comfortable. Jazzi's arms, however, felt like lead, like she might never be able to lift them again. They only took a short lunch break, even though the paninis were a big hit, so they could finish the ceiling by the time Gaff arrived. The guys were going to finish walling off the bathroom space while she was gone.

When she and Gaff reached Ronnie's grandma's house, the wind blew hard enough, Gaff put an arm under Jazzi's elbow and they leaned into the sharp gusts to walk up the sidewalk. When they knocked, a small voice called, "It's open."

They entered, and heat hit them hard. The woman had the furnace set so high, the air was stifling. Jazzi knew old people did that. When she was a little girl and visited her great-grandma, the house was so hot that Jazzi always left with a headache. Today, Ronnie's grandma sat in a high backed rocking chair, wearing a long chenille robe and heavy stockings with a blanket draped over her legs.

Jazzi's heart sank. The last time they'd seen her, she'd reminded Jazzi of a pert, little bird—small and quick with bright, alert eyes. Now her shoulders drooped and it looked like all the energy had drained out of her. She looked at Jazzi and shook her head.

"Ronnie wouldn't just go off and not tell me. He'd call from somewhere to let me know he was okay."

Gaff took a chair close to hers. "Did he talk about meeting anyone? Doing anything unusual?"

"He promised to bring me home some of them chicken wings from his restaurant. Knows how I like 'em. He didn't forget stuff like that. Somethin' happened to my boy. Somethin' bad."

"Did he ever have to hide out from anyone?" Gaff asked. "Did he have a spot he ran to when he was in trouble?"

"He came here. He knew I'd take care of 'im." She lifted a handkerchief to her eyes. "I ain't got no one else. His mama's off who knows where. My son moved to Atlanta, close to retirement now. Has a house and family of his own. He don't need me."

Jazzi glanced at Gaff. Maybe they should call her son, tell him what happened. Gaff must have been thinking the same thing. He nodded.

"Is there someone we can call to stay with you?" Jazzi asked. "You look like you could use some company right now."

The old woman smiled at her. "Ain't you a nice girl? My friend Pudding from church is comin' this afternoon. The church ladies have cooked me some nice casseroles and they're meetin' here for a prayer meetin' tomorrow. Don't think even prayer'll help my Ronnie, though."

"But it might help you." Jazzi thought the woman had been through enough having her daughter take off, leaving her to raise her son and then having that grandson go to prison.

"Pudding always makes me feel better." She pulled her blanket higher and rearranged it on her knees.

Jazzi leaned forward to pat her hand. "I'm being nosy, but how did your friend get the nickname Pudding?"

Ronnie's grandma smiled again. "First off, she loves the stuff. Second, she eats enough of it, she kinda has that same, soft feel to her. Ya know?"

Jazzi grinned, but Gaff stood more abruptly than usual.

"Are you going to be okay?" he asked.

"Don't you worry 'bout me. I been through enough bad times, I'll get through this, too."

Jazzi wished she could wrap the old woman in blankets of hugs, but her friends would be here this afternoon, and they'd help see her through this. She bent to kiss her cheek before she followed Gaff out the door.

Once in the car, Gaff said, "I'll call her son. I have the information at the office. Ronnie sure let that woman down, though." His voice was gruff. "And he probably isn't going to be around to make up for it."

Jazzi was thinking the same thing. That reminded her to tell him about Didi saying that the rumor about Gavin was that he'd killed two people but no one ever found the bodies. "Did you visit him this morning?"

"Sure did. He, his two brothers, and dad were all painting the inside of a house together. Own a company business. They do roofing in good weather and painting in bad. They were all smoking and joking because the jobs were so easy now that all four of them are out of the joint at the same time."

Jazzi blinked. "That's a rare thing?"

"For them. They go in and out like a revolving door. All built like refrigerators. All have nasty tempers. And they all like to drink."

The word refrigerator reminded Jazzi of going to Maureen and Ray's house last night. She told Gaff about Ray's eye and fingers.

Gaff shook his head. "His wife knows someone beat him up, but she didn't call me. Ray wouldn't tell me anything anyway."

"He must think he's safe now, that whoever did that to him doesn't think he was involved in whatever happened."

Gaff's scowl only deepened. "You'd think if the same guy who broke Ray's fingers killed his son, Ray would tell us."

"I'm not so sure about that." The words left her lips before she thought them through, but that was her gut feeling. "I think Ray cares more about covering his own fanny than avenging Donovan."

Gaff grimaced. "You might be right. For Ray, what's done is done. Or maybe, if the guy who visited him was Gavin, he was afraid if he ratted on him, his brothers would come for him or Maureen."

Jazzi hadn't thought of that. "Is Gavin married?"

Gaff turned toward the center of town. It wouldn't be long before she was back at work. "Married with two kids, eight and eleven. Bragged that his wife visited him every week and brought a carton of cigarettes. Got the feeling she didn't care much what he did as long as she had enough money to pay bills."

"Did you mention the rumor that he'd killed two people?"

"It came up when I told him about Ronnie disappearing. He just shrugged. Said I should check on Jarrett's schedule for that night. When I told him Jarrett had been with Brianne the entire time, he laughed and said any smart woman would say that. Guess two women filed restraining orders against Jarrett before he went to prison."

Jazzi let out a frustrated sigh. When every person seemed to be worse than the one before, how did you decide who did anything?

Gaff was passing Calhoun Street and glanced sideways at her. "Do you mind if I stop to talk to Ronnie's coworkers before I take you home? The restaurant's only a couple blocks away. They might remember if Ronnie said something the night he disappeared."

"Sure, it won't take long to talk to the cooks."

He turned and headed to a small restaurant on the fringes of town. It served ribs, wings, and fries as its specialties. When he asked at the front counter, the hostess led them to the kitchen. The two cooks were working double shifts today.

The one was precooking wings and looked up and saw Gaff. When the wings were ready, he took them out and added more, calling to his friend, who was working on fries. "We got company! Look sharp."

Their eyes lit up when they saw Jazzi and moseyed over to talk.

"You got a new partner, Gaff?" the first cook asked. "Looks like you moved up in the world."

Gaff grinned. "No, this is a friend of mine. She went with me to an earlier interview. She's good at soothing family members."

"She can soothe me anytime," the second guy joked. "What would you like to ask me, honey?"

She'd worked around enough men to appreciate these two. They both looked harmless. "We were hoping you'd remember some small thing that Ronnie said the night he disappeared that might help us find him."

The first guy swiped his face with his apron. The kitchen was steamy. The second man had a blue bandanna wrapped around his forehead to catch the sweat. Bandanna said, "We've been talking about Ronnie. Can't think of anything. We watched him get in his car and drive away. Told us he was going home. We liked the boy."

"Even though he had a police record?" Gaff asked.

Apron man shrugged. "I spent some time in jail. Drunk and disorderly. Jed here got picked up for his stash of marijuana. We've been trying to talk the manager into hiring Ronnie as a cook."

Gaff shook his head. "His probation officer came in a while ago, saw Ronnie drinking on his break."

Bandanna man chuckled. "Small time stuff. He'd get a slap on the wrist for that. We told him so. Might spend a weekend in jail, but we'd take him some cigarettes."

"The way we see it," Apron added, "is Ronnie was a criminal by default. He didn't have nothing better to do. If he became a cook, he could make a living. He'd never be rich, but he could always find a job."

"The boy swore he'd never go back to prison." The timer buzzed on the second batch of wings and Bandanna went to dump them out of the fry basket and add more.

Apron nodded. "He'd never make it there on his own."

Gaff started buttoning up his coat again. "Ronnie didn't say anything about meeting anyone or hiding out somewhere?"

They both shook their heads.

"Thanks," he told them.

They smiled at Jazzi. "You come back and see us anytime. We'll sneak you free wings."

She laughed. "I'll remember that."

Outside, Gaff held the car door for her, then drove toward the fixer-upper. "Thanks for going with me today. I wanted to make it as easy as I could for Ronnie's grandma, and the two cooks sure liked seeing you."

"They're decent guys."

"Yeah, they would have been good for Ronnie."

But Ronnie had never made it home, and his grandma would fret, not knowing what happened to him.

Chapter 21

It was hard for Jazzi to shift gears and get into home repairs again. But they were making progress on the Victorian. With any luck, they'd have the interior finished by the time the weather turned warm enough to work outside.

The guys were still busy finishing the walls for the attic bathroom, so she grabbed the tape to start finishing the ceiling's seams. It meant holding her hands above her head again. She was a strong woman, but that got to her back and neck every time. She was relieved when Jerod's cell phone beeped and they took a quick break. He walked a little distance away to hear better. When he returned to them, he said, "Franny says you and Ansel have been so nice to us, she'd like to have you over for pizza tonight. Can you make it?"

"Hmm, tough call. Great company. No cooking. We'll be there," Jazzi said. "But are you sure? Peter's still waking you up every night, isn't he?"

"That comes with the territory." He pressed his phone to his ear. "It's a go, babe."

When he hung up, Jazzi asked, "Can I bring anything?"

"Just yourselves. I have plenty of wine and beer. We're talking about a small menu."

"Perfect." She didn't need any fancy extras when pizza was on offer.

Jerod grinned. "I'll call in the order and pick up the pizzas on my way home. This isn't a hint for more, but we've gone through all your food, so Franny thought of pizza and then she thought of you two. We're more in the rhythm with Peter now, and Franny's not as wiped out from giving birth. Things are falling in place again."

"But Peter still doesn't sleep through the night?" Jazzi didn't think she could function on short rations of sleep.

"That would be a miracle, but no. Gunther and Lizzie didn't until they were six or seven weeks old. But when Peter takes his nap and the kids are in preschool, Franny gets a quick nap, too. We take turns sleeping in on the weekends, and Gunther and Lizzie watch cartoons until we get up. We're all adjusting."

He did look better. Regardless of what he said, though, Jazzi intended to make one more batch of food for them. For nights when things *didn't* fall into place.

Jerod nodded to the last few studs they needed to cover to finish the wall. "If you two finish that, I'll call in the order and we can take off at five."

Even better. Ceiling work could wait until tomorrow.

Half an hour later, Ansel carried George down the steps and to the van. Jazzi grabbed the cooler, but left the panini maker. It was going to be cold outside again tomorrow. Then they locked up and went their separate ways.

"Want to stop on the way and buy some ice cream for dessert?" Ansel asked. "It will take Jerod a minute to grab the pizzas."

Jazzi liked the idea. She grabbed some toppings, too—hot fudge, caramel sauce, and maraschino cherries. When they pulled into Jerod's drive, he was walking to the house, balancing the pizza boxes. Jazzi followed him with the grocery bag, and Ansel cradled George in his arms. It was a good thing Ansel had biceps like iron. The dog was no lightweight. She wouldn't be able to carry him as far as Ansel did.

Franny smiled when she saw them. Her carrot colored hair was pulled back in a bun, and dark circles still rimmed her eyes, but she did look better. "I'm glad you could make it at short notice. We're grateful for all the food you sent."

"Glad to help out." Lizzie ran and held up her hands for Jazzi to lift her. Ugh! Her arms were sore, but how could she turn down such a cute kid? Gunther went straight to Ansel. He put down George and reached for Gunther. They carried both kids to the table, and Jerod passed out paper plates, then flipped the lids open on the pizza boxes.

People talked over each other, the kids talking about their day at school, and Franny excited that she got to spend an hour refinishing a buffet she bought at an auction. Peter slept through it all.

"My mom told me not to tiptoe around when a baby naps. She said if you do, they'll wake up at every little noise. She was right. I run the sweeper and bang dishes while Peter sleeps, and nothing fazes him." Franny finished her third slice of meat lovers' pizza.

Jazzi liked Franny's mom. She didn't see her often, but Hilda struck her as a practical, cheerful woman. "Is your mom having a hard time staying away from the baby?"

Franny laughed. "She comes here every day she doesn't have to work. Of course, that's sort of rare." Hilda restocked the produce aisle at a grocery store and volunteered at a pet shelter. The woman knew half the people in River Bluffs, or it seemed that way.

"Has she volunteered to babysit yet?"

"She's ready. I want to wait till Peter sleeps through the night." Franny reached for a Pepsi. She never drank alcohol when she was nursing. "Right now, she's been fussing over a young guy she works with at the store. He sacks groceries and stocks shelves. He told her that he needed more hours and more money, and a guy offered him a side job, but he didn't feel good about taking it."

"What kind of side job?"

"The guy said he'd only need him once in a while but there'd be good money in it each time he called him."

Jazzi couldn't help but think of Ronnie. Those kinds of side jobs got you in a lot of trouble. "What did your mom tell him?"

"That if the money was too good, there was something wrong with it. She told the kid to steer clear of him. But she worries that the money will be too tempting, so she keeps checking on him."

"Your mom's one of the best."

Franny grinned and nodded. "She and Dad did a pretty good job with my three sisters and me."

Jazzi sometimes forgot that Franny had three sisters. Two of them lived in town, but Sandy had moved to Cleveland, and Jazzi had only seen her at Jerod and Franny's wedding.

Ansel swallowed his last bite of sausage and mushroom and got up to carry the ice cream and toppings to the table. "I'm surprised the kid at the store talked to your mom about that."

Jerod snorted. "Hilda's like Franny and Jazzi. People confide in them all the time, even people who hardly know them."

Ansel's gaze met Jazzi's. "That's true. Strangers tell Jazzi stuff that surprises me."

Jerod scooped two balls of butter pecan ice cream into Franny's bowl and doused them with hot fudge. "Our women look approachable, have that good listener look, like they'd sympathize."

Was that why people confided in her? Jazzi didn't *feel* approachable, but did anyone see himself the way others saw him? She wanted to know more about the kid. "Did the boy listen to your mom?"

Peter fussed, and Franny cocked her head to listen. When he was quiet again, she said, "The boy told Mom that he didn't know the guy who called and that worried him. I guess the kid's buddy met him and blabbed that they'd spent time together in juvie. The buddy's on parole."

"Why was his buddy on parole?" Jazzi drizzled both caramel sauce and hot fudge over her butter pecan.

"Got in a bar fight. Some drunk was pestering his girlfriend. They ended up in a brawl."

"And he got in trouble for that?" Ansel asked. "It sounds like the other man started it."

Franny nodded. "He wasn't twenty-one. He shouldn't have been in the bar. Had a fake ID. When the cop looked him up, he had a warrant for disorderly conduct."

"Well that explains it. Kids that age like to bend the rules." Ansel drained his beer bottle, and Jerod handed him a fresh one.

Peter's cry this time was more insistent. Franny gulped the last of her dessert, then hurried to the bassinet in the living room. While she nursed him, the rest of them finished up and helped clear the table, putting all of the extra pizza in one box to save. When Franny returned, she put Peter to her shoulder to burp. Jazzi couldn't believe such a loud noise could come from such a small body.

Ansel went to stare at him. When Franny offered to let him hold him, he gladly took the baby and held him to his shoulder, too. That's when spit up spewed all over his flannel shirt. Franny grabbed a napkin to swipe it off, but the smell was rank. Ansel shrugged. "When you work in a barn, it can be worse."

Jerod laughed and reached for his son. Jazzi and Ansel went for their winter coats and Ansel carried George back to the van. As far as Jazzi knew, George's paws only touched snow when they let him out to do his number.

When they got home, the cats hunched in front of their food bowls and meowed. Ansel and Jazzi hadn't come straight home after work, and the cats were hungry. While Jazzi fed and petted them, Ansel frowned at a missed message on his cell phone.

"Bain called."

"You'd better call him back." George came for a treat, too, and she gave him one. The pug hadn't begged for pizza, which had surprised her. But he tried not to get too close to Jerod's kids.

Ansel put his phone on speaker when Bain said, "Jazzi might want to hear this, too."

"How's the farm?" Ansel asked.

"We're getting caught up, but what I wanted to let you know is that I took Mom to the doctor in town. She's anemic and low on vitamin D. Both things they can fix, but she's diabetic, too. She needs to take a class to teach her how to manage her blood sugar. The doctor recommended that she takes a week off to rest and get stronger. She's so far behind on cleaning and cooking, I hired a local girl to help out for a week. I'm paying for her out of my own money. Dad isn't happy about it. He thinks that money could go into the farm, but Mom needs help. The doctor wants to see her three times a year until her numbers get stable. He says to think of it as maintenance."

Ansel's lips pressed together in a tight line. Sometimes, Jazzi knew, he'd like to throttle his dad. "Jazzi and I want to help out. We'll send money for the girl to stay an extra week."

"That's not necessary. I can cover it," Bain said.

"She's my mom, too. We want to." He glanced at Jazzi, and she nodded. "I'll tell Radley, and he might want to pitch in, too."

"Any help will be appreciated." Bain sounded sincere.

"We'll send it Quick Pay to your account," Ansel said. "Make sure Mom gets all the help she needs. And thanks for taking her in. Dad never would have done it."

"I know. I'm starting to see that side of Dad. And he's going to let me plant orchards and start beehives this spring, or else."

Ansel smiled. "Flex your muscles, bro. You have rights, too."

When they hung up, Ansel reached for her and held her close. They just stood and hugged, swaying together. Her Norseman needed some TLC, and she was happy to oblige.

Chapter 22

On Thursday, Jazzi decided to run to the store after she dropped Ansel at the fixer-upper. They'd intended to buy more deli meat and bread last night, but they'd forgotten after the pizza and Jerod's kids. The kids had a way of wearing them out. She didn't know how Jerod did it, but he swore when they were your own, it was different, you settled into a pattern. Still, no one would be happy with peanut butter on crackers for lunch.

Ansel was happy to let her drive to New Haven. The man felt no need to prove his manliness and was more than okay with letting her climb behind the steering wheel. When they reached the house, he leaned over to kiss her before he scooped up George and headed inside.

Alone, Jazzi turned south and drove farther to get to the store Franny's mom worked at. Jerod and Ansel would wonder where she'd gotten to. There was a store in New Haven only ten minutes away, but she was curious about the kid Franny had told them about. Franny had mentioned that her mom would be working today, and Jazzi wanted to ask her a few questions.

Hilda's store was a lot smaller than the superstore close to their house. Jazzi decided to do her shopping first, so it would be finished before she tracked her down. After buying ham and roast beef, she added a round of crusty bread from the bakery. For good measure, since she was taking longer than usual, she bought a chocolate cake, too. Dessert went a long way to tame the savage beasts, and both men liked chocolate.

Last but not least, she went to the produce aisle for lettuce and picked up red pepper relish on her way. They all liked it for a change of pace. Hilda was restocking boxes of mushrooms when Jazzi went to talk to her.

The minute Hilda saw her, she stopped working, staring at her in surprise. "I didn't think you'd make it here this fast. Franny said she wouldn't see you till Sunday."

Jazzi blinked, confused. "I saw Franny last night."

"She told me, and that reminded me that you work with a detective once in a while, don't you?"

"Gaff? I don't work with him, but I'm a tagalong once in a while."

"Good." Hilda motioned for Jazzi to follow her into a back room. "I want you to talk to Chad. I told him you knew a detective, and he's worried about his friend."

This was working out better than Jazzi had hoped. Hilda led her through a maze of pallets stacked with canned goods to a table and chairs in the center of the room. A young kid sat there, eating chicken nuggets and drinking a Coke. Hilda sat down opposite him and nodded toward Jazzi. "This is the woman I was telling you about, the one who works with a detective once in a while."

Jazzi opened her mouth to correct her. She didn't do police work, but decided it didn't matter. She smiled. "Hi, I'm Jazzi."

Chad narrowed his eyes. "Hilda thinks you might be able to help me."

"What do you need?"

"I'm worried about my friend. He's bummed that he's still on probation when he didn't do anything big. He's mad at the cop who sent him to juvie. Mad enough to do something dumb."

Hilda clasped her hands together on the tabletop. "Chad wants to make a deal with you."

"With me?" What in the world could she help him with?

Chad squared his shoulders. "If I talk to you, tell you what I know, would Gaff get my buddy off probation? Cut him loose? It isn't fair he's in so much trouble. The guy at the bar wouldn't leave his girlfriend alone."

"He should have complained to the bartender," Jazzi said.

"He lost his temper, okay? Anyway, he learned his lesson. It won't happen again."

Jazzi wasn't so sure about that, but what would it hurt if she asked Gaff to help the friend out? "I'll ask him, but that doesn't mean he'll agree."

Chad looked thoughtful. "Tell him that the guy wanted to hire him and me to move parts. If Gaff can help us, I'll tell him his name."

"Have you got a phone number so I can have Gaff call you?"

The kid took her cell phone and punched it in.

She jammed her phone back into her jeans pocket. "I'll call him when I get home. And good luck."

Hilda led her back to her cart, and Jazzi thanked her before heading to checkout.

When she got to the fixer-upper, the guys came to see what had taken her so long. While they made sandwiches for lunch, she told them about Chad and the deal he offered Gaff. George came to beg when he smelled deli ham, and Ansel tossed him some small bites.

Jerod wolfed down a sandwich, then started to make another one. It was a nuisance bending over the coffee table to work. Once they finished the drywall and framing upstairs, Jazzi was ready to work on the ground floor again. She wanted the kitchen installed.

Jerod took a bite of his second sandwich before saying, "If I were Gaff, I'd make the deal. The kid's buddy didn't do anything I didn't do when I was that age. Heck, I probably did more. It seems like a good trade-off to me."

Ansel frowned. "Will it get Chad or his friend in trouble with the guy who's trying to hire them?"

She'd worried about that, too. "Gaff should be able to work around that somehow. I know he'll take that into consideration." Jazzi opened the lid on the chocolate cake. Between the dessert and her news, the guys didn't mind the extra time she'd taken.

When they finished their lunch, Jerod gave Jazzi a nod. "Call Gaff and see what he says. I want to know before I leave for the night."

She'd picked up the phone to dial him when it rang in her hand. She glanced at the ID. "Gaff."

"Good, I wanted to talk to you," she said, answering it.

"What about?"

When she filled him in, he said, "I'll see what I can do. If it ties into this case—and it might—I'd like a name. I have bad news. We found Ronnie's car on a side road in the country. Someone called it in after it sat there so long. Ronnie's body was in a ditch across the road from it. A bullet in his head. I have to go talk to his grandma now."

She put a hand to her heart. It hurt. She could picture Ronnie's grandma pulling her blanket even closer to shield herself from the news. Poor Gaff. She didn't envy him his job. "Do you have the name of her friend?" she asked. "It was Pudding, wasn't it? Could you get her there when you tell his grandma?"

"That's a good idea. I'll see what I can do. I can call her church and see if someone can give me some names."

"It's a stinky job, Gaff."

"Comes with my line of work. Tell me the kid's number again so I can call him when I get back to the station."

"I don't want to get him or his friend killed." She felt bad enough that they'd talked to Ronnie and now he was dead.

"Whoever killed Ronnie expected us to question him. There has to be more to what happened. And I'll be careful with the kids."

"Let us know what happens?"

"Will do." He disconnected, and Jazzi told the guys the news.

Jerod took a deep breath. "I keep telling my kids to choose their friends wisely. One rotten apple can spoil everything he touches."

Ansel lowered his hand to stroke George's head—a habit of his when he was upset. "Whoever's involved in what's happening doesn't mind killing. I hate having two young guys in the middle of this investigation."

Jazzi could hear the worry in his voice. She put her hand over his. "Look at it this way. If Chad's friend hooks up with whoever's trying to hire him, I think his chances of being dead are even higher."

Ansel took a second to mull that over. "You could be right. Talking to Gaff's probably a safer risk than moving stolen goods."

Slightly more satisfied, they trotted upstairs to finish their work in the attic. By the end of the day, they were ready to wrap up and start on the kitchen tomorrow. First, they'd prime and paint. The three of them could finish that in one day. Then they'd install new floors. They couldn't save or restore the old ones. And then they could install the appliances and cupboards. For the Victorian, they'd chosen white Shaker cupboards with black hardware and butcher block countertops. They'd give the kitchen a warm, homey feel.

They were cleaning up when Jazzi's cell rang again.

"Gaff." She put the phone on speaker.

"Ronnie was shot at close range. Looks like he drove out to meet someone he knew. His grandma told me that an old friend had called him, and Ronnie told him he didn't want to work with him anymore. He meant to go clean. His grandma was proud of him. She heard him tell his friend that he might know someone else who'd want the job."

"Chad's friend?" Jazzi asked.

"Yeah, when I talked to the kid, he said that it was Ronnie who'd called him. They worked as busboys together at a restaurant once."

"So, you still don't have the name of who called Ronnie. Do you have Ronnie's cell phone?"

"The killer probably took it with him. We looked for it. The good news, Chad's buddy's out of probation and both of the guys should be safe. Ronnie never gave them his friend's name. There's no trail to follow."

"But the killer took Ronnie's phone. He could look them up."

"He knows better than that. Once Ronnie's murder hits the papers, he won't risk the kids connecting him to it."

That *was* good news, but it was a bummer Gaff hadn't found another clue. Still, Jazzi was relieved the boys were out of the loop.

"If I hear anything else, I'll pass it on." As usual, the phone disconnected. When Gaff was busy working a case, the niceties disappeared.

Jerod glanced at them. "I guess that means everything's wrapped up here tonight."

Ansel nodded, but didn't look happy. "I don't like it that somehow Didi might be wrapped up in this. I'm glad it's our Thursday night out. Maybe it'll take my mind off this mess."

Jerod shrugged into his coat. "That's the good thing about kids. Once you walk inside your house, you don't have time to think about anything else."

They locked up and left. George stared at them on the drive home. The pug knew it was Thursday and they'd leave him tonight. He'd suffer and pout until they returned. This time, Ansel's phone buzzed, and it was Walker.

"Didi heard about Ronnie." His voice carried in the van, and Jazzi listened in. "She's really upset. I don't want to leave her alone. Can you guys come here tonight for supper? I'll order in Chinese. Thane and Olivia are coming, too."

Jazzi tried not to be disappointed. She was looking forward to meeting Olivia at a Mexican restaurant, having a margarita or two. She didn't want to think about Gaff's case. But she couldn't shrug off Didi. She nodded and Ansel said, "We'll be there."

When he hung up, he didn't look any happier about it than she did. Thursday night was for going out, leaving your cares behind you. That wasn't going to happen this week. She called Olivia to share the news, and her sister said Thane and her would be at Walker's, too.

"Tonight sounds like a real downer, though," Olivia said.

Too true. But what could they do? They'd all show up to support Didi and Walker.

She and Ansel parked his van in the garage, then hurried through their evening routine—feeding the pets, showering, and changing clothes. They had to hustle to make it to Walker's at six. Ansel pushed a little harder on the pickup's gas pedal than usual.

Supper was a somber affair. Walker had ordered Chinese appetizers and four different entrees, but people only picked at their food. Even Ansel, who could usually eat regardless. Didi looked like a lit powder keg, ready to explode. River picked up on his mother's mood and was more quiet than usual.

Walker finally nodded at him. "Why don't you take your supper downstairs and eat while you watch TV?"

"I can do that?"

"Tonight."

River didn't need to be told twice. He grabbed his plate and took off. Soon, the sound of a video game drifted up to them.

Walker relaxed a little. "Good, he can't hear us."

Didi immediately blurted, "Gil always protected Ronnie! Always. I think whoever killed Ronnie, killed Gil. And that means it had to be someone they were in prison with, and I want Gaff to find out who did it."

Walker put his hand on her back and rubbed up and down to soothe her. He gave her a look of sympathy. "We *all* want this guy caught. He killed our friend, Donovan, and he didn't have anything to do with the robberies. He just walked in when the guy was trashing his apartment."

Didi relaxed a little under Walker's touch. "I can't figure out what he's looking for. Gil and I lived in my house before Gil went to prison, but he never brought anything home."

"Someone must think he did," Walker said.

Thane sat up, glancing around the table. "That makes me remember. Donovan's parents gave him the couch in his living room, the one that got slashed. I gave him a few things, but his mom wanted a new couch and talked Ray into letting him have their old one. Maybe the killer thinks Ray stashed something in it and sent it to Donovan's place to keep it safe."

Another connection. Jazzi would have to tell Gaff about the couch. "I thought all of the jobs Ronnie and his friends pulled were small time, not worth much."

"Gil never came home with a big share," Didi said. "Or at least, he never told me about it." She frowned. "But maybe he wouldn't't."

Jazzi mulled that over. "The only person who linked Donovan to the crimes is Ray. And Ray worked with Ronnie once. The last time I saw him, someone broke his fingers. Maybe Gaff should look into him more."

Ansel nodded. "It makes me wonder why the killer didn't hesitate to shoot Donovan and Ronnie, but didn't shoot him."

"Unless he thinks he needs Ray," Thane said. "He's the one with a truck, right?"

Walker's hand paused on Didi's back. "And he'd be the one who could move stuff that might make more money than sticking up a drugstore."

"Enough money to kill over?" Ansel asked.

"That's hard to believe." Didi pressed her lips together, clearly frustrated. "But then, what do these guys consider big money? How much would it take for them to turn on each other?"

"Whoever killed Gil didn't make any money off it at all," Jazzi pointed out.

That made everyone sit back and think.

Olivia glanced around the table, studying their faces. "You guys keep thinking there might be a good reason this killer does what he does. But maybe he's so violent, it doesn't take much."

Jazzi shivered and rubbed her hands up and down her arms to calm herself. That, unfortunately, struck her as very possible. From the expressions on her friends' faces, they thought so, too.

Chapter 23

Thank the heavens it was Friday. All Jazzi wanted to do today was prime and paint the fixer-upper, then have a fun night. That is, if today's weather didn't drown them first. Rain had started in the early hours and never quit. The week had started crappy and meant to finish that way. They all must have been ready for a break because the ceilings and walls were done before they broke for lunch. They'd decided on white ceilings and wheat colored walls to add warmth to the rooms. Splattered with paint, they cracked the windows for ventilation, then carried their sandwiches and George upstairs to escape the fumes. Ansel and Jerod had worn baseball caps to keep the paint out of their hair, and Jazzi had pinned hers up and wrapped it in a large bandanna style scarf.

Ansel grinned at her. "You'd make a gorgeous peasant."

She rolled her eyes. "You need to add horns on the side of your baseball cap to look like a Viking."

"They didn't really wear horns, you know." He sounded smug. "Some movie director must have thought horns were more dramatic."

"They should have worn them." She took a bite of her panini. "They were dangerous enough."

"Am I dangerous?" He lifted his lips in a half grin.

"Oh, yeah. Women should run from you."

"You didn't."

She shrugged. "The devil you know…"

Jerod shook his head. "Enough with the cute talk. Eat up so we can get back to work."

Her cousin wanted an early night. That said, they didn't linger. After washing down two sandwiches with coffee, the guys were ready to go again.

Jerod narrowed his eyes, studying the rooms, and nodded. "The place already looks better, but so far, nothing we've done has jazzed it up for curb appeal. We won't get any early offers."

They'd gotten spoiled. Houses were selling so fast lately, people had paid for flips before they'd finished them, but that was because they usually worked on the exteriors before the interiors. Impossible in winter weather.

"Let's at least get the downstairs ready to show. The wooden floors should sell it." They'd gotten the engineered maple planks on a closeout sale, and they were beautiful. They'd bought enough for the entire downstairs to match.

They trudged down the steps and pulled on their knee protectors. Jazzi couldn't wait to see how the floor looked when it was finished. This was the part of every job that excited her, when they could see how everything pulled together. After the kitchen, they were going to move to the far wall in the living room to lay the floor perpendicular to the kitchen's. That room spanned the entire front of the house. They had made it to the large arch to the dining room when someone knocked on the door.

They all waited for Gaff to push the door open and pop in, like he usually did. When that didn't happen, Jerod called, "It's open!"

A man they'd never seen before hesitantly stepped inside, leaving his umbrella on the front porch. "Hi, I live a couple blocks over, and my sister and her husband are moving back to River Bluffs. They're looking for a place on the east side close to me and my family. They asked me to look around for something big enough for them. They have four kids. Mind if I take a look at this place?"

Jerod's blue eyes flew wide in surprise. Talk about coincidence. None of them had seen this coming. He pushed to his feet. "Sure, we still have a lot to do, though."

As Jerod started the tour, the man held up his cell phone. "Mind if I take pictures of every room to send to them?"

"No problem."

The man strolled around the downstairs, capturing every space and the wooden floor. Then Jerod led him upstairs.

"We haven't gutted the second floor yet." Ansel reached for another section of flooring. "I hope the small rooms don't scare his sister away."

"Nothing we can do about that." Jazzi started work on the floorboard that joined his. "We didn't expect to show it to anyone this soon."

Forty-five minutes later, Jerod and the man returned. The man was excited. "My sister loved the third floor bedroom and bath," he told them. "She's thinking of making it into a dormitory for the three boys. Then they can put the master bedroom, their daughter's room, and an office on the second floor. How's the basement?"

"Solid. I'll show you." Jerod led him to the basement door and they disappeared again. The basement wasn't finished, but it was dry and in good shape. The ceiling was high enough that Ansel didn't have to stoop.

Ansel and Jazzi kept working. When Jerod led the man back again, he said, "My sister sent the pictures to her husband. Living in Chicago is so expensive, they can't believe how cheap houses are around here. They haven't liked anything else I've sent them, but they'd like to do a walk-through here tomorrow, if you can schedule it. If this works and they get it early enough, they can have some input on colors and stuff, can't they?"

Jerod hesitated. "I'm going to Franny's parents' house tomorrow. I won't be able to be here."

"We can," Ansel said. "What time will your sister want a tour?"

"Around one? Just after lunch."

Ansel glanced at Jazzi and she nodded. "We can do that."

Pleased, the man left.

"Can you believe that? We might already have a buyer." Jerod shook his head. When he and Jazzi started flipping together, a finished house could sit for a few months before it sold. He looked at his watch. "It's already later than usual. And you two have to come back tomorrow. Let's call it a day."

That sounded good to her. She gathered their things and Ansel grabbed George. They'd go home, take their showers, and go out to eat. It was surprising what a difference fifteen minutes made, though. Friday night traffic was always bad, but with stormy weather, it snarled to a crawl. March hadn't improved yet. Instead of snow, it dumped rain in torrents. They finally made it to the highway that led to their turn-off when a guy on a side street tried to zip into their lane and the driver in front of them couldn't brake fast enough. She crunched into the back door of his rusted SUV.

Ansel braked and waited to make sure both drivers were all right when the man in the SUV jumped out of his vehicle and stalked to the woman's car as she rolled down her window.

"Where did you learn to drive?" he bellowed. "Didn't you see me pull out?"

The woman's face froze with fear. She tried to roll her window back up, but the man reached in to grab the collar of her coat. Jazzi called 911 while Ansel leapt from the van and hurried toward them.

"You stay here!" he told her.

The man whirled on him when he approached, looked at his size, but didn't back down. Ansel glanced at the woman. "You're scaring her. Leave her alone."

"Keep out of this! If you want to be in one piece, get back in your van and drive away."

"And let you terrorize her? I don't think so. My wife just called the cops. Calm down. I'm staying to make sure they get the facts straight."

"You saw her hit me?"

"I saw you pull in front of her."

The man's face mottled with temper. "She was going too fast. I had plenty of time to make my turn."

"I was driving right behind her. We were both going under the speed limit."

The man's hands curled into fists, but Ansel had him by at least four inches. The arms of the guy's hoodie pulled tight over hard biceps as if he worked out every day. But Ansel didn't have a spare bit of fat on him. Every inch of him was muscle, and when he scowled like he was doing now, he looked intimidating. He planted his feet, ready for a fight.

The man looked him over again and took a step back. "Since you have to be a do-gooder, you can wait with the stupid woman. I'm going to sit in my car where it's warm."

He turned and stormed to his SUV, slammed it into reverse, and roared away. Jazzi took a photo of his license plate before he got too far.

When a police car finally came, Ansel and the woman explained what had happened. Jazzi showed him the cell phone picture, and the cop entered the license number in his car's computer. "Probably doesn't have any insurance." When he read the man's info, though, he shook his head. "You got lucky. If this guy calls either of you for any reason, don't deal with him. I doubt he'll risk it, but he just got out of prison a while ago."

The poor woman looked like she felt faint. Jazzi made a mental note to call Gaff. The only friend of Gil's she hadn't met was his cellmate, Gavin. And this guy fit the description Gaff had given her. Violent with a quick temper. Luckily, he hadn't gotten her or Ansel's names.

Once everything was settled, and Ansel was pulling back into traffic, he sighed. "Do you mind if we grab something on the way home and just call it a night?"

She nodded. "I've lost the mood, too. Let's keep it simple. I'm all for a quick supper and renting a movie."

So that's what they did, and it made all of them happy—George and the cats, too. It wasn't until they went up to bed that she thought of the accident again. If the driver who caused it was Gavin, as she suspected, she was glad she'd never met him. Hoped she never would.

Chapter 24

Jazzi hustled to clean the house before they had to leave to show the old Victorian in New Haven. While she scrubbed and dusted, Ansel damp mopped the wooden floors. The cats went back and forth, attacking the mop or chasing her dust rag. George, as usual, supervised.

It was a typical start to a Saturday, so all three pets glared at them when they finished lunch and went for their coats. George trotted after them, but Ansel shook his head. "Sorry, bud, but we're going to the store afterward, and we'd have to leave you in the pickup way too long."

George whined, offended. Ansel bent to pet him, giving him a quick pat before heading to the door. Inky jumped on the sink counter and swung his paw at the flowers by the window. He couldn't knock the heavy crockery container over, but the flowers were a few days old, and petals scattered across the stainless steel. He turned to gauge her reaction.

"Do your best, fur ball. I'm buying new ones today."

He could tell by her tone he hadn't upset her, so jumped down and stalked away. Jazzi slipped on her warm gloves and pulled the back door shut behind her.

They got to the fixer-upper fifteen minutes ahead of the man and his sister and her husband. Enough time to turn up the heat. When they left each night, they lowered the temperature. The paint had turned slightly lighter as it completely dried, and Jazzi was happy with the way it complemented the wood floor.

They put down a rag rug for when the potential buyers arrived for them to wipe their feet. The woman entered first and gave a slow smile as her eyes scanned the house. "We'd have so much room here."

Her husband, following her, nodded. "I like the layout and the colors."

The brother rubbed his hands, smiling from ear to ear.

Jazzi trailed them as Ansel gave them the full tour and explained what he, Jerod, and Jazzi still meant to do with each space. There wasn't much the couple wanted to change. They liked the idea of knocking out walls on the second floor to make two big bedrooms with two baths and an office rather than keeping the current four small rooms. The floors were decent, but not wonderful. Ansel explained that they meant to sand and refinish them, but the wife shook her head.

"We'd rather have carpet up here. It's warmer and quieter."

Ansel smiled. "Easier for us. The bathrooms?"

"Tile that's easy to clean."

Jazzi chuckled. With four kids, the woman preferred functional over decorative.

When they reached the basement, the husband wondered if they could make part of it into a playroom and asked for a small wine cellar to be walled off. When Ansel assured them neither would be a problem, the husband turned to his wife. When she nodded, he said, "We want it."

The wife quickly explained, "But we don't want to move in until the kids are out of school this year. We don't want to pull them out with only a few more months to the end of their classes."

Ansel looked relieved. "Good, then we won't be rushed trying to finish things up. We can't work on the exterior until the weather's better anyway."

They didn't quibble about the price, so by the time Ansel turned the thermostat back down, and he and Jazzi locked up, the house was sold.

They waved the buyers off, then started to the grocery. Jazzi called Jerod on the way to tell him the news.

"We should start looking for a new place right away." She knew he'd say that. "It'll take us at least another two months to finish the projects the owners want and rehab the exterior, but while we work there, we can draw up plans for the next project."

"We have plenty of time before they move in. Is it the end of May when kids get out of school?"

"Around here it is," he said. "Not sure about Chicago. They might go longer. Did the buyers have any specific colors they wanted inside or out?"

"They asked for dove gray in the master and soft rose for their daughter's room. They wanted taupe for the boys' attic."

"What the heck is taupe?"

She grinned. Her cousin wasn't too into the subtleties of shades. "Sort of light brown with gray undertones."

Jerod grunted. "What about the exterior?"

"Peach with white trim and rose details."

"Peach?"

"It will look pretty. It'll fit the house."

"If you say so. Are they going to give me a call later so I can do the paperwork?"

"Yup, I gave them your number." Jerod took care of the banking and she was in charge of lunches. It evened out.

They were almost to the store by the time Jazzi finished her call and returned her phone to her pocket. Ansel grinned. "Let me guess. He's ready to look for the next house."

"You know Jerod."

Ansel found a parking space three rows from the store's door, and they grabbed their list and slogged through the puddles to go inside. Bad weather put shoppers in stock up mode, so the aisles were full of carts to negotiate around.

"So, what's on the agenda for the Sunday meal tomorrow?" Ansel asked.

"I'm hungry for Mexican. Thought I'd make chicken tamale casseroles."

His blue eyes lit up. "Make extra so we have leftovers."

She knew he'd say that. She put three rotisserie chickens in their cart. It would take three casseroles to feed her family tomorrow and still have enough for them to eat later. "I want to make something quick for Jerod and Franny to take home, too. I'll cross them off my list once the baby sleeps through the night." Her family had been slipping extra money in the glass jar on Sundays to help her pay for the extra food—their way of supporting him.

Ansel grinned, and a woman with messy hair who looked half asleep, woke up to stare at him. She looked like she needed a bright spot in her day. Seeing Ansel would perk up any female. "What about stew? Then you can make some for us."

Why not? She tossed two packages of stew meat in the cart. When she made Jerod's, she'd make theirs, and then she could just reheat it some night for supper. Not much made Ansel happier than meat and potatoes.

Ansel tossed in things to make salads. They ate a fresh salad almost every night. They'd make big bowls of greens to go with the casserole tomorrow. "What about dessert?"

Before she could answer, his cell phone rang. It was Radley. "Hey, this is short notice, but I'm just asking. If it's too much, just tell me."

Ansel quirked an eyebrow, clearly curious. "What is it?"

"Could I invite Elspeth to the Sunday meal tomorrow?"

Ansel's shoulders relaxed. "Sure, we'll have plenty."

"See you then!" Radley clicked off.

Jazzi let out a long breath. "Maybe we should buy another folding table."

Ansel put three cartons of eggs into their cart. "We have room for two more people before we have to add another one."

"You set the table, so you'd know."

"Now, back to the important stuff. What's for dessert?"

"Bread pudding with whiskey sauce." It was one of Olivia's favorites.

They grabbed what they needed and checked out. The cats came running when they heard paper grocery bags in the kitchen. They loved playing in them once they were empty. George was always happy to see food enter the house, so they all settled in for a relaxing night, cooking together and chilling out.

She and Ansel were watching TV when her cell buzzed. She didn't recognize the number, but recognized Chad's voice the minute he started talking.

"Hilda told me about Ronnie," he said. "I feel bad that he couldn't find anyone to take his place, but I'm glad my buddy stayed out of this. I saw Tim today and when we started talking, he let a name slip. Ray. He didn't know if that would help you or not, but we both want whoever killed Ronnie to get caught."

"It will help," Jazzi told him. "I'll pass it on to my detective friend. And thanks for telling me. But don't do any more. Don't try to call Ray or ask questions."

"We almost didn't call you," Chad admitted. "But telling you this much shouldn't get us in trouble. That's all we can help you with."

"I appreciate your sharing. Thanks again."

After she told Ansel, she called Gaff. Plates and silverware mingled with voices in the background. He'd obviously taken his Ann out to eat tonight. "Sorry to bother you," she said before telling him her news.

"Thanks for the tip. I'll stop by to see Ray again on Monday," he said. "But this time, I'm going alone. If Ray's involved with whoever killed Donovan, Gil, and Ronnie, I don't want him to get any ideas about you."

"After meeting Jarrett and Gavin, I'd rather not meet them again."

There was a pause. "You met Gavin?"

She'd forgotten to tell him about the accident the night before. When she finished, Gaff's tone was even sharper. "Now you know what I meant when I said you should keep your distance from him."

"Works for me, but I'm interrupting your supper. Enjoy yourself and tell Ann *hi* from us." Jazzi hung up and snuggled deeper on her sofa, glancing at Ansel lying across from her. After having so much company for so long, it was a treat to have the house to themselves. For a while, if she could, she'd like to go to work every day, then come home and hibernate. With their house's security system and Ansel, she felt safe but would not run into surprises when she was out and about.

Chapter 25

Sunday morning, Ansel brought her coffee in bed. He loved to fuss over her, and she had to admit, it made her feel special. She scooched up to rest her back against her pillow and sipped while they talked. Ansel carefully lowered himself to the end of the bed so that he wouldn't jostle her.

"Morning, babe." He reached to push some of her loose, wild hair away from her face. "You look gorgeous with bedhead."

Yeah, right. Her teeth felt gritty and she didn't have any makeup on. She probably looked like she'd crawled out of a cave in some jungle. Her Norseman still wore his flannel pajama bottoms and a loose white T-shirt. His hair was mussed and his chin stubbly. Okay, he might be right. Rumpled could look delicious.

Inky came to rub his head against Ansel's arm. Ansel ran a big hand over the cat's back. "Thought we could enjoy a slow start this morning. All we have to do is reheat the tamale casserole and make the salad for the meal." Jealous, Marmalade came to sit on Jazzi's lap for attention. Ansel grinned. "Your cats are spoiled."

She glanced at George, snoring in his dog bed. "And your pug isn't?"

"You've got me there. Want me to run to buy a *New York Times*? We could spend the morning reading newspapers."

She shook her head. "*The Journal Gazette*'s enough for me. Maybe we can watch *Face The Nation*, too." She wasn't one of those people who listened to the news twenty four hours a day, but she and Ansel liked to keep up on what was happening.

She drained her coffee mug and Ansel stood to offer her an arm to walk her downstairs. She tugged on her robe, deciding to get dressed later. Draped on the sofa with her second cup of coffee in her hand, she felt totally pampered.

They didn't get moving until noon, and then she zipped upstairs to pull on her good jeans and a lightweight sweater before going to the kitchen to heat the casseroles. Ansel was already tearing greens for the salad, and she made a quick dressing for it. The bread puddings and whiskey sauce were already made. She and Ansel even had time to take another quick break before Jerod and his family arrived. While Franny removed Gunther and Lizzie's coats and unwrapped little Peter, her cousin went straight to the kitchen island for the cheese ball and crackers. He immediately noticed the extra place setting at the table.

"Who else is coming?"

Ansel handed him a cold beer. "Radley's bringing Elspeth, Donovan's girlfriend. They've been hanging out a little, crying on each other's shoulders."

"Sure they have." Jerod reached to spread more cheese on another half dozen crackers. "It has to be more than that or he'd let her family deal with her on weekends."

"Jerod!" Franny gave his arm a soft punch. "Some men are more sensitive than you are."

"Bull pucky." He was unrepentant. "When I wanted to be nice to a girl I wasn't interested in, I caulked around her windows or brought her takeout for supper."

Ansel chuckled with a nod of his head. "My brother must definitely be interested in her."

Before Franny could argue, Walker and Didi arrived with River. River went to kneel next to the baby carrier to gaze at Peter. Gunther and Lizzie crowded next to him.

"Does he cry a lot?" River asked.

"Only when he's hungry or needs his diaper changed," Gunther said.

River frowned. "Do you like having him?"

Lizzie gave him a hard stare. "He's our little brother. We have to like him."

Jazzi smothered a laugh. That was probably the most honest answer she'd ever heard.

A knock sounded on the door and Olivia, Thane, Mom, and Dad walked in. Her sister wasn't the last one here two weeks in a row. That honor went to Radley and Elspeth. Elspeth was visibly nervous, and Radley wrapped his arm around her waist.

After introductions, Ansel made it easy for them. "We're all here now. Let's eat."

People went to the table and grabbed plates to line up at the buffet on the kitchen island. When everyone settled, people started talking on top of one another. Her friends and relatives were in good moods. It was a warmer day than usual and the weatherman predicted temperatures in the fifties all week. No rain. Everyone looked more tired than usual, too. It had been a busy time for all of them, especially Olivia and Thane, planning for their wedding. Mom was more hyper than usual. If it was possible, she acted more excited about the wedding than Jazzi's sister.

"What about you?" Olivia asked Jazzi. "You've been going at top speed, too, haven't you?"

Jazzi nodded. "But we're invited to Isabelle and Reuben's spring fling party next Friday night. That will be fun. It's a dress up affair." Jazzi's old upstairs neighbor didn't know how to do casual, and since he'd married Isabelle, his parties were even fancier than before.

"Spring fling?" Mom asked.

"March nineteenth's the official equinox this year, but that's a Thursday night, so they're celebrating on Friday. It's an annual event."

Olivia pouted. "I wish we knew someone who gave parties like that."

Thane wrinkled his nose. "Dress up? I'd have to wear a suit."

Gran glanced at Samantha, the woman who'd moved in with her after both of their husbands died. "Olivia's wedding's coming up on April second. This house has seen a lot of wonderful get-togethers. It's going to be the perfect place for the reception."

Didi nodded. "If I ever get married, I'd be happy to celebrate someplace like this."

Gran turned and narrowed her eyes to study her. Uh-oh, Jazzi knew that look. Something unexpected was about to pop out of her grandma's mouth.

Gran raised her wine glass in a toast. "Congratulations, dear."

Didi stared. "For what?"

"You'll finally get the little girl you've always wanted."

Walker's jaw dropped. "Are you pregnant?"

Didi sputtered, and he reached to pat her on the back. "I thought I was just late."

Gran shook her head. "I can always tell. I see the mask." She turned to River. "You'll be a big brother by Christmas."

River turned in his chair to look at the baby carrier and Peter. His expression reflected his mixed feelings. He obviously wasn't sure what to think.

Walker tossed his arm around the boy's shoulders. "Someone else to love. Pretty cool, huh? You'll be one of the best big brothers ever."

River's shoulders relaxed. "Maybe."

Jazzi admired how easily Walker had comforted him. She wondered how soon Didi and Walker would announce their upcoming wedding. They clearly were meant for each other.

Gran looked straight at her, and she tensed. "Ray's wife should leave town for a few weeks and not tell anyone where she's going."

Chills raced up and down Jazzi's spine. She didn't doubt Gran. She was always right. "How soon should she leave?"

"Tomorrow or the next day." Gran finished her wine and went to the refrigerator for another glass. She dug out a few cookies to sneak to River on her way back to the table. When Jazzi raised her eyebrow, Gran said, "He's not a fan of bread pudding."

Having people help her bake wasn't working out the way she'd thought. Since they'd pitched in, they felt entitled to snag more than their share.

Since Gran had mentioned dessert, people lined up for theirs and Jazzi cleared away their dirty plates. Ansel helped rinse them. An hour later, their stomachs full and conversation winding down, people started to gather their coats to leave.

Once they were alone in the kitchen, all of their company gone, Ansel scrubbed a hand through his hair. "Walker's going to be a dad."

Jazzi loaded the last plate in the dishwasher. "Do you think he'll marry Didi before the baby comes?"

"He'll want to. I'm sure of that. Let's hope she's easier to convince than you were."

"Hey, I had some legitimate concerns."

"Silly woman, you thought you were my rebound girl, but I fell for you the minute I saw you." He kept insisting that was true. All she could say was that he must have a thing for women who wore tool belts.

He turned out the kitchen lights and led her to the living room and their favorite couches. "Everything's done. Time to relax." He was still thinking about Didi and Walker though, she could tell. Jerod and Franny had just had Peter and now Walker and Didi would have a baby girl. Were they putting him in the baby mood? Luckily, his cell phone rang, jostling him out of his reveries. He glanced at the ID. "Bain." He put it on speakerphone.

Bain hurried into speech. "I wanted to let you both know that Greta moved in with us late this afternoon. She'll take care of things until Mom's stronger. She cooked salmon for us for an early supper, and I heard Mom laughing with her in the kitchen. I can't remember the last time I heard Mom laugh. Dad's not happy I'm paying for her, but that's not his decision."

"How old is she?" Ansel asked.

"Thirty-seven. A home nurse. Sort of dowdy, but pleasant and calm. Dad doesn't intimidate her at all." Bain sounded surprised.

"We sent money to pitch in. Did you get it?"

"Yep, thank you. Radley sent money, too, so Dad can't gripe too much." Curious, Jazzi had to ask, "How's Stubs?"

A chuckle answered her question. "That cat thinks he owns the barn. If I don't squirt milk in his mouth every time I hook up the cows, he yowls and fusses."

They talked a few minutes more before Dalmar's voice bellowed in the background. Bain sighed. "Have to go. Dad needs help with a fence."

When Ansel hung up, he gave a rueful smile. "My brother had better watch out. He respects this Greta, and she can cook. Bain's been coping with Dad a long time. It sounds like this girl is good for him and Mom."

They settled back on their couches, but Ansel sat up again. "I forgot. You need to call Gaff and tell him what Gran said."

He was right. Jazzi felt bad about bothering Gaff again on the weekend, but he'd want to know. When she explained about Gran's prediction, he didn't argue with her. He'd worked with Gran before. "I'll tell her and try to convince her to leave, but I can't make her."

Jazzi was worried about that. "All we can do is warn her."

And somehow, that felt pretty inadequate. But there really wasn't anything else.

Chapter 26

Jerod called them first thing on Monday morning. His dad had told him about a Queen Anne for sale in Auburn. That was farther than they usually ventured, but his dad assured him it looked solid and was going for a good price.

"What if I pick you guys up and we take a look at it before we start work on the Victorian?"

"Fine with us." Auburn would be a long drive for her cousin, but they lived on the north side of River Bluffs—about a twenty minute drive—and they'd be on Jerod's way.

"I'll drop you back at your place when we're done, and then we'll drive separately to the fixer-upper."

Even better. If they timed it right, they could eat lunch at home instead of dragging it with them in the cooler.

Jerod honked when he pulled in the driveway, and they climbed in his pickup. Twenty minutes later, they reached Auburn. Jazzi liked the small town. At one time, the city was home to a factory making Duesenberg cars—the big shiny showboats that still impressed. The Auburn Cord Duesenberg Automobile Museum was a favorite place for her to visit. After looking at the gleaming cars on display, she liked to drive up and down Main Street to see the big old houses that the city's elite lived in.

The Queen Anne for sale was off the main drag on a backstreet, and Jazzi fell in love with it on sight. Brick with a turret on the side and a deep porch, it spoke of glorious yesteryears. It needed a new roof, and maybe that was part of the reason the price was so reasonable. It would be a bear to put on new shingles.

"The owner can't meet us, but told me the numbers to punch in on the entry keypad," Jerod told them. "We can take a good look inside."

Jazzi could hardly wait.

The house didn't disappoint. It was empty, so it was easier for her to imagine how it should flow. The bad news? Whoever had lived here before had installed drop ceiling tiles for the entire ground floor and painted all of the woodwork to modernize it, but they'd coped with drop ceilings before. Nothing a day of ripping off and tossing out wouldn't fix. It would take a lot longer to sand the woodwork.

For once, Jazzi didn't think she'd tear down one wall. An arch connected the kitchen and dining room, and the living room was cavernous. The wide staircase boasted beautiful railings. They needed to be refinished, along with the treads, but once done, they'd be showstoppers.

On the second floor, three large bedrooms opened off a wide hall. Once again, all of the woodwork was painted and bold wallpaper hung in each room. It would have to go. A narrow staircase led to a high ceilinged attic. Everything looked easy to repair until they descended into the basement, musty smelling and cold. The cement walls and floor crumbled. They'd have to waterproof them and apply layers of new cement. The gravity furnace was old-school with giant arms radiating from it. Another expense.

Jerod led them back upstairs to the kitchen—aged and inadequate—but if they gutted it, they had plenty of room to add an island. "Well, what do you think?"

"If we can get it for a little less, we have a great fixer-upper," Ansel said.

When Jazzi nodded agreement, Jerod grinned. "Good, I really wanted a go at this one. I'll see what I can do."

On the ride back to their house, Jazzi said, "Why don't we eat lunch before going to New Haven? The sandwiches are all made, and I'll bring out a bag of cookies."

"Cookies?" Jerod glanced in the rearview mirror at her. "Have you made the spice cookies yet?"

She shook her head. They were his favorites. "Sorry, but I have plenty of others."

"Any cookie is better than no cookie," he told her. He pulled in their driveway and once inside the house, headed straight to the coffee pot. The temperatures had warmed up, but no one would call it a heat wave outdoors.

They'd left George at home and he gave them a dirty look. The cats were surprised to see them this early on a weekday and shamelessly begged for scraps. Between the two guys, most of the cookies in the bag disappeared. After they ate, Ansel lugged the pug to their van, and they followed Jerod to New Haven.

The appliances were being delivered late in the afternoon, so the three of them tossed their coats over the stair railing and got to work on installing light fixtures. Jerod had sent pictures to the new owners, and they'd chosen what they wanted.

At three, Gaff knocked on the door and wandered in. Jazzi was upstairs when he called to her. She came down to meet him. "What's up?"

He went to the card table and chairs and took a seat. They joined him. "Your gran's warning spooked me, so I went to see Donovan's mom, and she blew me off. Said she couldn't leave till the end of the week because another lunch worker had taken time off and they were shorthanded. I couldn't change her mind, so I went to visit Gavin."

Ansel frowned. "Which one is he? I keep getting the ex-cons mixed up."

Jazzi said, "He works with his family doing roofing and painting. He was Gil's cellmate."

Gaff nodded. "He wasn't working today, stayed home with his wife and kids. Had a few beers in him and wasn't in the best mood. When I asked him about Ronnie, I got an earful. He told me that he hated Gil because if he hadn't always had Ronnie's back, somebody would have pounded the kid and taught him some life lessons. According to Gavin, no one could stand Ronnie and resented Gil for protecting him. But he swore he didn't kill Gil. Said he wanted out too bad to risk it, that everyone would think he did it."

"What do you think?" Jazzi asked.

"The man's so violent, I don't believe anything he tells me."

Ansel wiped his hands on his work jeans. "Did people want to kill Ronnie, or did they just want to knock him around?"

Gaff stared at the few cookies still on a paper plate and Jerod got up to bring them to him. He chose a chocolate chip before saying, "Gavin said Ronnie got the crap beat out of him once Gil died. He thought someone had been waiting to do that for a long time and Gil got in their way one time too many. He told me that if Gil would have thrown the little punk to the wolves, he'd probably still be alive."

A gloomy thought.

Gaff reached for a chocolate crinkle cookie. "After I saw Gavin, I doubled back to see Donovan's parents again. Ray wasn't home the first time I went, and I wanted to talk to him. I asked why Ronnie would mention his name when he was talking about pulling a new job."

Jazzi poured herself another cup of coffee. "What did he say?"

"Swore he didn't have a clue. Said the company where they worked together let Ronnie go. Too many products 'fell off the trucks' when he helped load them. Said he still worked with Ronnie once in a while when he had especially big deliveries, but the company only agreed if Ray promised to keep an eye on him." Gaff went for a cup of coffee, too. Looking thoughtful. He paused before pouring. "Donovan's mom looked more and more upset the longer Ray talked, so I told Ray about your gran's sight. I mentioned that whoever hurt him might come back to hurt her, hoping Ray would talk."

"And?" Ansel's eyebrows furrowed with curiosity.

"He just laughed at me and said no one hurt him, a refrigerator slipped . . ."

Ansel pushed to his feet. "If that woman gets hurt, it's his fault."

Gaff looked at them and shook his head. "I've done everything I can." He reached for the last cookie.

Just then, the delivery truck arrived with the kitchen cabinets and appliances.

"I'm out of here," he told them. "The place is starting to come together."

They stayed later than usual to install the top cabinets. Tomorrow, they'd install the lower ones and the pantry before installing the farmhouse sink, the island, and stainless steel appliances. Jazzi had talked Jerod into pantry doors with glass in the top half to give the feel of a china cupboard. The countertops were scheduled for Wednesday.

They were dragging a little when they left for the day.

"Maybe since we've warned Ray and his wife, Gran's vision will come out differently," Jazzi said on the drive home.

"Warnings only make a difference if people listen to them." Ansel wore his brooding scowl, the one that made him look intimidating. "It just doesn't make sense to me. It still feels like this whole mess revolves around money, deals gone wrong, but if Ray gypped someone somehow, why wouldn't he just give them their share when they got out of prison? Why risk it?"

Jazzi had wondered about that herself. "Maybe he doesn't have the money anymore. Maybe he spent it."

Ansel's hands clenched on the steering wheel. "Then they couldn't have made much. It sure doesn't sound like they're rolling in dough."

They didn't live in a ritzy area, that was for sure. And their cars were newer but nothing expensive. She scrubbed a hand through her hair, messing it. She reached to tame it, but Ansel shook his head.

"I like your hair when it gets wild." He was an unreliable critic. He swore she looked good when she knew for sure she didn't.

She turned to stare out the window while her thoughts tumbled. She finally said, "Gaff can check on bank accounts and finances, can't he? Maybe he could see if Ray, Ronnie, Gavin, or Jarrett socked more money than usual away a short time before the three of them went behind bars."

"It's worth a shot." Ansel turned onto their street. "You might want to call Didi, too. She's mostly concentrated on why Gil got killed in prison, but Donovan and Ronnie might not be related to that. Having her house searched might, though."

He was right. Once they got in the house, Ansel fed and petted George and the cats while she walked to the sitting area and made her phone calls. When she finished and joined him, he was seasoning chicken breasts to sauté, along with mushrooms and asparagus. She started the rice.

"Any luck?" he asked.

"Didi said Gil was worried about Ronnie before they were sent to prison. He was in on a job where they robbed expensive parts from a high tech company, parts that brought a lot of money, and rumor was that the money disappeared. When Ronnie and Jarrett got caught pulling a similar heist at another company, cops suspected they pulled the first job, too, but no one spilled where the money was."

"And Gil wasn't part of those jobs?"

She stirred a pat of butter into the rice and replaced the pot's lid. "No, but Didi said Ronnie came to visit Gil about that time and asked him to run and grab some beer for them. She's been thinking about it ever since she found her sofa slashed to pieces. Ronnie was alone in their house for half an hour. She's starting to worry he stashed the money somewhere to keep it safe."

Ansel nodded. "And if Ray was involved somehow, someone might think he hid it, too. The couch in Donovan's apartment came from his parents, right?"

"Oh, jeez. Donovan wouldn't have even known it was there if that's what happened."

Ansel nodded to her phone. "You might want to call Gaff again."

After she explained their idea and hung up, she said, "He's going to look into it."

When they sat down to eat, they both felt a little cheerier. Maybe they'd get lucky and Gaff would get a break on this case. Hopefully before anything happened to Donovan's mom.

Chapter 27

Jazzi glanced out the bedroom window when she got up on Monday and stopped to stare. Green sprouts poked their heads above ground in her flower beds, and crocuses were ready to bloom. When had that happened? Mid March was offering up the promise of spring. The temperatures had climbed a little, but it was still coat weather.

She hugged herself. The earth was awakening and stretching from under its blanket of snow. Regular sandwiches wouldn't cut it today. She'd have to take something for lunch to celebrate.

She had to laugh at herself. Why was everything in her life related to food? But she couldn't help it. Spring deserved a lighter touch, more fresh vegetables. She hurried down to the kitchen and spread Crescent Roll dough onto a cookie sheet. She sautéed sausage and mushrooms, added a teaspoon of fennel seeds and shredded mozzarella cheese, rolled the filling in the dough, then sealed it. After twenty five minutes in the oven, it would be done.

When she finally sat at the kitchen island with Ansel, he shook his head at her. "What brought that on?"

"Flowers are coming up in our backyard."

"That puts you in a cooking frenzy?"

She raised an eyebrow. "Not a frenzy, but it puts me in the mood to celebrate."

"In that case . . ." He stood and pulled her into his arms, then began to waltz around the kitchen. When they returned to their stools, he bent to give her a proper kiss. "Let me know if you need more."

140 *Judi Lynn*

She could think of a few things, but they'd be late for work. The timer buzzed and she pulled their lunch from the oven. Gulping down a mug of coffee, she got ready to leave.

When they reached the Victorian, she stalked around its yard, looking at the flowerbeds. No luck. No spring shoots. When she walked inside, Jerod smirked at her. "You always had a thing about flowers and birds."

True. That's why she'd hung birdfeeders at home where she could see them from the kitchen window.

"Hey, if daffodils make her want to cook special lunches for us, I say we plant more bulbs." Ansel gently lowered George close to his dog bed. The pug only had to take a few steps before he curled and got comfortable enough to supervise their work.

Jerod went to remove the cardboard box from an upper kitchen cupboard. "Let's hope spring gives her more energy to hold these up for us."

A not very subtle cue to get busy. They buckled on their toolbelts and got to work.

They'd installed the upper kitchen cabinets and the pantry before lunch. George liked the idea of fancier fare than usual and begged for scraps. Ansel tossed him a few and then patted his head. "That's enough, buddy. You'll have to wait for more until dinner time."

The dog flopped on the floor, placing his head on his paws, and whimpered. Jazzi smiled, waiting to see if Ansel would give in. And yes, he did. The man was putty in the dog's paws.

They were back to working on the appliances when Gaff tapped at the door and came in. He looked as disgruntled and upset as Jazzi had ever seen him. They all stopped and automatically went to him. He stood inside the door, his shoulders hunched.

When they waited silently, he cleared his throat and said, "Ray's wife is in Lutheran Hospital. Someone attacked her in the school parking lot and beat her so badly, she's unconscious. One of the other lunch ladies walked out and found her on the ground near her car."

Cold crept through Jazzi's veins. She rubbed her arms, trying to warm herself. "Does Ray know?"

"He's at the hospital with her. I got the call when I was talking to a driver Ray used to work with. The guy told me he only worked with Ray on one job and that was moving appliances out of a warehouse Ronnie worked at. He didn't know much, but it means that Ray helped Ronnie move stolen goods at least once."

The news slid out of Jazzi's head as though it had landed on Teflon. She couldn't stop thinking about Donovan's mom. "Did this finally persuade Ray to talk to you? To tell you who broke his fingers and gave him a black eye?"

"He told me, but I understand why he stayed mum. He said two guys he'd never seen before showed up. One held him while the other guy asked him where the money was. At first, Ray didn't know what money they were talking about, but when they told him it was from a job he'd done with Ronnie, Jarrett, and Gavin, he said that he'd taken his share of the cut and given the rest to Ronnie to pass on. They'd already visited Ronnie, and he told them that Ray kept it all. They decided to help Ray's memory and when he couldn't tell them anything else, they said they'd be back and if he said anything to anyone about what happened, they'd question his wife instead of him."

"And they grabbed her anyway." Jerod shook his head. "What did they think would happen if they beat her this bad? They'd have to think it would make Ray mad enough to talk to you."

Gaff shrugged. "I'd guess whoever's looking for the money is losing his cool. Maybe he didn't send hired thugs this time but went himself and got a little too carried away."

Jazzi couldn't imagine a man beating up a woman, but she read about it all the time in the newspapers. "Didn't you say Jarrett had two women file restraining orders against him?"

Gaff nodded. "I plan on stopping to see him again, but the guy's been in and out of jail most of his life. He holds his cards close. Anyway, I'm telling you this because you share so much information with me. If you hear anything else, keep me informed, will you? But whatever you do, stay away from Gavin and Jarrett."

"No worries. I don't go looking for trouble." And she didn't. It just sort of showed up, unexpected. "Do Radley and Elspeth know?"

Gaff shook his head. "Didn't think about calling them. You can if you want to."

"They were close to Donovan. They'll want to know." But she didn't reach for her cell phone. She fought down anger and frustration instead. Why hadn't Ray or his wife listened to them? Gran had warned them this might happen.

Gaff pressed his lips together, then turned to leave. "If either Radley or Donovan's girlfriend have heard anything, pass it on, will you? Gotta go. I have to get back to the station."

When the door closed behind him, Ansel reached out to hold her. "Sorry, babe. You tried to warn her. You going to be okay?"

Jerod stomped to the counter and poured himself a cup of coffee. He gripped the mug's handle so tightly, she was afraid it might snap. It took a minute to collect himself, then he nodded at her. "If anyone laid a hand on Franny, I'd want to kill him. You'd better call Radley. He deserves to know."

She walked into the other room to make her calls. When she returned, she said, "Radley's going to pick up Elspeth, and he wants me to go to the hospital with them to visit Ray and his wife."

"Go." Jerod put his empty mug into the newly installed deep sink and motioned to the stainless steel stove. "Ansel and I will finish this job and install the kitchen island. I need to work."

Ansel went to join him. Jazzi helped until Radley's van pulled to the curb. With a wave to the guys, she ran out to join him and Elspeth.

On the drive to the hospital, she said, "I always forget Ray's wife's name. What is it?"

"Maureen," Elspeth told her. She had her light brown hair pulled up in a knot today and wore only the minimum of makeup. Her pretty smile was missing, her expression anxious. "I hope she's going to be all right, that there's no permanent damage."

Jazzi's hands balled into fists. Did it take two thugs to beat up a middle-aged woman, or had whoever was behind this done it himself? And why send two guys after Ray? Because Ray would recognize whoever paid them?

At the hospital, she braced herself for the visit. How bad did Maureen look? Would there be tubes circling her hospital bed? She was glad for Radley and Elspeth's company. When they walked into the room, Jazzi was relieved to see that, even though Maureen's face and body were covered with bruises, she was awake. That had to be a good sign, didn't it?

Ray sat next to her bed, holding her hand. When he saw them, he looked relieved. "She could use someone to talk to besides me."

Elspeth went to stand on the other side of the bed and fidgeted nervously. "You don't know me. We never met. I'm Elspeth. I was Donovan's girlfriend before he . . . died."

Maureen's left eye was swollen shut, but she studied Elspeth carefully. "Donovan talked about you every time he called. He thought the world of you." The words came slowly and slurred. Her cracked and puffy lips made it hard to talk, and her two front teeth were missing.

Tears misted Elspeth's eyes and she blinked them away. "I liked him, too." She turned to Radley. "This is Radley. He worked with Donovan and they were friends."

"It was nice of you to come." Maureen looked back and forth between the two of them. "Have you become friends?"

Elspeth's shoulders sagged. "We got together to remember Donovan, and we've sort of . . . well, gotten to like each other."

Maureen tried to smile and winced. "Donovan would like that. He wanted the people he loved to be happy."

Radley shuffled his feet, frowning. "Do you have any idea who did this to you?"

Maureen shook her head, wincing again. "Sorry. It hurts to move. I have two fractured ribs."

"Did he punch you in the stomach?" Anger tainted Radley's tone.

"No, in the face. He kicked me when I was down."

Jazzi wished she knew who did this. More, she wished she could hogtie him, drag him into a basement, and give him to Thane, Jerod, Radley, and Ansel. Let him see how much fun it was to be beat up. She came to stand closer to the bed. "Was there only one man or two?"

Maureen tried another smile. Failed. "I was hoping you'd come. One, wearing a ski mask and gloves. He hit me before I could look for his car. I couldn't tell Detective Gaff anything that might help him."

"Was he tall?" Jazzi remembered both Jarrett and Gavin were over six feet.

"Taller than Ray."

She'd guess Ray didn't quite reach six feet.

"Did he say anything to you?" Jazzi asked.

"He told me to tell Ray to give him his money, or the next time, I'd be dead."

Ray gave a frustrated sigh. "I don't *have* the money. I told the guys that who broke my fingers. I bought us each a new car with my share."

Maureen's bottom lip quivered, and she gingerly pressed a finger to it. "You told me you won that money with a lottery ticket."

"What did you want me to say?" Ray demanded. "I'm not proud of what I did, okay? But we were short on cash and we both needed new cars, couldn't even afford to put them on payments."

"That doesn't make it right." She glared.

"Look, if I could take it back, I would, but I can't. I never thought it would lead to any of this. Everything worked out like the four of us thought it would, and everything would have been all right, except I'm thinking Ronnie, the little weasel, played fast and loose with the stash. I did what I was supposed to, took my share and gave the rest to him to pass on. Except he didn't."

Maureen started to argue, but turned her head instead, raising her hand to wipe away tears.

Ray stood and began pacing. "Ronnie, Gavin, Jarrett, and I have known each other for years. I'm telling you none of us would do any of this crap. But they all ended up in prison, pulling another job, and I'm thinking one of them blabbed to a cellmate or fellow con, and this guy thinks he can rattle the money out of us. If it was one of us, we'd know it was probably Ronnie who ripped us off. We'd never kill him because he probably took the secret of where he hid it to his grave."

That was a new thought. And what he said made sense. Why kill Ronnie? If he knew where the money was, it was gone now.

A nurse stuck her head in the room. "Maureen's had enough visitors for now. The doctor's coming to see her soon. You might want to say your goodbyes."

Elspeth reached out to touch Maureen's hand gently. "Do you need anything? Would you like us to bring something up for you?"

Maureen shook her head. "I'm fine. Ray's taken time off to stay with me. It was nice meeting you, though. And thanks for thinking of me."

It seemed precious little to do, but they turned to leave the room. They didn't talk in the elevator ride down to the lobby. They waited until they were back in Radley's van, headed home, before Radley said, "Well, this whole mess stinks. Donovan died for nothing."

"That makes it worse, doesn't it?" Elspeth agreed. "Someone shot him because he walked into his apartment at the wrong time, and there never was any money in his old sofa."

Jazzi thought of the murders she'd been involved with before. Most of them seemed pointless. She decided then and there that killing was different than murder. Soldiers killed to protect their country. Cops killed to protect themselves and civilians. Murder was a selfish, generally stupid endeavor. And this murderer seemed worse than usual.

When she reached the fixer-upper and told Ansel and Jerod about the visit with Maureen, their moods tanked again, too.

Ansel grimaced. "I get it now. Ray was trying to protect her. He's still no prize, but at least he's not as bad as I'd painted him."

"It doesn't sound like he even knew the money disappeared until his buddies in crime got out of prison." Jerod stared into space, frowning. "It's hard to piece everything together, but what Ray said makes sense. Who'd kill Ronnie if the money trail stopped with him? No one who knew him. So maybe there's one or two players involved who weren't part of the original group."

Jazzi groaned. Just what they needed. More suspects. With a sigh, she said, "Do you think people would mind if we called off cookie baking tonight? It's short notice, but I don't think I can work myself up for it."

"I'll take care of it." Ansel reached for his cell phone. "Want to cancel or reschedule?"

"Can we make it tomorrow instead?"

"Whatever works for you."

"I enjoy seeing everybody to bake together. It might lift my spirits. We'll make it Wednesday if that works for them."

Two phone calls later, Ansel reached across to lay his hand on hers. "Done. Everyone understood. They'll see us tomorrow."

Relieved, she settled back to regroup and have an easy night. She had plenty of soup in the freezer to thaw for supper. They'd watch TV and maybe head upstairs early. Spending time in bed with Ansel always made things better. He made everything better. She thought about Ronnie's grandma. Alone. But she had a network of solid friends to rely on. Everybody needed someone.

Chapter 28

They all threw themselves into work the next day and made a lot of progress. Each completed job boosted their morale. They finished the maple floor. The kitchen appliances and island were put in place, and the dining room stretched, large and spacious, with a plate railing on three walls and three white shaded pendant lights hanging above where the owners' dining room table would eventually go. They installed a new mantle over the fireplace in the living room, and curtains and drapes went up. As far as Jazzi could tell, the ground floor was completed. Now all they needed to do were finishing touches on the attic before starting to knock out walls on the second floor to convert it into two large bedrooms with baths and an office. She'd already removed all of the trim, so a week's worth of heavy framing should see how the layout worked.

"Well? What do you think?" Jerod asked, coming to study the finished first floor with her.

"I love it. The living room's large enough for two sitting areas, like ours." She hadn't been quite sure what they'd need with two of them, but when they gave big parties—like their wedding and Olivia's upcoming reception—she'd noticed the men congregated in one area and the women in another. It worked out well.

Jerod sounded pleased. "It's going to be great for a big family."

Ansel nodded in agreement. "The only thing I still can't picture is how to make a playroom and wine room in the basement, but we'll get there."

"That basement is going to make this house," Jerod said. "I can hardly drag my kids upstairs out of the playroom you guys helped me with."

Jazzi wasn't concerned about the kids' area. "The basement's dry and the cement floors are in good shape. All we need to do is drywall, install indoor-outdoor carpet, and hang a ceiling. We'll add built-in benches on the short wall with storage underneath and bookshelves opposite those with space for a TV screen."

"What about the wine room?" Ansel asked. "We've never done one of those before."

Jazzi pushed a strand of hair that escaped her ponytail out of the way. "We'll have to do some serious measuring to see what we can fit where. They want a laundry room down there, too, right?"

"We can build that right behind the wine room," Jerod said.

Satisfied with their plans so far, they trudged upstairs to mark measurements for their work tomorrow. Then they grabbed sledgehammers and got busy. Nothing like knocking down walls to get your mind off things. Even with their white masks covering their noses and mouths, it was dirty work. The scarf that protected Jazzi's hair was so stiff, she wondered if the dust would wash out. They were finishing for the day when Jazzi's cell phone buzzed. She looked at the ID and frowned. "It's Donovan's ex-girlfriend, Brianne."

The girl jumped straight into speech when she heard Jazzi's phone click on. "I need to talk to you. That detective friend of yours is drilling Jarrett right now, and Jarrett's getting in a scary awful mood. I don't want to be here when Gaff leaves. Meet me somewhere? I'll swap new info if you keep me out of Jarrett's way for a while."

People were coming to bake cookies and make candy tonight. "Company's coming to my house in a couple of hours."

"I could meet you there. Please. If Jarrett's mad enough, he doesn't mind cuffing me once or twice."

Jazzi didn't really want Brianne to know where she lived, but then she remembered that Jarrett had already pounded on their door. If he knew, she knew. And if Brianne had something new to tell her... She bit her bottom lip. She didn't like the girl, didn't even trust her, but she didn't want her to get hit either. "You can't stay long. We're pretty far north, and I can only see you for half an hour before our company comes."

"I'll be there at five fifteen. I'm leaving our place right now, and I promise, I won't stay."

"Okay, see you then." It would be cutting it close, but she could cook while she talked to Brianne. For cookie nights, she kept the food simple. She'd already browned hamburger with taco seasonings, diced plenty of toppings, and bought tons of Mexican chips to throw everything together for nachos.

Ansel's frown spoke volumes. "Really? You invited her to our place?"

She quickly explained, and he settled down a little, but he still wasn't happy. "I guess we can't pass up a chance for new information if she actually has some."

Jazzi nodded. "Even if she tells us something, Gaff had better check it out. I don't peg Brianne as very reliable."

Jerod pulled his white mask back in place. "Let's finish this wall and call it a day. Peter's been fussy the last few nights, and Franny could use a little TLC. I'll stop on my way home and grab something for us to eat."

Forty minutes later, they dusted themselves off as best they could and headed home. The first thing on Jazzi's agenda was a shower. She'd love to supervise Ansel's, too, but there was no time for play.

When they walked inside their house, though, she'd miscalculated. The *first* thing on the agenda was the care and feeding of a starving pug and two naughty cats. *Then* she and Ansel went upstairs to clean up.

Her hair was still damp when she layered all of the ingredients onto four large rimmed cookie sheets to heat up the nachos. When she cooked while her hair dried, it had a tendency to get messier than usual, but there was no help for it tonight. She was rushed. A chip fell on the floor in her hurry and Inky pounced on it, then began batting it around the kitchen, Marmalade chasing after him. They were having a good time until it got too close to George, and he ate it. Inky arched his back and hissed at the pug, but George showed no shame. He looked around for another chip and when none was in sight, closed his eyes again.

Jazzi began lining up ingredients to make peanut butter cookies, along with pinwheels and sugar 'n' spice—Jerod's favorite. She had out her heavy saucepan and candy thermometer to make caramels when there was a knock at the door. Ansel went to answer it.

"Well, hello there!" she heard Brianne say.

Ansel stepped aside for her to enter. "Jazzi's expecting you." He motioned toward the kitchen.

Brianne gawked on her way in. He was wearing his worn jeans and a thermal shirt that showed off all of his muscles. When she tore her gaze away, she studied the house. "Jeez, girl, I didn't know you had it so good. Is this your fine looking man?" She looked Ansel slowly up and down.

"Yup, he's mine. I snagged him before he knew better." Jazzi motioned toward the coat tree near the back door. "Sorry, but I have to get things ready while we talk."

Brianne shrugged out of her coat and came to sit on a stool at the kitchen island to watch her get ready. Tonight, she had more blue streaks than before in her ink black hair. And her eyes were rimmed with plum instead of black. "What are you making?"

"Cookies and candy for Easter. I make them two or three batches a week and freeze them to deliver later." She stopped for a minute to study Brianne. As far as she could see, there wasn't a bruise on the girl. "Did you get out before Jarrett got nasty?"

"I left when Gaff left. He'll drink a few beers and settle down before I get back."

"What upset him so much?" Jazzi reached for the vanilla out of her corner cupboard, but the bottle on the lazy Susan was almost empty. She went to the extra cupboard to get a new one. When Brianne saw all of the vinegars and wines for cooking in there, her eyes went wide.

"How many people do you feed?"

"A lot, and Ansel and I like to cook together. We like to keep everything well stocked."

Brianne's eyebrows rose. "The hunk cooks, too?"

Ansel stopped scooping sour cream into a fancy bowl to scowl at her. "Jazzi and I are partners at work and at home."

"Do you ever hit her?"

Ansel stared. "Wouldn't be safe. She'd hit me back. Maybe when I was sleeping."

Brianne threw back her head and laughed. "If I touched Jarrett, he'd beat me till I couldn't raise an arm."

"And you still stay with him?" Ansel was clearly puzzled.

"I like a guy who won't take any guff from me."

"To each his own." Ansel shook his head.

She smirked, amused. "I know how to handle him. A couple of his girlfriends didn't."

Jazzi joined the conversation. "Are they the ones who filed restraining orders against him?"

"Stupid, right? If Jarrett was ticked enough, he'd go after them anyway."

"Did he go after Maureen and beat her up?"

Brianne sat up straighter, her shoulders stiff. "Jarrett's not like that. He'd never kick a woman when she was down, especially an old broad like Maureen."

Jazzi wasn't sure what to make of that. Jarrett only beat women he knew personally, and then only if they were young enough?

Brianne went on. "After talking to Gaff, Jarrett thinks someone talked when they were inside. Having two guys rough up Ray made him worry. Two guys came into the garage a few days ago and jumped him. Newbies.

He wiped the floor with them before they took off. He thought they were after the money in the cash register, but now he thinks they were looking for the stolen cash."

"Could he give a description of them?" If they had records and mug shots, Gaff might be able to track them down.

"Yeah, Gaff brought in a guy who draws stuff like that. Jarrett was happy with how the pictures turned out. Said it looked like them."

Good. Little by little, they were making progress. *If* Brianne was telling the truth.

Brianne looked at the clock. "Guess your friends will be here soon, but it's still too early for me to go home. I'd stop at a bar and hang out if I had money." She gave Jazzi a knowing look.

What the heck? Jazzi reached for her purse, but Ansel beat her to it. He opened his wallet and handed her a twenty-dollar bill. "Knock yourself out."

She cocked an eyebrow at him. "You wanna miss all this funfest and hang out with me?"

"Not a chance." He added a five-dollar bill for her.

She grinned and went for her coat. "If you ever feel a little frisky on the side, let me know."

He didn't answer, so she let herself out. "That girl has a lot of nerve."

"She thinks she's a badass, but that's not doing herself any favors. She kicked Donovan to the curb to run back to Jarrett."

"That says it all." He pushed the sour cream to the end of the kitchen island near the shredded lettuce and diced tomatoes, then began filling another bowl with sliced black olives.

A few minutes later, Walker, Didi, and River came through the back door.

"It smells good in here." Walker helped River take off his coat and reached for Didi's to hang on the coat tree.

"Supper got a little rushed," Jazzi said. "Nachos."

"I love nachos!" River went to the junk drawer to pull out the cats' string and play with them. Inky and Marmalade came running.

Didi shrugged. "He loves anything messy—spaghetti, goulash, tacos..."

"He's a kid." With a smile, Walker watched him run, dragging the string behind him.

Once again, Jazzi was struck by how much the man loved the little boy. She had no worries that when Didi had his daughter, he'd love both kids equally. "Does your mom know that you're going to be a dad in nine months?"

"She knows I'm a dad now, and our family will get bigger soon. She can't wait to come for Easter to meet Didi and River."

Didi twined her arm through his and leaned her head against him. "Is he the best, or what?"

Jazzi motioned toward Ansel. "The men in our family—and you guys are like family to us—aren't too shabby."

Didi laughed. "Right now, I feel more like freeloaders. We'll have to have everyone over to our house sometime. We finally have enough room and dishes to entertain."

Our house. Jazzi couldn't stop a smile and Didi hugged herself.

"I don't know how I got so lucky, but Walker wants me for keeps. We're putting my house up for sale and having a small wedding. It all feels like we're going too fast, but I can't imagine life without him. I just can't."

Fast was right. A whirlwind might be a better description, but Walker and Didi looked like a perfect fit the minute they met. Jazzi gave her a warm hug. "I'm so happy for both of you."

Just then the door opened and Gran and Samantha came in. Samantha was carrying a stack of cardboard cartons full of fresh eggs from their farm. "We thought we'd contribute something to the cookie baking," she said. "And just so you know, the asparagus poked above ground this morning."

It was too soon to pick, but Gran had enough asparagus and rhubarb plants to share. Jazzi started thinking about different dishes she could make for Sunday meals soon.

"Where's the food?" Gran asked. "And my wine?"

Just like Gran to get right down to the important matters at hand. Jazzi and Ansel spread the cookie sheets filled with nachos on the butcher block countertop and put the lettuce, tomatoes, and other toppings within reach. To make things easy, they were using paper plates. No one worried about formalities and grabbed their food to settle at the dining table. The women drank wine and the guys grabbed beers. River and Didi drank soda. When the food was gone, the women started baking while the guys did cleanup, and soon batches of peanut butter dough were ready for the ovens.

River took off to the living room with Ansel and Walker while Jazzi and Samantha stirred ingredients for the sugar and spice cookies and Gran and Didi mixed the dough for the date filled spirals. When the timer sounded, and the first batch of cookies came out to cool, River swooped back in to be near Gran for the handoff of fresh cookies from the oven.

Didi shook her head. "No wonder he wants you to adopt him as your grandson."

Gran chuckled. "That boy can spend a day on the farm with us anytime. Both Samantha and I will spoil him rotten. We never get to be around kids anymore."

When Jazzi pulled Didi to the stove to make caramels with her, the rest of the women finished the baking. By the time the caramels were cooling, so were the cookies. Jazzi loaded two plates for people to take home.

"No caramels?" River begged. "I've never had real ones before."

Jazzi rolled her eyes. If Gran could cheat, why couldn't she? She cut off three squares of them to send home with Didi, one for each of them.

"I've never had real caramels either," Gran begged.

Now that was an out and out fib, but Jazzi wrapped two more squares in wax paper to send home with her.

When she and Ansel were finally alone, he came to help with cleanup, then surprised her by dropping to one knee and holding his hands out, palms up, like Oliver in the Charles Dickens novel. "Please, Jazz. I've never had a real caramel either."

She busted out laughing. "Just every year since we've known each other, but what the heck? Cut one for yourself." She'd made two batches. She knew her Viking.

After she counted out forty of each cookie to freeze, she dished up extra sugar 'n' spice to put in a Ziploc baggie to take to Jerod for lunch tomorrow. She'd be lucky if anyone here could even *look* at a cookie near Easter, they'd already eaten so many, but then she shook her head. Who was she kidding? No one else in her family baked. The more cookies, the better.

They finally started turning out kitchen lights and headed to the couches to watch TV. Ansel stretched out on his with George by his feet and she lay on hers with both cats.

"It's been a long night," Ansel said. "But baking cookies is worth it."

Her Norseman loved his food. And she loved him. She was happy for Didi and Walker. If they were as happy as she and Ansel were, they were lucky. And hopefully, even Jarrett would be happy enough tonight not to cuff Brianne when she returned home.

Chapter 29

Jazzi didn't want to get out of bed Thursday morning. The alarm buzzed and Ansel flipped it off. He threw back his blankets and padded to the bathroom. It didn't matter if the man only got two hours of sleep, when his alarm went off, he was alert. She didn't get that gene. She closed her eyes, dug deeper under the covers. Inky, pressed against her side, stretched and jumped to the floor. She heard him stop, then start back to her. He knew their routine. Ansel got up, then so did she, but she wasn't moving this morning. He jumped back up, moving to her pillow, and batted her hair with his paw. She put up a hand to stop him, and he licked it with his sandpaper tongue. Not a sign of affection. He was purposely trying to annoy her. She tugged her hand back under the blanket and he grabbed a clump of her hair with his teeth and pulled.

That did it! She sat up and glared at him. He blinked, free of shame, and jumped to the floor, looking back to make sure she'd follow him. The fur ball wanted to be fed. With a sigh, she gave in ungraciously. When Ansel exited the bathroom, it was her turn. Inky ran ahead of her. The beast had a thing for the running water in the sink when she brushed her teeth. He sat on the counter and leaned forward to drink. When she bent to spit, he jumped in the bathtub to play with the chain for the plug while she washed her face.

When she exited to start dressing, he raced ahead of her to bother Ansel while he tied the shoestrings of his work boots. Marmalade had her proclivity and didn't leave the softness of the bed until she and Ansel booted her off to make it. Then Ansel picked up George and they all went down to the kitchen, Inky and Marmalade running ahead of them. While Ansel plopped pumpernickel bread into the toaster, Jazzi spooned half a can of wet food into each cat's bowl and refilled their dry food. George whimpered and she fed him, too, then he went to the island to beg for a few crusts of toast from Ansel. While they sipped their coffee, he stayed to beg for bits and pieces of deli roast beef when Jazzi made sandwiches for lunch.

Their morning routine done, they pulled on hoodies and grabbed the cooler to go to work. If they got lucky, they could start framing new walls today.

Jerod was way ahead of them. When they got to the house and climbed the steps, he had already started cleaning so they could frame.

"You're a little early this morning, aren't you?" Ansel asked. He carried George to a clean corner to put him down, but the pug whined. He didn't like all the dust and hammering, so Ansel carried him back down to the kitchen where his dog bed was. George would supervise out of sight today.

When Ansel returned, Jerod said, "Peter got up at five thirty this morning and wouldn't go back to sleep, so I stayed with him until Franny got up to get Gunther and Lizzie ready for preschool. I thought about trying for a little more shut eye but gave up and drove here early."

"The joys of fatherhood." Ansel shook his head. "Not sure I'm ready for that yet."

Jazzi heard that with relief. When they'd first gotten married, Ansel made noises about wanting kids. Little did she know the best birth control in the world was actually being around a baby.

"Take your time," Jerod told him. "Once you have one, you can't send it back."

Another surprise. Usually, her cousin teased her about beating her ticking biological clock. He must be especially tired this morning.

They quit talking and strapped on their toolbelts to get to work. They had both bedrooms framed when Jazzi's cell phone rang. She glanced at the screen. "Gaff."

There was no place to get away from the noise on this floor, so she zipped downstairs to talk to him.

"I'm going to Ronnie's funeral today," he told her. "Thought you might want to come along. His grandma was pretty partial to you."

"The funeral's today?" How had she forgotten that? She'd watched the paper for the announcement a couple of days and then got busy. The notice got lost in the shuffle.

"His grandma's son meant to come home for it, so they waited, but it fell through."

"I didn't bring anything to change into. I'm in my work clothes."

"His grandma won't mind. She'll just be happy you came. Want me to pick you up?" Gaff was being too nice about this. He must be hoping the old woman would tell her something she might not tell him. But Jazzi *did* have a special fondness for the woman.

"Sure. What time?"

"The funeral's at two thirty. What if I pick you up at two?"

"I'll be ready, but I won't look very good."

"See you then."

She rejoined the guys upstairs and told them she'd have to leave. They both nodded. "Mrs. Reynolds took a liking to you," Jerod said. "She'd want you there."

Jazzi wasn't so sure. Ronnie's grandma had lots of close church friends, but she'd put in an appearance anyway. The woman deserved all the support she could get.

They worked even harder after the call and waited to have lunch late so that they could frame in the bathrooms, too, before Gaff came. Then they hurried down for sandwiches and had just finished when Gaff pulled to the curb in front of the house.

Jazzi grabbed her hoodie and ran to his car. On the drive to Creighton Street, Jazzi shook her head at her dirty jeans and work boots.

"You're fine," Gaff told her. "Mrs. Reynolds will know you came straight from work."

But when they walked into the towering old brick church where the funeral was being held, Jazzi felt her spirits plunge. The black women in the pews all wore dresses, heels, and hats. The men wore suits. "I want to sit in the back pew," she said.

When Mrs. Reynolds saw her, though, she waved for her to come forward for a hug. Jazzi felt eyes following her progress as she went to the front of the church. If she could shrink and become invisible, she would. She blurted, "I'm so sorry. I didn't have time to change into something better."

"No matter, baby." Mrs. Reynolds wrapped her thin arms around her and pulled her close. Then she looked at her friends in the pews and said, "This is the pretty white girl I told ya 'bout, come straight from her job, the one who's been so nice to me."

A woman jumped out of her pew and came to pump Jazzi's hand. "Heard all about you. I'm Pudding. We got plenty of food in the basement. Why don't you and the detective fill a plate with us after the service?"

Jazzi started to say she had to get back to work, but Gaff talked right over her.

"We'd love to. Thank you."

Yup, this was a setup. Gaff was fishing for new information.

The preacher walked up to the microphone, and everyone took their seats. Mrs. Reynolds gripped Jazzi's hand and didn't let go, so she and Gaff sat in the front pew with her. There was lots of preaching and lots of music before the service was over and everyone wandered to the basement to eat.

Mrs. Reynolds leaned against Jazzi's arm and whispered, "Thank ya for comin', girl. I know ya probably didn't want to, but it sure made me feel good."

She looked so small, so fragile. Jazzi wanted to wrap her in bubble wrap and tuck her somewhere safe. "Are you going to be okay by yourself in your house?"

Ronnie's grandma waved that off. "Oh, honey, Ronnie spent more time in jail than at home. I'm used ta takin' care of myself."

"If there's anything you need..." Jazzi reached into her purse and pressed one of her business cards into the old woman's hand.

"I 'preciate that, I do, but I got friends that'll help me out, lots o' them. Good people." She tucked the card in her purse, though. Shaking her head, she said, "Ronnie told me he'd found God this last time in prison, but I guess not even God could keep 'im outta trouble. The boy liked his pot and beer." She wrinkled her face in thought. "There are worse things a boy can do. I thought he'd still be okay, 'specially when them cooks tried to get 'im hired to work with them. Made the boy mighty proud."

Gaff cleared his throat. "Any idea why Ronnie tried to find guys to do a job with an old friend?"

She shook her head. "He didn't want to do it. Told me so. Tried to find someone else. Maybe that's what got him dead."

The preacher came upstairs to look for her, and Mrs. Reynolds got to her feet. "Time to show you folks what good cooks we are. You ain't gonna eat this good for a long time."

Smiling, Jazzi and Gaff went downstairs to join in the funeral dinner. And Mrs. Reynolds didn't exaggerate. The food was delicious, the people fun and friendly. By the time they had to leave, Jazzi had quit worrying about the old woman. Her church took care of its own. She'd be fine.

"You can still come and see me once in a while," she told Jazzi. "And I sure don't mind a bit o' chocolate now and then."

"I'll remember that. You take care now." With a hug, Jazzi left her.

On the drive back to New Haven, Gaff said, "I don't see why someone killed Ronnie. It keeps bringing me up short. It seems like he really did plan to go straight, don't you think?"

Jazzi nodded. "He turned down the job someone offered him, that's for sure."

"That shouldn't have gotten him killed, though." Gaff sounded as though he was talking to himself as much as to her. He grimaced. "When I talked to Jarrett, he couldn't figure things out either. I'm missing something. We'll have to keep at it."

He reached the old Victorian and parked at the curb. She reached over and patted his shoulder. "You'll find the answers. You always do."

"Not always." He sounded frustrated.

Jazzi understood, but she had nothing new to tell him, so she climbed out of the car and waved him away.

When she went in the house, she heard the sound of nail guns upstairs. She went to see how Jerod and Ansel were doing. They'd framed the office. She studied the layout and smiled. "Looking good." They'd have to patch and match a few floorboards, but they could manage that.

Jerod stopped working and wiped sweat from his forehead. "We'll start drywall tomorrow."

Ansel stopped, too. "How was the funeral?"

Jazzi filled them in while she helped with clean up. That done, they started down the stairs to grab their hoodies and go home.

"I haven't gotten to spend much time with you lately. Alone." Ansel picked up George. "And tonight's girls' night out. I'm starting to get lonely."

She snorted. "Right. Where are you, Thane, Radley, and Walker going?"

Jerod sniffed, starting to his pickup. "I'm grabbing a box of fried chicken, stuffing my face, and hitting the couch. I'm going to bed when Gunther and Lizzie do."

Her poor cousin was dragging. Little or no sleep will do that to you. She hoped Peter slept through the night tonight.

While Ansel loaded George in the van, Jazzi asked again, "Where are the four of you off to tonight?"

"*Five Guys* for burgers and fries."

She shook her head. "Bulk. You get lots of food there, right?"

"We can handle it, and it's all good."

All four men were big. Half pound burgers were just the right size for them.

On the drive home, Ansel asked, "Where are you and Olivia going?"

"Our standby—Henry's."

When they pulled in the drive, they hurried more than usual to get ready. They'd worked a little longer at the fixer-upper than they'd meant to. George lowered his head onto his paws with a sigh when they both walked to the door. He knew the Thursday night drill. They climbed into their vehicles and drove their separate ways.

When Jazzi walked through Henry's doors, she saw Olivia waiting for her at a booth. She'd already ordered wine for each of them. Jazzi took a sip and asked, "How's it going?"

Olivia raised a blond eyebrow. "Do you want to know what my stupid boyfriend wants to do for our wedding?"

Uh-oh. Olivia's brown eyes sparkled with temper. Her sister was more spontaneous than she was, probably more fun, but her temper was quicker to surface, too. Jazzi grimaced. "Do I want to know?"

"He doesn't want to rent tuxes for our wedding. He wants to wear suits. He needs a new one anyway, so this is his brilliant solution."

"Ansel wore a suit for our wedding and looked yummy."

"You got married at home. It's different."

The waitress came and Olivia glared at her.

"I can come back." They usually had the same waitress, and she was used to them.

"No, I'm hungry now." Olivia pointed to the shrimp wrap-up. "I'm watching my weight for my wedding, so I'll have coleslaw with it instead of fries."

"And you?" The waitress looked at Jazzi.

"The filet sandwich, medium. And fries." Henry's made some of the best fries in town.

With a nod, she left and Olivia returned to venting. "Have you seen my wedding dress?" She pulled the picture from her purse and stuck it in front of Jazzi. "It's gorgeous. Thane's going to look like a poor relative if he stands next to me in a suit."

Olivia took fashion seriously. She and Reuben's wife, Isabelle, had actually driven to Chicago for a long weekend of shopping a few weeks ago. Jazzi wasn't quite so style conscious. "Have the bridesmaid dresses come in yet?" Olivia had informed her that she'd be her maid of honor and Isabelle was a bridesmaid. She'd taken both their measurements and was waiting for the dresses she chose to arrive for final tailoring. The cost of the dress almost made Jazzi faint, but Ansel had told her it would be worth it. If it made her sister happy, she should pay the money and shut up, even though she'd never seen what Olivia chose.

"Easy for you to say," she'd told Ansel. "You get to try on your tux. You won't have any nasty surprises."

"You look good in anything, so relax. This is all about your sister."

And Olivia had taken full advantage of that. "You won't want to wear anything I pick," she'd complained. "But you don't get to vote on this. You and Isabelle will both look gorgeous in the color and style. If you hate it, you can give it to Goodwill once Thane and I are on our honeymoon."

Lucky ducks. They were taking off an entire week to celebrate.

But now Thane didn't want to rent a tux. She tried to picture him in a penguin suit and couldn't. "It doesn't matter what he wears if he doesn't do something with that wild auburn hair of his."

"What's wrong with his hair?" Olivia's eyes narrowed. "I don't want him to cut it."

Oh, boy. She'd hit a nerve. "I don't either, but maybe he could pull it back in a ponytail."

Olivia relaxed. "That would work."

The food came and Olivia concentrated on her wrap. She ate like she was starving. Jazzi frowned. "You're not trying to lose weight for the wedding, are you? Because you look great, as is."

Between bites, Olivia said, "I'm being more careful than usual, that's all. But I'm hungry all the time."

"No wonder you're grouchy."

Olivia glared. "I'm not grouchy. I'm ticked at Thane."

"I'll side with you on this one." Jazzi wanted her sister's wedding to be as wonderful as she dreamed it would be. "I've already bought most of the food for the reception."

"Have you?" She drank the last of her wine and motioned for another glass. "I'm starting to get nervous. There are so many things to think about."

Jazzi shrugged. "It's going to be a piece of cake. You're going to be a beautiful bride and Thane's going to be a doting husband."

Olivia smiled. "That's the main thing, isn't it?"

"Absolutely. Have you heard about Walker and Didi? They want to get married, too, before Didi starts to show too much."

"They do?" Olivia stared at her, then broke into a huge grin. "Wouldn't it be wonderful if we had a double wedding?"

"What?" Jazzi shook her head. "They didn't want to announce anything and take away from your big day."

Olivia dug in her purse for her phone. "That's silly. A double wedding would be even more fun." She called Thane and asked him about it. When she squirmed with happiness, Jazzi decided that Thane must have liked the idea, too.

Why had she gone and opened her big mouth? "You're having the reception at our house. You've already invited a lot of people."

"How many people would Walker and Didi invite? It couldn't be that bad. Let's find out!" She dialed Thane again before Jazzi could protest. With her hand over the phone, she whispered, "Thane's with Walker and Ansel right now. He can ask him."

It took longer to get an answer this time, but when she did, Olivia looked thrilled. When she hung up, she reached across the table and grabbed Jazzi's hands. "You're brilliant, sis! Walker called Didi and they said yes. Thane even agreed to go with Walker to rent a tux. Isn't it wonderful?"

"Wonderful." Jazzi tried to sound sincere. She'd have to get a new number of guests and buy more food. They had a perfect house for entertaining, but she was beginning to worry that it would be standing room only.

"You okay?" Olivia looked repentant. "I didn't even ask you if you liked the idea, did I? I just sprang it on you."

"Things might be crowded."

Olivia's grin returned. "The more the merrier, right?"

"We'll make it work." And they would. Somehow.

Chapter 30

On Friday, George chose to curl in his dog bed in the kitchen when they reached the Victorian. Probably a smart choice. They headed upstairs to work on drywall, but when Jazzi looked at the office's ceiling, she frowned. "The ceilings in the other rooms are fine, but moving walls around made cracks where some of these seams join. We can re-tape them, but what if we put up a beadboard ceiling instead? It would make the office feel special."

Ansel glanced at the square room. "The owners want carpet up here, so a wooden ceiling would look nice. It wouldn't cost that much since this room's smaller."

Jerod cocked his head, trying to picture it. "It would be just as easy to do beadboard as to re-tape the whole room."

"Then it's a go?" Jazzi asked.

He nodded. "It will be a nice touch, but first, all of the rooms need drywall."

They couldn't finish it in one day, but they'd do as much as they could.

Jerod grabbed a sheet and asked, "How's Olivia? Is she going nuts trying to get everything ready for the wedding?"

Jazzi's shoulders sagged. "Olivia and Thane have decided to have a double wedding with Walker and Didi."

"That's great!" He looked at her face. "Maybe."

"That means there'll be even more people at our house for the reception."

"Aah, now I get that worried look. When will you know if you're going to sink or swim cooking enough food for the party?"

"Walker told Ansel he'd call him tonight. If we have to, I can call in Gran and Samantha for backup to help out."

"Gran would love that."

Jazzi started to feel better. Gran would. And they'd figure out how to get everything done and make it work. Ansel put an arm around her. "We might want to fix up our basement someday like Jerod's to have more room."

She rolled her eyes. "I thought I'd never have to worry about that when I left my apartment. I thought I'd have so much room I wouldn't know what to do with it all. Who knew?"

Jerod laughed. "When we moved into our farmhouse, we swore we'd never have enough pots and pans and dishes to fill the kitchen cupboards. Look at us now. Filled to the brim. We even ran out of space for the kids to play."

Jazzi shied away from a mental picture of her entire house filled with folding tables and kids running amok. "Our families are growing bigger."

"See?" Jerod strapped on his toolbelt. "Everything's relative, cuz."

Relative. Right. What would happen when Radley got married and had kids and Olivia and Thane brought theirs? How many people would have to crowd around tables for the Sunday meal? She shut her eyes, blocking the vision. When the inevitable happened, they might have to change things up.

They pushed harder than usual to finish as much as they could, but even taking a short lunch, they still had one bedroom to go. Then they had to tape and plaster, sand and prime. Only then could they install the beadboard ceiling.

Jerod unhooked his toolbelt. "It's Friday. I'm ready to go home."

Jazzi wasn't going to argue with that. They trudged down the steps and she shrugged into her hoodie. Ansel hadn't even worn a jacket, the weather was so mild—a perfect day for Reuben and Isabelle's spring fling tonight. And Jazzi would gladly celebrate the equinox. She was ready to say goodbye to winter.

Ansel collected George to carry to the van, and Jerod pulled away when they did. Her cousin wanted to take Franny and the kids out shopping. They always bought new dress clothes for Easter, not that they attended church regularly, but Franny dragged them to it once a month.

Ansel placed George on the backseat and they were pulling out of the Victorian's driveway when his cell phone buzzed. He pulled to the curb and frowned at the ID. "Brianne."

Why would Donovan's ex call Ansel? Jazzi could tell from his expression that the conversation was serious. Near the end of it, he said, "We'll be there. It will take us about twenty minutes."

He pulled from the curb and headed south. "Brianne gave me directions to Jarrett's garage. Jarrett had the day off and they went out. When they got back, his apartment was trashed. The owner and customers were in the garage, but they didn't see anyone go up the outside stairs to their place. Every piece of furniture is ripped open. They don't have renters' insurance. Jarrett's furious and Brianne's trying to convince him not to go pound somebody."

Jazzi gulped. "So we're going to talk to him?"

"Yeah, she's worried he'll get himself in trouble, he's so mad."

Ansel was six-five of all muscle, but Jarrett was a big man, too. And he didn't seem to mind starting a fight with someone bigger than he was. He probably fought dirty.

"If he throws a punch, call Gaff," Ansel said.

It would take Gaff ten or fifteen minutes to get there. By then, the two men could be wading in a blood bath. "I don't like this idea."

"Neither do I, but Jarrett is mad enough that maybe he'll talk. I'd like to know what the heck is going on."

"It's not worth a broken nose and a black eye."

Ansel raised an eyebrow. "I can take care of myself. I played football in high school and one of the guys had it in for me. It didn't go well for him."

Jazzi stared. Guys seemed to establish pecking order with their fists. "Did you and your brothers fight a lot?"

"We had our moments, but Ethan, my best friend through middle and high school, was on the wrestling team and took boxing lessons. I sparred with him, one way or another, every weekend."

All of a sudden, it made sense that Ansel never seemed worried about handling trouble. "Why is this the first time you've told me this?"

He shrugged. "It never came up."

A reasonable answer. She didn't talk to him much about her two BFFs, Leesa and Suze, either. By the time they pulled near the side of Jarrett's garage, a CLOSED sign hung in the front window. They climbed the steps to the upstairs apartment and Ansel gave a quick knock.

"Come in!" Brianne's voice sounded stressed.

Ansel turned the knob and they walked inside. Jarrett was alternately pacing and punching the wall. Brianne was hovering close to him, trying to calm him down. She looked at Ansel and Jazzi. "Help me!"

Jarrett squared his shoulders, glaring at them.

"Can we help?" Ansel asked. "Brianne said it was a mess."

An understatement. Someone had even slashed the drywall, leaving deep gouges. This was more than a search and trash. It looked like anger and destruction.

When Jarrett didn't answer, Ansel said, "We're fixer-uppers. We can help you put up new drywall."

Finally, the fight seemed to go out of Jarrett. He sagged down on his broken couch and put his head in his hands. "I kept my trap shut all through prison. Figured I was stupid enough to trust people I shouldn't have. I never expected to see the money when I got out. All I wanted to do was keep my nose clean, my head down, and start over. And this. The owner came up, took one look at it, and fired me. I don't even have a job anymore. Brianne and I have to move out by April first."

No fair. It wasn't Jarrett's fault someone did this to him. But the owner probably worried that the trouble wouldn't stop there. She felt sorry for Jarrett for the first time.

Ansel must have, too. "If we fix the place up, will he change his mind?"

"No way. He took a chance on me and it blew up in his face. I don't blame him. I'm not sure what to do next, though."

"Let us ask around." Ansel leaned against the wall. The couch and chairs were all gutted. Their stuffing littered the floor.

Jarrett shrugged. He obviously didn't hold out much hope.

"Care to tell us who might have done this?" Ansel asked.

Brianne went to sit next to Jarrett's feet and he absently reached out to rub her back to comfort her. "No clue. I even got together with Ray to talk about it, and we can't figure it out. He thought the two guys who jumped him were probably ex-cons, doing a favor for somebody. We're thinking someone on the inside heard that we had money stashed away for when we got out, but who that person would be, we don't know. Ray doesn't know where the money is. Neither do I. They shot Ronnie when he couldn't give them an answer."

Jazzi believed him when he'd talked to Gaff, and she believed him now. The man looked like every last hope had been knocked out of him. She decided to ask Jerod if his dad needed any help in his garage. Jarrett was no expert like Eli was, but she knew that everyday maintenance needed to be performed on some of the cars there.

At the moment, though, Jarrett and Brianne just needed a bed to sleep in and a place to stay. "We have air mattresses at our place that we could bring over," Ansel said.

Jarrett shook his head. "We can go to the Salvation Army and buy a used couch, maybe some sleeping bags. We'll manage for now. But thanks."

"If you need us for anything…" Jazzi hesitated. She rummaged in her purse for one of their business cards and handed it to him.

He pushed to his feet. "We'll be all right. Guess we might as well start cleaning up and buy a few things for tonight. Thanks, though."

There wasn't anything else they could do. They went down the steps and settled in the van.

"I feel sorry for him," Ansel said.

"Me, too." It had taken some of the fun out of going to the party tonight.

Ansel shook his head. "Look. It's Friday. Let's have a good time tonight with our friends. Tomorrow, we'll put our heads together and see if we can help Jarrett out somehow. But that's tomorrow. For now, we push him out of our mind and enjoy the party."

A good plan. There wasn't anything they could do now anyway. Jazzi gave a quick nod. "I'm shifting to spring fling mode."

"That's my girl. Me, too." And they drove home to get ready for a wonderful night of celebrating.

They fed pets and pampered them with attention before going upstairs to get ready. Jazzi took more time than usual with her hair and makeup. Ansel's phone buzzed and he went downstairs to stay out of her way while she dressed. She decided to wear a dress she'd ordered online—the French Film Star Travel Dress in hunter green—with black heels. It had a touch of glamour she liked and showed off her curves. When she came down the steps to join him, Ansel was wearing a charcoal colored dress shirt with black slacks. The dark colors complemented his white blond hair and blue eyes. At six five with broad shoulders, her Viking could vie for any woman's fantasy.

"We clean up pretty well." His gaze never left her.

"The dress dips lower than I expected. Do I look all right?"

"Better than all right. Hon, all of your parts are good. I like looking at all of them."

She made a pledge to dress up a little more often, he liked it so much. He held his arm out to lead her to the pickup.

On the drive to West Central, Ansel said, "That was Bain who called earlier. He's starting to take Greta out to eat once in a while so they can talk about Mom and Dad without arguing with them."

"Is that the only reason?"

"She only comes once a week now to clean and cook a pot of soup for Mom to eat during the week." He grinned. "She *does* come to cook supper for Bain once in a while, though, and to visit with him."

"I bet that gets your dad going."

"Dad's on a rampage. He told Bain he's going soft. First, he moved Stubs into his house with him and now he's seeing Greta. Greta loves the cat as much as Bain does."

"Your dad probably sees money going up in flames."

"That's what it always comes down to for him. He already told Bain that if he decides to marry Greta just because she's the only girl who'll have anything to do with him, he'd better go to a lawyer and get a prenup, because she's probably just after his money."

Jazzi laughed. "Dalmar sure has a way of making someone feel special."

Ansel snorted. "Yeah, he has a knack, doesn't he? But I've been thinking. The big bedroom upstairs would be easy to divide into two smaller rooms with double beds so more people can come and visit."

She put down her coffee cup. "Your parents?"

"Mom might come. And Adda and Henry. And if things go well, maybe Bain and Greta."

She couldn't complain. Ansel welcomed her entire family every Sunday. She could tolerate his family once or twice a year. She actually really liked his sister and her husband. "The one guest bedroom *is* way too big. It wouldn't be hard to make it into two."

He reached across to take her hand. "Thank you. I know my family's not as much fun as yours."

She shrugged. "They're family. You get what you get."

He pulled to the curb in front of Reuben and Isabelle's house. Cars lined the street. He got out and came around the truck to hold the door for her. "No more serious talks tonight. Time to have fun."

As they walked to the deep porch, Reuben came out to greet them, a drink in each hand. He held them out for them to take. "Cheers, old friends! Fling your cares away. This is a party! To spring's return!"

And that's the way the rest of the night went.

Chapter 31

They might have celebrated a little too much. They didn't even stir until ten on Saturday morning. The pets glowered at them. They rarely slept so late.

Ansel sat up and groaned. He pressed a hand to each side of his head. "What did Reuben put in the drinks last night?"

Jazzi went straight to the bathroom to down two aspirins with a glass of water. She'd only had one glass of Reuben's concoction, but mixed with the wine she drank, it was enough. Her mouth felt as dry as the Sahara. She brought back two aspirins and water for her Viking. "Reuben's favorite drinks are martinis. We should have known better than to believe him when he said the drinks were light on alcohol."

Ansel winced when he tipped back his head to swallow. "They probably were light for him. I'm sticking with beer at his place from now on. I drank water for the last two hours of the party so I could drive home."

Jazzi had felt pretty good when they left, too. She'd spaced her drinks, but she should have drunk water before going to bed. Talk about being dehydrated!

Ansel gingerly stood up. "I need coffee. Did you set the timer on the pot last night?"

"For nine. It might be cold by now."

"I'll nuke mine. Want me to bring you up a cup?"

"No, I'm right behind you." She stood, too, and the cats raced for the stairs.

When Ansel bent to scoop up George, he grunted. "My eyes hurt."

She patted him on his glorious fanny on his way out the door. "All we have to do is clean the house and go to the store today. There's no rush."

"I want to check on the riding lawn mower, make sure it's in good shape. I might have to mow soon."

It wasn't even April yet. The man and his grass! "Your choice. I'm going slow today."

Ansel put George down next to his bed in the kitchen. Then he poured them each a cup of coffee and heated them up. Jazzi made toast while he carried the mugs to the kitchen island. She felt a little more alive sipping her coffee, and the toast settled her stomach. They lingered over their breakfast longer than usual. The cats fussed at her and wound around her ankles. She usually fed them first. When she finally rose to divide a can of wet food between them, they settled down. George, who'd patiently waited, came to his dog dish and she gave him a little extra for good behavior.

They took their time straightening things up and were ready to head back upstairs to get ready for the day when Jazzi's cell phone rang.

Walker sounded annoyingly cheerful. "My mom and Gene can make it to the wedding. One of Didi's sisters is coming. That's about it for us. We won't make a lot more work for you."

She blinked. "That's it? Three people?"

"Fine with us. We were just going to go to the courthouse with River. This is three more than we thought we'd have."

How could he be so chipper on a Saturday morning? She rubbed her left temple. "Can Didi find a dress with such short notice?"

"We did that last night and rented a tux for River, too. Thanks for thinking of us, Jazzi. This is a lot nicer than we expected."

"No problem. It was Olivia's idea."

"Well, we sure appreciate it."

When she hung up, she felt guilty for ever grouching about it. Walker and Didi felt almost like family, and she was happy for them.

Ansel asked, "They're only inviting three guests?"

"That's what they want. We don't have to buy more of anything for that small of a number. We'd already counted Walker, Didi, and River as guests."

He nodded and grimaced. "I hope my head feels better by lunch time."

She did, too. Ansel wasn't used to sitting around. He'd get antsy and drive her nuts. By the time they finished their showers and got dressed, though, they were both feeling better.

"Do you have a big grocery order this week?" He looked outside at the gray skies. "Maybe we should go to the store before it rains. I'll help you clean later in the afternoon."

"Not a bad idea. I want to buy some things ahead for Easter—a twenty-pound ham and a nine-pound prime rib. We can put those in the spare fridge in the basement." It usually held beer, but there was plenty of room for Easter goodies. Right now, their kitchen refrigerator was full of food for the wedding reception.

Ansel nodded. "Sounds good to me. Easter's two weeks after the wedding, right? We can stock up a little at a time. Walker and Didi won't be here for that. They're driving to his parents' house."

Smart man. Their house would be full to the brim again, and he might be ready for something smaller after the wedding.

The air was warm when they walked to the garage, but dark clouds were gathering in the west. They'd have to hurry or they'd get caught in the storm.

Their cart was heaped with groceries when they left the store. It took them multiple trips to carry all of the bags into the house. The cats loved it, racing back and forth to keep an eye on things. George supervised from his dog bed.

They still had more to go when Radley pulled into their drive. He went to the van to help them carry the rest of the things inside. They were on their last load when the first splats of rain fell.

"Thanks, you came at the right time. We didn't have to get wet." Ansel went to the refrigerator to get his brother a beer. He poured more coffee for himself. "What brings you on a Saturday?" Radley usually came for their Sunday meal.

"Someone broke into my apartment when I was shopping with Elspeth today." When Jazzi gasped, he hurried to say, "Nothing's missing, but then I don't have much. The burglar dumped everything, though, even my flour and sugar canisters. Elspeth helped me clean everything, but I was wondering. Would you mind if I start bringing her over every once in a while on Sunday? She visits her family in Peru some weekends."

"Ooh, it must be getting serious," Jazzi teased.

Radley grinned at her. "She just lost Donovan. She wants to take it slow. I'm fine with that. I can wait."

It *was* serious. And it was about time Ansel's older brothers found some nice girls. She put the milk and new beer in the refrigerator and smiled. "Bring her along. We always have plenty of food."

"I'll put extra in the money jar," Radley told her.

"Just remember my tip."

He laughed. "I'll bring an extra quarter."

"You're the second house that's been broken into," Ansel said, reverting back to the break-in. "Jarrett and Brianne's apartment got torn apart yesterday."

"Torn apart?"

"Yeah, the burglar even jabbed gouges in their walls."

Radley shook his head. "I got off lucky then. He was probably in a hurry. People on my floor work odd hours. They're in and out a lot." He pinched his lips together. "Someone new is moving into Donovan's apartment this week."

"Is that hard for you?" Ansel put the ham and prime rib on the counter to carry to the basement later.

"A little. Part of why I wanted to stay out of the building more than usual. I met the new guy. He's nice enough, but it's going to take a while not to think of 2D as Donovan's place." He took a deep breath and blew it out. "Well, I'd better get going. Elspeth's cooking me supper tonight and I promised to hang a shelving unit for her."

They waved him off.

Ansel started putting frozen foods away. "I get what Radley said about seeing someone move into Donovan's. It has to stir up memories." He flipped on some music while they dealt with the rest of the groceries.

The upbeat songs put them in a silly mood, and soon, Ansel wrapped his arms around her and they started dancing around the kitchen. He dipped her, and they were laughing when Jazzi's cell phone buzzed. With a sigh, Ansel righted her and turned off the music.

"Hello?" Jazzi answered.

Someone mumbled on the other end and she couldn't make out what they said.

"Sorry. I didn't catch that. Can you repeat it?"

"H...lp." The voice was so weak, she could hardly hear it. She frowned and looked at caller ID.

"Brianne?"

"H...p." There was a thud when the phone dropped and went dead.

"We're on our way! Hang in there." She wasn't sure if Brianne could hear her. She hung up and told Ansel, "Brianne's in trouble. She needs us *now*."

They zipped out of the house so fast, George didn't even have a chance to whine. Ansel pushed the speed limit on the way to Jarrett's apartment and Jazzi called 911. Then she called Gaff. They raced up the outside steps and shoved the door open. Jarrett pulled in beside their van and frowned up at them.

"Brianne!" Jazzi called.

He raced up after them.

Brianne's body sprawled on the floor, bloody and unconscious, her cell phone next to her outstretched hand. Jazzi knelt beside her and felt for a pulse. When Ansel stared, she gave him a reassuring nod. Jarrett reached to hold her, but Ansel shook his head.

"Don't move her. Something might be broken. It's not safe."

Bruises were forming on her face and arms. Jazzi remembered that the man who'd attacked Maureen had kicked her when she was down, fracturing ribs. Had he hurt Brianne even more? She wrapped her arms around herself. How could someone do this to a fellow human being, someone who didn't threaten them at all? She shut her eyes, trying to block out the image. She wanted to do something to comfort Brianne, frustrated with a feeling of helplessness. It felt like hours before a siren sounded in the distance, and they all breathed sighs of relief when medics hurried up the stairs.

While the two men checked Brianne over, Jarrett reached for his cell phone to scan it. He frowned. "She tried to call me. I met some friends at a pool parlor. I turned my phone to silent because it was so loud in there, I'd never be able to hear if someone tried to reach me. She needed help, and I didn't come."

His words brought back Ansel's lecture when Jazzi was in danger and he was mowing around the pond. He was frustrated that he hadn't been in the house when she was in trouble. But at least, he'd come at the last minute and nothing had happened. "No one can be there for you twenty-four hours a day," she told Jarrett.

Ansel leveled a look her way, but it was true.

As the medics loaded Brianne onto a stretcher to take her to the hospital, Jarrett asked, "Will she be all right?"

"She has a broken arm, but we didn't feel any other broken bones. She could have internal injuries. The doc will have to check her over."

They took separate vehicles to follow the ambulance to the hospital. They waited with Jarrett until a doctor came to tell him that Brianne would be all right. "Other than her arm, she has a fractured jawbone, but there's no internal damage. You can stay with her when she gets to her room."

Jarrett jerked a nod at Ansel and Jazzi. "Thanks for staying with me, but we'll be okay now. I'll call you when they let her go home . . . if the cops let us back in my apartment. And I'll let you know how she's doing."

He'd rather they left. Jazzi understood. Once they got in the pickup, though, Jazzi called Gaff to fill him in on what happened. He and the crime techs had come as the medics were loading Brianne into the ambulance. They'd stayed at Jarrett's apartment, checking for evidence. As usual, they hadn't found any.

"Our burglar wears gloves, knows how to get in and out without leaving anything behind," Gaff told her.

Jazzi was curious. "Jarrett and Ray have both had burglaries. So have Didi and Radley. Ronnie was shot. Has anything happened to Gavin?"

"When his wife went to pick up their kids from their grandma's, their house was trashed. So was their garage."

She sighed. So much for that theory. "Has anyone tried to rough up any of them?"

"When I asked Gavin that, he laughed. Said if anyone laid a finger on his family, he and his dad and two brothers would tear River Bluffs apart to find out who did it, and that person would never walk or use their fingers again."

Pitting yourself against Gavin's rough family would be enough to deter her. She told Gaff about Jarrett's theory that it was someone from the pen who'd heard more than he should have who was terrorizing them.

"I checked into that," he told her. "The only people who got out around the same time they did live in other states. And I followed up on that. They all went home. They're still home."

"Will Jarrett and Brianne be able to go back to their apartment? I don't think they have anywhere else to stay."

"Not tonight," he told her. "We might want to give it another look tomorrow, but we'll try not to keep them out too long."

She wondered where Jarrett would spend the night, but Ansel said, "I think Jarrett was planning on sleeping on the foldout chair in Brianne's room. He wanted to be there when she woke up."

Jazzi nodded and passed that on to Gaff. She hung up, frustrated. They kept running into dead ends. But eventually, they'd have to catch a break, wouldn't they?

Chapter 32

When Jazzi and Ansel got home, George turned his head, ignoring them. A first. The pug was snubbing them. He'd probably learned that from Inky, who was a pro at ducking his head to avoid petting when he was irritated with her. Ansel went to scratch his ears and make amends while Jazzi took four chicken leg quarters out of the refrigerator. She wagged a finger at George. "Shape up or no more beer for you!"

The pug trotted over to make nice with her. He knew who the disciplinarian in the house was. Ansel was a bust when it came to rules. While the sheet pan dinner was in the oven, she was going to start working on food for the Sunday meal. Ansel was excited because it was warm enough, he could grill.

Once they slid the chicken, potato quarters, onions, and carrots into a hot oven, Ansel came to help her skewer cubes of steak, kielbasa, and shrimp between thick slices of zucchini, red peppers, mushrooms, and onions. They seasoned those, covered them with Saran Wrap, and slid them in the fridge. They'd bought enough fresh asparagus for him to grill, too, and Jazzi planned on making yellow rice with peas on the side along with Ree Drummond's cheat peach dumplings for dessert. When she'd seen them made on *The Pioneer Woman* with crescent rolls and Sprite, she knew she was going to make them…often.

"Are we still going to take off Friday this week to get ready for Olivia's wedding?" Ansel asked.

Jazzi nodded. "Olivia and I cancelled going out on Thursday night. Too much to do, so we'll have plenty of time to get things together for the reception."

"Has your dress come in yet?"

She shook her head. "There was some kind of delay, but the shop promised Olivia they'd get to her house late this week."

"That's cutting it a little close, isn't it?"

"I think Olivia did it on purpose. Then if I hate it, there's nothing I can do about it."

He chuckled, the deep rumble she loved. Then he grew serious. "You know, after the break-ins today, I've been thinking about Gil getting stabbed in prison. Killing Gil might have been about the money, too, or why search Didi's place?"

"You think the killer planned that far ahead?"

"Why not? Gil wasn't the type to let someone trash Didi's house or threaten Ronnie. He'd have started digging for answers."

They finished their prep work and were eating supper when Jarrett called. Jazzi wasn't sure if he'd really keep them informed or not, so she was grateful he did.

"Brianne woke up long enough to tell me that a tall, bulky man wearing a ski mask and gloves kicked in the door when she was alone. He kept hitting and kicking her and told her to give me a message. He wants his money, or she's dead the next time he sees her."

One man. The only reason he'd send two thugs after Ray must be because he thought Ray would recognize him, even if he wore a mask. "Can she remember what the man was wearing?"

Brianne had struck Jazzi as a woman who loved clothes and fashion as much as Olivia did. She'd notice details.

There was a pause while Jarrett turned away from the phone to talk to Brianne. When he came back, he said, "A dark navy hoodie that zipped up the front. He wore the hood up over a navy ski mask. Carpenter jeans and light tan work boots with red laces."

"Red laces?"

"She said you couldn't help but notice them."

Good, something that stood out. Another thought struck her. "Has Gaff learned any more about the two ex-cons who beat up Ray and came for you?"

"Yup, they shared yard time with Gavin when they all worked in the laundry room with Ronnie. He wants to question them, but word is they've skipped town."

"Thanks, Jarrett. Do either of you need anything?" she asked.

"Not right now. They're not keeping Brianne long. I don't have any insurance and can't afford for her to stay here. Gaff said it's okay to use our apartment when she gets discharged."

Medical costs. Jazzi wondered how long it would take him to pay off her bills. She, Ansel, and Jerod had to pay for their own insurance, too, and it wasn't cheap.

When she hung up, Ansel took her plate to the microwave to reheat her food. "I heard most of the conversation. I have to give Jarrett credit. He's hanging in there for Brianne."

"Neither of them is exactly what I'd call a prize, but they seem to be right for each other, and they're trying."

When the microwave beeped, he carried the plate back to her. "I wish them well."

"Me, too." George bumped her leg with his head. The pug had a thing for chicken. She pulled some off the bone and tossed it to him. She was a lucky woman. She had Ansel, a house she loved, and was surrounded by love. She got the feeling Jarrett and Brianne had never been able to say the same. She hoped once all of this calmed down, they'd have a happy life together.

Chapter 33

When everyone arrived on Sunday, it took two folding tables—one on each side of the farm table—to have enough seats. Jerod and Walker went out to grill with Ansel. Radley stayed inside with Elspeth. She came bearing a small gift bag for each family. They waited to open them together. Inside each bag were leather coasters with embroidered decorations in the centers, one for each person in that particular house. Jazzi had never seen anything like them.

"Thank you. These are beautiful." Hers and Ansel's had pink lily blossoms in the center with pink embroidered hems.

Elspeth grinned. "I made them myself."

"You sewed through leather by hand?"

She shook her head. "No, I have a fancy sewing machine that can sew through any fabric. I can download patterns from online for the machine to stitch."

Amazing. "I never learned to sew," Jazzi admitted. "I was lucky I passed home ec class in high school."

Elspeth laughed. "My mom can make anything—men's shirts, prom dresses, you name it. She taught me everything she knows—which is a lot. My favorite things to make, though, are quilts."

"I love quilts!" Jazzi planned on dragging Ansel to Shipshewana in the summer to look at the Amish quilts for sale in some of the small shops.

"My mother made me a queen-size sunbonnet quilt that I cherish. I'm making a patchwork quilt for Radley right now."

Jazzi was jealous. "And you love to cook?"

Radley nodded. "She's as good as you are. How I met two such wonderful cooks, I don't know, but I consider myself a lucky man."

Elspeth laughed. "You have to say that. You want me to keep feeding you."

He gave a sheepish grin. "That's true, but I really do love your meals."

"Uh-oh, now the pressure's on." Jazzi motioned to the guys carrying in the kebabs. "Hope you like them."

"No worries, Radley raves about your food." People were already lining up at the kitchen island, so Elspeth went with Radley to take their place for the buffet. Jazzi added the rice and peas to the spread, along with the grilled asparagus, and people began loading their plates.

Ansel carried a glass of red wine to the table for Gran once she got settled, and she nodded her thanks. She looked around the table at all of the couples and grimaced. "It's time Jarrett appreciates that silly girl of his and settles down. He's ready to. He wants change."

Jazzi blinked. She never knew what would come out of Gran's mouth, but this was completely off topic. It was the perfect lead-in, though, for her to tell them about Jarrett's apartment getting trashed and him losing his job.

When she finished, before she could even ask, Jerod's dad—Eli—asked, "How good is he as a mechanic? One of our guys is moving to Pennsylvania to be closer to his wife's family. She's going to have their first child. Sid mostly does oil changes, tires, that kind of thing. We could use somebody."

"That's pretty much what he did at the garage he worked at." Jazzi gave Jarrett's number to Eli. "He was dependable, but the owner didn't want any trouble from whoever trashed his apartment."

"That wasn't Jarrett's fault," Thane said. "It doesn't seem fair. Look. Radley and I just installed a new heating-cooling unit in an old apartment building off Spy Run. The owner was looking for a part-time caretaker who could repair leaking faucets, that kind of thing, in exchange for free rent. The guy who used to do it retired and moved to Florida, but he only fixed things on the weekends or in the evenings, part-time. The place isn't fancy, but it's clean. The area is a mixed bag, so the owner pays for a security system. If anyone tries to break in, a silent alarm goes off and the cops show up."

"That sounds perfect." Jazzi gave him Jarrett's number, too. She felt better. She never thought it was possible, but she felt sorry for the ex-con. She turned to Gran. "Can you see who's behind the robberies, Gran?"

Gran shook her head. "I only see what I see. I don't ask questions. Things just come to me." She pushed away her empty plate and got up to pour herself another glass of wine. She liked wine with her meal and another glass with her dessert.

Jazzi took the hint and stood to clear the table, and Ansel rose to help her. Jazzi raised an eyebrow when she caught Gran opening a bag of cookies to slip one to River. "You can quit stealing chocolate chips for him. I have everyone's boxes of cookies and candy ready to take home today."

Gran laughed and handed River the cookie anyway. "Just this one," she promised.

They waited for Gran to take her seat, then she and Ansel carried two 9 x 13 pans of the cheat peach dumplings to the table and put them within easy reach of everyone.

Ansel handed Jerod, Walker, and Thane cartons of vanilla ice cream and scoops. He kept one and started topping the dessert bowls close to him. Jazzi put two coffee pots on the table for people to pass around.

When Walker plopped one scoop of ice cream in River's bowl, the little boy hesitated. "Can I have two?"

Walker glanced at Didi, and when she nodded, he scooped out another one.

Dessert always disappeared fast, and this was no exception. In half an hour, every dumpling was gone and the ice cream cartons were empty. People visited another half hour, then got ready to go. Jazzi and Ansel handed out boxes of treats at the door.

When Radley took his, Jazzi said, "I added two of each cookie and candy for Elspeth, too."

Elspeth blushed. "That was so nice of you."

Ansel grunted. "Just make sure Radley doesn't eat your share."

When they were finally on their own, Ansel pulled her into his arms and kissed her. Her breath caught in her throat and everything tingled. His kiss topped off everything. "What's that for?" she asked.

"This was an especially nice Sunday meal."

She'd have to let Ansel grill more often. There was nothing better than being pressed against his chest and body. "You ready to relax?"

"Right after we finish in the kitchen."

Jazzi rinsed and Ansel loaded dishes into the dishwasher. In twenty minutes, they headed to their couches to watch TV. Sunday was the only day Ansel watched sports. Jazzi sat across from him and glanced at the game occasionally while she read a book. When the game ended, Ansel stood and stretched. He held out his hand for her and asked, "Ready?"

Wasn't she always? They headed to the stairs and when George started to follow them, Ansel said, "Later."

The pug sagged onto the floor, his head on his paws. He didn't pretend to suffer, though. He'd gotten so many scraps of steak and chicken from

Ansel during the meal, he looked satisfied with himself. He closed his eyes and before they reached the top step, Jazzi heard him snoring.

Inky and Marmalade didn't even jump off the couch where they'd been curled with her. "The pets aren't in any hurry tonight," she said.

Ansel grinned. "Good, because neither am I."

Promises, promises . . . but Ansel was a man of his word. Jazzi shivered with anticipation just thinking about it.

Chapter 34

Monday morning, they were back at the old Victorian, sanding walls. Jazzi had made wraps instead of sandwiches for lunch since it was warm outside. They felt lighter, even though she wasn't sure if they were actually healthier or not, especially since the guys ate so many of them. George supervised work and begged from the kitchen. After they'd eaten, they trudged upstairs and got busy on cleaning up the dust and mess.

With the three of them working together, soon the upstairs was in good shape. That left them free to start installing the beadboard on the office ceiling. That went fast, too. Jazzi was staining it while the guys installed trim when Gaff called.

"Can you meet me at Ronnie's house? You'll never believe what happened."

Her stomach tied itself in knots. "Did someone trash it or beat up Mrs. Reynolds?"

"No, no. Sorry. Nothing like that. But you'll have to hear this for yourself."

"I'm on my way."

She told Jerod and Ansel about the call, then drove to Creighton Street to meet Gaff. Ronnie's grandma opened the door and the tiny woman looked like someone had lit her up, she was so agitated and confused. She led Jazzi into the living room and motioned for her to sit in the chair beside Gaff's. Once she got comfortable in her rocking chair, she said, "Ronnie's lawyer called me today. Didn't know he had one. State paid for one when he went to prison."

Jazzi frowned. "Why would he need a lawyer after he got out?"

Gaff smiled. "He left Mrs. Reynolds a lot of money, and the lawyer's been keeping an eye on it."

Jazzi couldn't hide her surprise. "Ronnie kept everyone's money so that he could give it to his grandma?"

Her lips trembled. "A fool thing to do. I'd rather have my boy than his money. Don't want no blood money for me or my church."

Gaff tried to change her mind. "Ronnie served time for it and it cost him his life. The tech company already collected insurance for it. I'm betting they'd offer a reward for its return."

She rocked harder, shaking her head. "Every penny would make me think of my Ronnie. I have everthin' I need. House is paid for. I don't drive. Only thing I pine for is to visit my sister in Georgia, stay with her a while."

Jazzi wondered how old her sister must be. Did she still live in her own home, too? "Is she younger than you?"

Mrs. Reynolds chuckled. "No, baby, four years older. Women in my family don't die till they have to."

"Can she still get around? Keep up a house?" Jazzi tried to picture Ronnie's grandma four years from now.

"Sure 'nuff. We go till we drop. You get me and Henrietta together with a little moonshine, and we know how to have a good time."

Gaff leaned forward, pressing his hands together to gesture at her. "There. See? That's a great idea, a way to use a little of Ronnie's money to honor him! That would help us tremendously. If we book you a flight and you leave this house, we can leak the news of your new inheritance to bait a trap. Whoever killed Ronnie will show up, looking for it."

She stopped rocking, frowned at him, suspicious. "Using that money would help you catch the man who hurt my boy?"

"It's worth a try," Gaff said.

She sat back in her chair, a determined expression on her wrinkled face. "If that money will catch my boy's killer, it'll bring me peace."

Gaff turned to glance at Jazzi. "Tell her. We can't try out my plan if she's in town. It's too dangerous. She could be hurt. I won't have that on my conscience."

"He's right," Jazzi said. "Ronnie's killer is ruthless and brutal. He's put two women in the hospital."

Her eyes went wide. "He hits women? No man should lay a finger on a woman or child."

Jazzi didn't try to keep the anger out of her voice. "This killer doesn't care who he hurts. It seems to me he enjoys it."

The old woman sighed. "Okay, I'll go. But if you can, give the rest of the money to the people Ronnie shoulda give it to. Seems to me, they've paid for their sins over and over again." She brightened. "That'd be a good way to catch this crook, wouldn't it? If I called 'em and said Ronnie's lawyer gave me his money, but they can have it all? I don't want it."

Gaff rubbed his hands together, excited. "Actually, that's perfect. You get the arrangements made to visit your sister and right before Jazzi drives you to the airport, you call Jarrett and Gavin. You leave, and I'll stay at the house with two of my men to stake it out."

Jazzi blinked when he volunteered her but didn't disagree. If this plan worked, it would be worth losing time to get Mrs. Reynolds on an airplane and out of town.

Mrs. Reynolds liked the idea and reached for her cell phone. "I'll call Pudding. She buys airplane tickets all the time to visit her boy in the army."

Gaff nodded, satisfied. "Call me when you know when you're leaving, and we'll come back when you're ready to make the phone calls and drive you to the airport."

When they stood to leave, Mrs. Reynolds came to Jazzi for a hug. "You take care now. You're always runnin' 'round, tryin' to help people."

Jazzi smiled. "Only people I like. And I get lots of love in return."

The old woman nodded. "Now that's a good thing. Maybe sometime you can bring your man to meet me, too. I been kinda wonderin' what kind of fella you hooked up with."

Mrs. Reynolds had enough curiosity to spare. "I'll have him come with me to see you off at the airport."

Satisfied, Ronnie's grandma settled in her rocking chair and waved as they left.

Walking to their cars, Gaff grew serious. "The sooner she's out of this house, the safer I'll feel. It would only take one punch from our killer to send her on her way."

Jazzi agreed. She was relieved when later that night, while she and Ansel watched TV before bed, Pudding called to tell her that she'd found good tickets for Mrs. Reynolds and she'd be leaving on Wednesday morning.

"Thanks, Pudding."

The woman laughed. "Don't thank me, hon. I'm the one who usually picks people up to give 'em rides to the airport. Don't mind having you spell me one bit."

Ansel was relieved when Jazzi told him the news. "We'll let Jerod know tomorrow. Maybe he can stay home Wednesday morning, and we'll all go into work late."

Chapter 35

Ansel drove to pick up Mrs. Reynolds early Wednesday. The sky looked like an artist had painted it robin egg blue. Big, puffy white clouds dotted it—the kinds kids drew on crayon projects. Mrs. Reynolds was dressed in her Sunday best—a black dress with white polka dots, black lace-up shoes with a small heel, and a black straw hat. Her kinky gray hair was pulled back in a bun. She was a small woman, but standing next to Ansel, she looked downright tiny.

Gaff walked her to their van, passing her off to Ansel. He looked at Jazzi. "She made the calls. Did a good job, too. Both Jarrett and Gavin know the money's hidden in the house somewhere. If you two are ready to take her, I'm going to meet with my team and get ready to keep watch on this place."

Ansel held out a hand to help Ronnie's grandma onto the front seat.

She looked up at him. "My, my, my, you did good, girl," she told Jazzi. "Good-lookin' and a gentleman, too."

Jazzi smiled. "I'm thinking of keeping him. He's nice to have around the house."

Mrs. Reynolds threw back her head and laughed. "You do that, baby. But he done all right, too. You're plenty special."

"Thank you, Mrs. Reynolds." Jazzi settled on the backseat with George. They'd thought about driving her pickup, but the step up into it was probably too high for the old lady.

Mrs. Reynolds oohed and aahed at the scenery on the way to the airport. "When did River Bluffs get so danged big?" she asked. "Houses have sprung up everywhere."

"You should drive north or southwest," Ansel told her. "The city's grown a lot."

When they pulled to the drop off area at the airport, Jazzi got out to help Mrs. Reynolds with her suitcase and to walk her inside the terminal. The boarding line wasn't too long, so she stayed with her to get her ticket and walk her to the security area.

When the security agent asked her to take off her shoes, Mrs. Reynolds gave him an evil glare. "Why would I do that?" she asked. "They won't fit no one here."

The man smiled. "We have to scan them for weapons. The world's changed, ma'am. We do our best to keep our passengers safe." He looked at Jazzi. "You can't enter with her, but I'll walk her through everything and make sure someone helps her onto the plane."

"Thank you." Jazzi gave the old woman a quick hug. "Enjoy your sister."

Mrs. Reynolds turned back to the nice man helping her remove her shoes. "You seem like a nice boy."

Jazzi left while Ronnie's grandma schmoozed her way through security.

Once back in the van with Ansel, she sighed. "She's in good hands. I'm glad she's leaving town. She'll be safe in Georgia. I just hope the killer breaks into her place while she's gone and the whole thing's settled before she gets back."

"Me, too. I never pictured her as so small and frail."

Jazzi snickered. "She might look frail, but that woman has lots of stamina."

They returned home to eat lunch before driving to the Victorian. Jerod pulled into the drive behind them. Walking inside together, they went upstairs to give the second floor one final scan. Satisfied, they climbed the steps to the attic bedroom and were happy with it, too. All the two spaces needed were coats of paint and carpet. After that, they could focus on the basement and the house's exterior.

They all wanted the work done. If they could put in long hours, they might finish the painting tomorrow. Then they'd take Friday off to get ready for Olivia's wedding on Sunday.

They put down drop cloths, covered their heads, and started on the ceilings. Those went quickly, so Jerod packed up and left at five thirty to get home to help Franny watch the kids and make supper. Ansel and Jazzi decided to stay longer to tape around windows and woodwork. Jazzi hated that job, but it had to be done. Better tonight than tomorrow.

When they finally put the last blue tape strip on the attached bathrooms, Ansel took off his baseball cap and grabbed a rag to wipe dried paint splatters off his face. His blond hair was damp with sweat. He still looked good. "I'm done in. How about you? Let's stop and grab something to eat on the way home."

Jazzi untied her scarf. "I'm whipped. It's going to be an early bedtime for me."

Ansel's grin sagged at the edges. "I'd take advantage of that, but I'm too tired."

Laughing, they went to fetch George and head home. They grabbed a bucket of fried chicken and sides on the way. The pug and cats wound around them when they settled at the kitchen island and tossed them scraps.

At nine thirty, they'd hit a wall. Ansel picked up George to carry upstairs and the cats chased after Jazzi. By nine forty-five, the entire household was asleep.

Chapter 36

Gaff didn't call Thursday morning. Jazzi found herself glancing at her watch every half hour, hoping she'd hear something. What if their plan didn't work? What if Jarrett or Gavin didn't pass the information along that Ronnie's grandma had the money? What if Jarrett was right and it was some unknown person in prison who'd overheard Ronnie talk about the money? Would the news reach him or the two goons who'd beat up Ray?

Jazzi had canceled going out with Olivia tonight so that she could get a head start on food for the wedding. She, Jerod, and Ansel had arrived at the Victorian earlier than usual to try to paint the upstairs and attic walls. Surely, Gaff would call during the day.

But it took them until five thirty, and no call. Like last night, Jerod left the minute they'd cleaned the paintbrushes. They stayed to roll up drop cloths and sweep the floors. When they walked out of the Victorian, it's main living spaces were in perfect shape.

They got home before seven, ate a quick supper, and stretched out on their couches, the pets stretching beside them. Jazzi placed her cell phone on the coffee table between them, within easy reach. No call. They let themselves relax, but Jazzi's mind couldn't help returning to Gaff's stakeout. Why hadn't the burglar broken in last night? Would he try tonight once it was dark?

She thought she'd fret when she went to bed, but she was mistaken. She slept so hard, she woke on Friday morning and checked her cell phone to see if she'd missed a message. Nothing.

"Give the guy time," Ansel said, ruffling her hair on his way to the bathroom.

"But what if it's not Jarrett or Gavin? What if it's one of the thugs, and he doesn't hear about Ronnie's money?"

"He'll hear. Maybe he's waiting for the weekend."

She threw her legs over the side of the bed and stretched. Her muscles felt tight. "Why the weekend? More people are home then who might notice him."

"Maybe he works during the week and doesn't want to throw suspicion on himself by taking a day off."

She relaxed a little. That was a possibility. Then her thoughts flew to Jarrett. He'd started his job at Eli's garage, and he and Brianne had moved into the new apartment building where he did part-time maintenance. She bit her bottom lip. She didn't want it to be him.

Ansel reached for her hand and tugged her off the bed. "Give it time. It'll happen. And in the meantime, we have plenty to get done today. Hop to it!"

He was right. She tossed on old clothes and went to report for kitchen duty. They had lots of food to make.

They were on their third pot of coffee and had finished the chicken salad, skewered the beef satays, baked the sausage parmesan palmiers and broccoli 'n' cheddar dip when Jazzi's cell phone rang. "Gaff!" Her voice rose with hope when she said, "Did you catch him?"

She put the phone on speaker.

Gaff sounded disappointed. "No, but a cop saw the two thugs from Jarrett's artist's sketch and picked them up. Once we had their wallets, we looked up their credit cards. They left River Bluffs after Jarrett pounded them and didn't come back until last night. They admitted to beating Ray and trying to shake down Jarrett but swore they'd never touch a woman. Beyond that, they're not talking."

Ansel scowled in frustration. "So they won't say who they were working for?"

"Clammed up the minute we asked."

Jazzi sighed. More waiting.

Gaff heard her and said, "Our guy knows Mrs. Reynolds is only going to be gone a week. If he doesn't move by then, Jarrett or Gavin will come for their share."

True, if the killer wanted it all, he'd have to steal it now.

"Thanks for telling us," Ansel told Gaff.

"Don't give up yet. I'm thinking our guys returned to River Bluffs to break into Mrs. Reynolds's place. They had one phone call from lockup, and they didn't call a lawyer."

"You think they called whoever hired them," Ansel said.

"Wouldn't you? They wouldn't want him to think they grabbed the money and ran."

True. He'd come after them. And he must scare them enough, they didn't want him mad at them.

Gaff hung up, and Ansel and Jazzi started cooking again. They'd pulled four large sheet cakes from the ovens when Olivia called.

"The bridesmaid dresses finally came. You have to come over and try yours on right away. Isabelle's coming, too. If they don't fit, the seamstress at the shop swore she'd alter them on Saturday."

The dresses had been making Olivia crazy. "We're on our way." Jazzi kept her fingers crossed the fit would work.

Isabelle's car was already in the drive and Ansel parked Jazzi's pickup next to it. The minute Jazzi walked into the house, Olivia grabbed her hand and tugged her toward the bedroom. "Come on. I have to know now."

Jazzi frowned. "Is Franny coming?"

"She's already been here and gone. Peter's fussy tonight."

Jazzi had remembered to bring heels with her to make sure the dress was hemmed at the correct length. She slid out of her jeans and T-shirt and pulled the dress over her head. It was a deep rose that hugged her figure before flowing into a bell shape at the bottom. Her voice reverent, she said, "I love it."

Olivia smiled. "I knew you would. Rose is one of your favorite colors. Heck, you painted your bedroom a dark rose." She glanced at Isabelle. Her dress was the same style but in a soft green—a shade Isabelle favored. "And you?"

"I'm keeping mine forever. Whoever took our measurements fitted these dresses perfectly."

Olivia looked relieved. "No fitting sessions or tailoring. We got off lucky."

They had indeed. Jazzi couldn't have chosen a gown she liked more. And from the look on Isabelle's face, she felt the same.

Olivia clapped her hands. "Quick. Take them off. I want to hide them in the closet so the guys can't see them."

Jazzi and Isabelle reluctantly removed them and pulled on their regular clothes. Jazzi had to admit there was something to be said for dressing up and feeling special every once in a while. When they returned to the kitchen, Ansel raised his blond eyebrows in question.

"It's perfect," Jazzi said.

"Something you could wear some place special?"

She shook her head. "We don't go to any parties where we have to dress up in formal gear, but I'll model it for you every once in a while if you're a good boy."

He grinned. "I can be very, very good when I have to."

Olivia rolled her eyes. "Enough already. How's my wedding reception coming?"

It was back to business. "We got a good start today," Jazzi said, "and have plenty of time to finish tomorrow."

Everyone stayed long enough to share a drink, and then they all scattered again. Everyone had plenty to do before the official ceremony.

Chapter 37

Jazzi and Ansel gave the house a quick clean Saturday morning before planting themselves in the kitchen again for a full day's work. People came in and out while they cooked, delivering flowers, rented gold-rimmed dishes and silverware for the reception, and a dozen other things. They finished the last dish they could make ahead by four. That gave them plenty of time to shower and change for the rehearsal at six thirty.

Ansel glanced at the decorated sheet cakes and cake rolls. He patted Jazzi on the back. "They're pretty close to professional. I didn't know you could do all the frosting swirls and flowers."

She was happy with the results herself. "I only do the easy scrolls. I sent Olivia to Country Kitchen for frosting tips, and we bought the flowers ready-made."

"Well, whatever you did, they look great."

His praise pleased her. Almost everything he did made her happy. She wove her arm through his. "We have some extra time. Let's go upstairs and see how you look with your apron off."

She didn't have to ask twice. He scooped her up and sprinted up the steps. At six, they were dressed and ready to go. George trotted to the door to go with them, but Ansel bent and patted his head. "Sorry, boy, not this time."

Head hanging, shoulders drooped, doggie nails dragging across the floor, the pug returned to his dog bed. He deserved an academy award for his performance, he looked so dejected.

Ansel smiled. "He's good, isn't he?"

"One of the best." If there were a class in how to manipulate humans, George could teach it.

On the drive to the church for the rehearsal, Ansel said, "You don't think Thane will try to prank us, do you? It's April first, April Fools' Day."

"I wouldn't put it past him. Jerod's the one to watch out for, though."

When they stepped out of her pickup, Jazzi caught their reflection in its front panel. They looked pretty good. Ansel wore his dark slacks and a sky blue dress shirt. The blue brought out the color of his eyes. She wore a top with a low scooped neckline, a flowered skirt that fell past her knees, and strappy sandals. Olivia would be proud of them.

When they stepped inside, Jerod and Franny were already there. So were Isabelle and Didi. Walker was talking to Thane near the lectern. Ansel went to join them. Olivia came through a side door, saw her, and came to pull her up to the other women. Olivia had kept the wedding party small. Jazzi, Franny, and Isabelle would stand with her and Didi. Ansel, Jerod, and Radley were groomsmen for Thane and Walker. Radley came in at the last minute.

"I waved Elspeth off when she drove to Peru to see her family," he said.

The minister cleared his throat and the rehearsals got underway. A short time later, everyone loaded into their cars to drive to a nearby restaurant. A hostess led them to a side room for small parties. Jerod held out a chair for Franny, then came to hold out a chair for Jazzi. When she sat down, a long fart sound made everyone stop to stare. Jazzi stood and held up a whoopee cushion. Jerod threw back his head and laughed.

Franny just shook her head. "Sorry, folks," she said to the room.

Ansel sat next to Jazzi, smiling. "Better you than me. You look pretty when you blush."

Jerod would pay for this. She didn't know how or when, but she'd exact her revenge.

Two waiters came in with their food and they settled down to eat. Her sister had decided to go with chicken Alfredo and a romaine salad for the meal. Olivia could be a little tight with her money, but at least, she hadn't ordered pizza for all of them. It didn't matter to Jazzi. She was so tired of cooking right now, she was just glad someone else prepared the meal.

No one was in a hurry, so it was two hours before they finished their sorbet and broke up to go home. Jazzi and Ansel had changed into their pajamas and were getting comfortable on their couches when Jazzi's cell rang. She grabbed for it and put it on speaker. "News?"

All they heard was the sound of a loud whack on the other end of the line. Then the line went dead.

A shiver raced down Jazzi's spine. Her arms felt cold. "Something happened to Gaff."

"We should call 911. Ask for someone to go check on him." Ansel reached for his phone. But Jazzi wasn't so sure.

"What if we're wrong? What if Gaff's catching the robber, and we call, and cops rush there and ruin the stakeout? Gaff won't be happy with us." She dialed Gaff's number but he didn't pick up. "We should go to Mrs. Reynold's house and drive past his car to see if he's alright."

Ansel raised a blond eyebrow. "And what if he's not? You're not going into that house after the robber. Neither am I. That's not smart."

"If he's hurt, *then* we'll call 911. He has two other cops with him. I wish I had their numbers, but I don't. We'll find one of them, tell him what happened."

Reluctantly, Ansel agreed. They tossed on clothes and hurried to Jazzi's pickup. For once, Ansel pushed on the gas, speeding into town. He slowed when they reached Mrs. Reynold's house and spotted Gaff's unmarked car. He parked on the street beside it, and Jazzi gasped when she saw Gaff slumped against the car's window, a gash bleeding at his hairline.

"There should be another car parked close by. We'll tell that cop what happened." She pointed when Ansel passed an alley and said, "There."

Ansel stopped the pickup and Jazzi leaped out to hurry to the man's window. He was slumped on the front seat, too. When she returned, she punched in 911 and explained what was happening. When she finished the call, she told Ansel, "They're on their way."

Ansel returned to Gaff's car and parked behind it, doors locked, waiting for backup.

"Do you think I should go to Gaff? Try to help him?" Jazzi asked.

"We shouldn't move him. A medic should look at him first."

Jazzi fidgeted. "Help should be here soon." Before anyone arrived, though, something hard smashed into Ansel's window, shattering the glass. Gavin stood there, wielding a crowbar and a gun.

"Get out!" he barked. "Your girlfriend, too."

Ansel carefully stepped out of the truck, placing his body between Gavin and Jazzi when she came to join him.

"Where's the money? I know you know, blondie. Where did the old lady hide it?"

"If I tell you, you'll shoot us. You killed Donovan and Ronnie. You won't let us go now that we can identify you."

"But I'll make it fast. If you don't talk, I'll shoot your hunky boyfriend one spot at a time. Do you know how much pain it causes to lose a kneecap?"

He was cruel enough to carry through on his threat. But Jazzi thought he might prolong their misery anyway if she told him the money was safe in a bank. Gaff just used it as bait. But no one was going to shoot Ansel. Her mind made up, she steeled herself and dove sideways.

Just as she'd expected, Gavin followed her movement with his gun, chasing a moving target, and at the same time, Ansel threw himself on him. The men grappled, Ansel trying to wrench the gun from Gavin's grip. Gavin dropped the crowbar to fight him, and Jazzi rushed to grab it. Gavin's entire attention on Ansel, Jazzi stepped behind him and swung hard. The crowbar hit him across his shoulder blades, and he crumpled. When he fell to his knees, Ansel shot an uppercut at his jaw, and Gavin went down. Jazzi scrabbled for the gun when he dropped it and gave it to Ansel.

When four squad cars raced to them, sirens blaring and lights flashing, cops jumped out and circled them, guns drawn.

"Which one of you is Jazzi?" one of them asked.

Wasn't it obvious? But she raised her hand. "I am, and the man with the gun is my husband. That's Gavin." She pointed to the man sprawled on the cement. "Gaff's in his car. Is he all right?"

A cop opened the door to check on him, and Gaff groaned, blinking and out of focus. He pressed a hand to his forehead, squinting to see her better. "Jazzi?" His gaze went to Ansel. "What are you doing here?"

Jazzi nodded at the alley. "Another cop's over there. He's unconscious, too." One of the men stalked in that direction.

With a grunt, Gaff tried to stand up. Couldn't. "Let my men take it from here."

"Gladly." Ansel handed Gavin's gun to one of them and went to pull Jazzi close. He was so tense, his muscles felt like rock. They waited until a detective came to question them. When they were finally free to go, Ansel grimly loaded her in the truck to drive home. On the way, he gritted out, "That's the last time we're ever driving to the rescue again. Got that?"

"Agreed." She couldn't make her hands stop shaking. She'd never been so scared in her life. If anything had happened to Ansel, she'd never have forgiven herself.

His voice sounded strained. "I can't lose you, Jazzi. I just can't."

"And I can't lose you. We're too good together."

His shoulders relaxed a little and his grip on the steering wheel loosened. He let out a long, harsh breath. "The wedding's tomorrow. I don't want tonight to ruin it for us."

She reached across to touch his arm, and she could feel him tremble. "Everyone's going to be alright. Gaff caught Gavin. We can put this whole thing behind us."

He gave a brisk nod. "Never again."

"Never again," she agreed.

Chapter 38

Gaff called early the next day. Jazzi put him on speaker. "I know today's the wedding, but I wanted to catch you up on everything. When we dragged Gavin downtown, we pulled his two thugs into another interrogating room and told them if they didn't fess up, we'd charge them with accessory to murder for protecting him."

"And?"

"They spilled. They didn't know anything about Donovan or Ronnie. Gavin only asked them to rough up Ray and Jarrett."

"That's a start."

"But we've nailed Gavin on everything. When we took his picture to Donovan's apartment building, a custodian remembered seeing him there. Gavin's work boots matched the print we found in the mud when he dumped Ronnie's body in the ditch. *And,* his work boots have red shoe laces."

"What about his house? Did he hire the thugs to trash it?"

"No, they think he trashed it himself so that he wouldn't look like a suspect."

"I bet his wife loved that."

"She was his first call and when she came to see him, he asked her to pass the word around to his family and to dig up the cash to hire him a lawyer. When I told her that he'd probably never step out of prison again, she shrugged. Said she'd still visit him once a week and bring him cigarettes."

Jazzi shook her head in disbelief. "And she's okay with that?"

"Seemed to be. Doesn't seem to expect much from their marriage except a steady paycheck."

Jazzi thought a minute. "Did Gavin say why he killed Ronnie? I never understood why he'd do that when he didn't know where the money was."

"I asked. He said Ronnie threatened to report him for threatening him. Gavin knew if Ronnie followed through on that, we'd look into him for killing Donovan. He had to shut him up."

"One more question. What about Gil? Did he know who killed him?"

"He spewed so much garbage about Gil, I'd guess he did it himself. He'll never admit it, but one of the prison buddies he hired watched him do it. No way anyone would take the guy's word for it, so we can't prove it, but he wanted to pressure Ronnie about the money in prison. Gil kept getting in his way. Then he got suspicious that Gil was hiding the money for Ronnie, and that really set him off."

"It doesn't take much, does it?" Ansel asked.

"The man's a walking bundle of violence." Gaff hesitated. "I want to thank you for your help. He'd have gotten away last night. I never saw who hit me. But I never want you two to put yourself in danger again. Never."

"We didn't do it on purpose," Ansel told him. "But we've learned not even to dabble in your business. I never want to go through something like that again."

"Good. It's my job, and I'd rather never repeat it either."

Jazzi asked, "Did you call Ronnie's grandma?"

"Yup, she knows she's coming home to a safe house. It took a lot of worry off her mind."

"Thanks for calling us, Gaff. How do you feel today?"

"Horrible. I have a headache that won't quit, but no concussion, and I'm going to live."

"Thanks again," Jazzi said.

He sighed. "I hope my next call is to ask if my Ann and I can come swim in your pond this summer."

"So do I. And the answer is yes."

When they hung up, Ansel pulled her so close, she could hardly breathe. "It's over. Let's switch gears. All we have to do now is enjoy the wedding."

And that, she was sure, was a slam dunk.

Chapter 39

The wedding was at two in the afternoon. When the music started playing, Jazzi was the first person to walk down the aisle. Her gaze focused on the men standing near the altar. Thane had pulled his wild, auburn hair back into a low ponytail. He looked more polished than Jazzi had ever seen him. Walker, tall and handsome, stood next to him. And then Ansel, Radley, and Jerod formed a line.

She'd never seen Ansel in a tux, and he looked so good, she simply stared at him for a moment. How did she get so lucky? When he smiled at her, her heart fluttered. Radley was nearly as good-looking, and then there was Jerod. There was just something about him. Her cousin was plenty eye-catching, but his blue eyes always had a sparkle.

When she reached the front of the church and turned to take her spot, she watched Franny and Isabelle make their way toward her. Franny's powder blue gown went well with her carrot orange hair. Instead of being twisted into its usual knot, her hair hung in loose waves past her shoulders. Jazzi glanced at Jerod. He looked like he might pop with pride.

When Isabelle reached the back pews, Reuben twisted in his seat to watch her. As usual, with her dramatic coloring, she looked stunning. Last, but not least, River—dressed in a tuxedo—walked down the aisle, carrying a satin pillow with Didi's ring cradled on it. And then, the wedding march started.

Didi came first in a soft, flowing wedding dress that matched her personality—sweet and generous. Finally, Olivia came down the aisle in her sophisticated gown with a scooped out back, and it was everything she'd said it would be.

The rest of the ceremony slightly blurred for Jazzi as her emotions peaked and threatened tears. Her sister looked beautiful. So did their mom in her mother of the bride gown. Walker's mom chose a gown similar in color to Mom's. It was all so perfect, Jazzi's throat closed and she had to swallow down pride.

At the end of the ceremony, Ansel came to escort her down the aisle. He wove his arm through hers and pulled her close. They stood next to each other to meet everyone who attended and shake hands. Lots of pictures followed that, and finally, it was time to drive to their house and party.

Everyone pitched in, arranging food on the butcher block counter of the kitchen island. The kitchen and living room, draped with ribbons and filled with flowers, glowed in the flickering fire of lit tapers in candelabras. Ansel flicked on background music, and the house swelled with friends, family, and laughter.

Champagne flowed, food disappeared, and before the men moved furniture to make room for dancing, tuxes were hung in the foyer closet. Then the real fun began. Radley spun Elspeth around the living room, and Jazzi smiled, watching them. Would they be the next to tie the knot? Or would Bain beat them to it with Greta? Maybe she and Ansel would be hosting another double wedding.

She went to the kitchen to pour herself another glass of wine and grab a beer for Ansel. She raised a brow when she saw George, under the long farmhouse table, tipping back the end of someone's lager. The pug would be lucky if he didn't have a hangover in the morning. Watching Gran pour herself another glass of champagne, she was glad to see that Samantha wasn't drinking. Gran would be lucky to be headache free tomorrow, too.

The party kept going until close to midnight, and then people started to drift away, ready to head home. River fell asleep on one of the couches, and Walker lifted him to carry to Didi's car.

"Thanks for everything," Didi said. "It was a fairytale night. It was perfect."

"Congratulations." She and Ansel walked them to the door.

Olivia and Thane came next. "You did it again, sis." Olivia hugged her in a crush of happiness. "This was the best wedding present ever."

In half an hour, the last guest had gone. Ansel closed and locked the door, then shook his head at the remnants of their fun.

"Tomorrow," Jazzi said. "Jerod said to skip work tomorrow. We can recover then."

He grinned. "Weddings always put me in a romantic mood."

"They do, do they?"

He took her hand and started for the stairs. "Later, George."

The dog actually sagged onto the floor. He couldn't quite focus. Jazzi laughed. "You're going to have to carry him, for sure, tonight. Your pug's had one beer too many."

Even the cats flopped down, exhausted. Too much fun and too many people.

Ansel still looked like he had plenty of energy, though. The pets might not make it to bed until the wee hours of the morning. On their way upstairs, Jazzi's thoughts returned to Radley and Bain. She hoped there'd be two more weddings in their future, soon, and no more murders.

Chicken Tamale Casserole

Heat oven to 400 degrees. Spray 9 x 13 casserole dish.
For bottom layer: in a large bowl, combine:

1/3 c chicken stock
1 large egg
1 t ground cumin
1/8 t cayenne
1 can cream-style corn
1 (8.5 oz) Jiffy cornbread mix
1 (4 oz.) can chopped green chiles

Pour into sprayed pan. Bake 15 min. or until set.
While bottom bakes, shred meat from 1 rotisserie chicken
into a large skillet. Add:
Salt and pepper to taste
1 c. chicken stock
1 c. salsa

Cook on medium heat until combined together and liquid is all soaked
into meat.
When you take bottom layer out of oven, poke the entire surface with
a toothpick.
Pour 10 oz. can of red enchilada sauce (I like Old El Paso) over entire
surface.
Let it soak in a few minutes, then layer shredded chicken on top.
Sprinkle with 1 c. shredded sharp cheddar cheese
Bake for another 15 minutes or until cheese melts.
Let stand for 5 minutes. When ready to serve, top with a dollop of sour
cream (optional). I serve with a tossed salad.

Kitchen Sink Soup (to use leftover Easter ham)

In Dutch oven:
2 or 3 T. olive oil to coat bottom of pan
Heat and add:

5 small Yukon gold potatoes, chopped
3 stalks celery, sliced
1 bag of frozen corn, nuked for 6 minutes to thaw
1/2 c frozen green peppers
1/2 c frozen chopped onions
1 bag of baby carrots, chopped
1 bag frozen peas, nuked for 5 minutes to thaw
Season to taste with salt and pepper while cooking.
Then add:
3 c chopped leftover ham
1 (32 oz.) box of chicken stock
1 (13.5 oz.) can lite coconut milk (I can't have milk) OR
equal amount of milk
2 t. minced garlic
1 t. thyme
Splash of soy sauce
Season to taste with salt and pepper.

Bring to boil in a soup pot until vegetables are tender, then lower heat and cook for 20-25 minutes until potatoes are tender. If you want a thicker soup, add a little sprinkle of instant mashed potatoes, a little at a time, until desired consistency.

Sausage and Cabbage Soup

Spray bottom of soup pan or Dutch oven.
Cut up 4 long links of smoked sausage. Add and brown:

1 coarsely diced onion
2 t. minced garlic
6 new potatoes, quartered
3 carrots, chopped

Cook till tender
Add:
4 c. beef stock
3 c. chicken stock
6 peppercorns or a dash of coarse ground pepper
2 whole cloves
2 bay leaves
1 15 oz. can diced tomatoes
6 cups very coarsely chopped cabbage

Bring to boil, then simmer till cabbage is tender.
Remove whole peppercorns, cloves, & bay leaves.

My Dad's Peanut Butter Fudge

Mix together in large saucepan:

    2 c. sugar
    2 T cocoa

Add to pan:

    1/3 c. white Karo
    2/3 c. milk

Mix and cook on low heat until candy thermometer reaches soft ball temperature (235 degrees).

Add 2 T. butter and remove from heat.

Add 1 c. of peanut butter (I use creamy) & stir until mixed. Don't take too long or it will harden when you try to pour it.

Pour into a buttered or sprayed pie plate.

Printed in the United States
by Baker & Taylor Publisher Services